Totally Bound Publishing books by Cassandra Hawke:

Demolition of the Heart

I0542420

DEMOLITION OF THE HEART

CASSANDRA HAWKE

Demolition of the Heart
ISBN # 978-1-78430-174-3
©Copyright Cassandra Hawke 2014
Cover Art by Posh Gosh ©Copyright July 2014
Interior text design by Claire Siemaszkiewicz
Totally Bound Publishing

DEMOLITION OF THE HEART

Dedication

To Elek, Phil and John
for pleasures shared

Chapter One

Kayla slipped on her new gown, feeling the sensual swish of the satin lining slide over her freshly washed skin. The tight bodice clung to the fullness of her breasts and the delicate green chiffon drapes swirled around her knees in featherlight caresses. With the current heat wave, she was glad she had chosen a short dress with a low neckline and little beaded cap sleeves. She pulled her long auburn tresses up into a neat chignon, attached her sassy little fascinator with its sparkling peacock feathers to the side of her head, and slipped on her strappy slides. *There. All done.*

Despite the remnants of jet lag that still clung to her mind, she was determined to enjoy herself today. Her early return from Scotland and attendance today at the annual Melbourne Cup Luncheon meant a lot to her dearest friend, Jessica. She wanted to express support for her as she struggled to find a positive outcome in her younger brother's cancer diagnosis. While her parents dedicated their lives to supporting Robbie, Jessica worked tirelessly to raise funds to support the organization that had supported her family during their crisis.

When they arrived, the function room was buzzing and Jessica held her arm tightly as they made their way through the swirling crowd. They were barely seated when a short, matronly woman rushed up and hugged Jessica.

"Oh, my dear, it is so nice to see you here today. How's our darling, Robbie?"

"He's doing okay, Mrs Lindsay-Jones," Jessica replied.

"And this is your friend…" Mrs Lindsay-Jones waved her hand slightly to indicate Kayla.

"Yes, this is Kayla Mackenzie. Kayla, Mrs Lindsay-Jones." Jessica smiled from one to the other as she made the brief introduction.

"Well I hope she won't mind, but I am going to steal you away for a short time. There is someone I want you to meet."

"Kayla?" Jessica inquired.

"You go, Jessica. I'll have a look at the silent auction while you're gone and see if anything takes my fancy."

While Jessica was dragged into the milling throng by the older woman, Kayla made her way to the silent auction. There were some impressive items, and this was just a sideline to the main fundraising auction to be held between the main course and dessert.

Keen to make a contribution she picked up the pen and bent over the bidding sheet for a couple of bottles of good Barossa wine. She sensed someone close behind her.

"A nice drop." The male voice was deep and well-modulated.

With her name signed she straightened and his tangy aftershave wafted tantalizingly around her. She felt the heat radiating from his body as she turned and looked up into a pair of golden hazel eyes that were attractively emphasized by fine lines crinkling the corners.

She held out the pen. "It's for a good cause. Are you going to place a bid?" she asked.

He reached out and took the pen, his fingers brushing delicately over hers as they closed around the writing instrument. Kayla stared up at him, her light-hearted animation shimmering into a liquid shower of awareness under the mischievous spark in his eyes. He slowly let his gaze slide from her face, over her breasts, and down the length of her body, right to the strappy slides on her feet.

"Of course," he replied. His grin blossomed into a genuine smile that tugged his wide, shapely mouth into a generous curve that accentuated the fullness of his bottom lip and molded the slightest of dimples on his cheeks.

The deepening lines on both sides of his mouth added strength to his angular jaw that was lightly dusted with designer stubble. He stepped around her, sliding past in a sinuous dance step, not touching her, but so close the force of his movement ruffled the chiffon of her skirt. Involuntarily, she stepped back as he bent over in front of her to reach the bidding sheet and scrawl a bid. The masculine aura that emanated from him held her entranced as she openly studied the muscular curves of his back and shoulders and his neat derriere, stretching the seat of his trousers before they hung lightly over long muscular legs. There was something familiar about this man, as if she should recognize him or had met him before, but she couldn't put a name to the face.

Frustrated by her inability to recall where she knew him from, she dragged her blatant ogle away from his derriere just in time to meet his when he straightened and stepped to the side of the table.

"Now that I have completed my obligations to the cause, perhaps you would indulge me in a circuit of the dance floor," he asked.

"I'm not much of a dancer..." she murmured.

In response to her trailing silence, he held out his hand. "Wade Faxton — a client of Douglas, Moore, and Associates."

She flinched and almost snatched her hand from his. Of course...Wade Faxton, the gambler and loan shark's son — the one she had the hots for in university, but stayed away — not because he was the boy from the wrong side of the tracks, but because she had still been smarting from her bitter break up with her childhood sweetheart.

She took a deep breath and slipped her hand into his warm, encompassing palm. "Kayla Mackenzie," she announced.

His clasp was firm and the shake controlled, but there was no overly masculine posturing that had in the past left her with numb fingers. As he shook her hand, she studied him — the impressive height, his unruly, collar length hair, the designer stubble that accentuated the square chin indented with the slightest of clefts, and the gold earring in his left earlobe. He was an assured, confident man most women would sneak a second glance at. As she looked back up into his eyes, she realized he had not released her hand.

"Ah, *the* Kayla Mackenzie, the one who wouldn't date me in uni because my pedigree wasn't prestigious enough…"

Her face seared hot. "That's not true, Wade. It had nothing to do with who you were…"

He raised his eyebrows. "Really, but that's what all the society girls said," he murmured. A sardonic grin distorted the line of his mouth ever so slightly.

"Well, in my case, it's true," she said. "I was nursing a bitterly broken heart. It was a bad time in my life. I didn't have any room for romance in my heart when I finally snapped out of it, you'd graduated."

He gave a genuine beam of pleasure now and a little bow. "Well, seeing it is bad manners to argue with a lady I will accept your explanation but in exchange, will you indulge me in a dance or two? Just to show there are no hard feelings," he asked.

In an effort to break the spell he seemed to have cast over her brain, she laughed lightly, glanced at his shoes, then back to his face. "If you do not value your toes, Mr Faxton, the answer is yes. I will join you on the dance floor."

"Never mind my toes, and please, call me Wade. I think we go back far enough to dispense with formalities."

She smiled and nodded as she allowed him to lead her toward the dancers.

His palm rested with deceptive lightness on the bare skin of her back as she reached up to his shoulder. With practiced ease, he clasped her hand in his as he swept her onto the crowded floor. With ease they glided between the other dancers in perfect rhythm, he drew her closer until their bodies touched with the lightest of contact. A glowing spark of uncertain sexual awareness slipped uninvited through her body and she found herself nestling into his embrace as they moved as one.

The band transitioned seamlessly from one tune to the next. They floated across the floor under the mesmerizing blur of the swirling lights. Kayla was drawn inexorably under the spell of his masculine sensuousness, the smooth lithe movement of his hard body in time with the rise and fall of the music. Held so close to him, she magically found it easy to follow his movement, like floating on air as her feet moved of their own volition, somehow smoothly following his expert lead.

The warmth of his breath ruffled her hair, his fingers curled around hers, tightening ever so slightly each time their hips slid, with whisper gentleness, against each other. She wanted this man, badly. She had always wanted this man.

The silence was deafening as the last note echoed hauntingly around the room. Their gliding halt seemed abrupt and brutal when they stopped moving and applauded the band. Her knees threatened to sag and her back still sizzled with the imprint of his hand, and her fingers spontaneously reached to be entrapped in his clasp again. She peeked up at him and offered her arm so he could escort her back to her seat, just in time for soup.

"Thank you, Kayla. I will be back shortly and would be very happy if you would grant me another dance…as you can see, my toes are perfectly intact."

She smiled up at him as she sank into her chair, knowing full well she could not refuse his request — didn't want to refuse his request. "Of course, Wade…that would be lovely," she said.

Then he was gone across the room and through the doors that led outside. She watched him go until he disappeared from sight.

Jessica slid in beside her. "Sorry I was gone so long, but at least you seemed to be getting taken care of. Who was that hunk you were cuddling up to on the dance floor?"

"I wasn't cuddling up, Jessica. You know me." Kayla laughingly replied.

"Well, some would believe you, Kayla. Anyway, who was he?" Jessica asked.

"His name is Wade Faxton."

Jessica shrugged screwing her face up into a perplexed expression. "Nobody I know. Did you give him your number?"

Kayla shook her head.

"Silly girl. Anyway, let's eat. I'm starving."

* * * *

Her bowl had barely been removed when Wade was by her shoulder.

"Another dance, Kayla?" he asked softly.

She took his hand and rose from the chair. She smiled at Jessica by way of apology for leaving her alone. Her friend just grinned back.

Wade guided her into the circulating dancers and pulled her close. Every inch of her began to tingle with awareness. His hard masculine angles caressed and teased her feminine curves — every move, an invitation to dance a more intimate dance. Her body hummed with desire, her pussy already molten with heat. Her mind shied away just a little at the suddenness of her capitulation, but she wanted him. In reply to his suggestive caresses, she moved closer her acquiescence obvious.

Still moving to the music, she was aware they were gradually drifting toward the edge of the dance floor and the wide glass doors to the foyer. With just the slightest of fumbles, Wade opened the door and guided them through. He continued to dance with her, but he was closer now. She felt his arousal as his body pressed against hers. She turned her face up to his. He smiled down at her. It was a hungry smile. Then his lips were on hers – hot, moist, and delicious. It was a commanding kiss that explored her whole mouth – caressing, demanding a response. The sparks flashed between them. Her body flushed with sexual warmth and her pussy became liquid fire.

They paused a moment until the lift doors slid open. The moment they closed behind them Wade hauled her hard against him and began to kiss her neck and cleavage. Kayla was barely aware they had exited the lift and were weaving erratically down the corridor. She heard a click and they gracefully swayed into a luxury suite with a king-size bed. The urgency between them imploded into a frenzied battle to find naked skin, to join and satisfy a long awaited desire.

He lifted her skirt, cupping her buttocks as he pressed her against the wall. His kisses were hotter, more invasive, and she responded, hungrily devouring all he had to offer. She fumbled with his belt and fly, but finally managed to release his cock from its enclosure. She grasped his hard length firmly, feeling the heat radiating from the turgid flesh. Her body ached with the need to have him inside her – to feel the length and heat filling her. She was wet, hot, and very, very needy. He pressed her hard against the wall, covering the swell of her breasts in his hands through the thin material of her dress and bra.

"Oh God, Kayla, I have wanted you for so long," he moaned against her mouth.

Wade fumbled with one hand to lower her knickers. Then he eased his hand between her legs, feeling her wetness and caressing her clit for a brief moment.

She pushed her hips toward him. She was on the verge of climaxing. Her body sizzled and throbbed. "Take me, Wade. Now. I want you," she muttered.

He ran his hands over her hips and lifted her slightly. She opened her legs. The head of his cock pressed against her opening. Her body quivered in anticipation of the hot length entering her. He paused just a moment to slip on protection then thrust swiftly into her. His solid hardness slipped easily into her tight wetness. She shuddered with desire as it filled her. Her legs quaked and she rocked toward him. She moaned against his mouth, struggling to breathe as he sank his full length into her heat she gasped. The unbearable tension in her pussy disintegrated into a series of all-encompassing waves of sensation that shook her body. She cried out and clung to his shoulders as her flesh convulsed again and again. He penetrated deep, withdrew, and went deep again. She felt his climax shudder into hers. She gasped for air. The intensity of her release shook her and melted her bones. He was pressing against her, holding her and himself upright, with hands pressed hard against the wall as their joint release sapped their bodies of substance. Wade was struggling to catch his breath as nuzzled into the curve of her neck.. She clutched his shoulders and buried her face in the sweet silken layers of his hair. She was aware of her perspiration blending with his and the smell of sex wafting between them.

Wade lifted his head and peered down at her. His eyes were filled with a dark and mysterious expression, a slight smile danced on his mouth. He leaned in and kissed her very lightly then pulled away. "All right, Kayla?"

She stared directly into his eyes. She knew he wasn't asking if the sex was good. He wanted to know if she had any regrets, fucking the notorious kid from the wrong side of the law.

She smiled, stretched up and kissed him lingeringly. "No regrets, Wade," she said firmly.

He pulled away from her then. She nearly slumped to the floor, but he held her steady.

"We better get back to the party before we are missed," he said quietly.

The small edge of regret in his voice echoed hers. She would've loved to stay and explore the explosive awareness that simmered between them. Even now, it shivered along her skin.

It took her barely a moment to smooth her ruffled persona back into cool, calm elegance, but she couldn't quite eradicate the sparkle that shone in her eyes. Wade appeared perfectly composed as he escorted back to the function room and through the twirling dancers and back to her table.

The main course was delicious and accompanied by the opening patter from the auctioneer. He was one of Australia's best, having won the Golden Gavel Award the last two years. He was entertaining, funny, and had a knack of wangling a few more dollars out of each bidder's pocket with his witty one-liners and undeniably persuasive and cajoling chatter that was aimed directly at any potential big spender's wallets.

There was plenty of heckling and good natured bantering back and forth as the bids came thick and fast for items such as Bradman cricket memorabilia, collectable wines, and overseas holidays.

"Now, ladies and gentlemen, I have lot number fifty-two — two exquisite paintings in oils, Seascapes by Australian pioneer artist Eloise McLeod. Do I have an opening bid?"

Kayla stared. The familiarity of the paintings slapped at her as she was sucked into a vortex of disbelief. The room receded. The chatter silenced. All that existed was the paintings.

Her paintings. They belonged on the walls of Ainsley House. A roiling surge of emotion swept over her. The best two seascapes of all Grandma Eloise's paintings had held pride of place in the reception area of her artist's retreat. They were the treasured gems of her private collection.

"What is this, Jessica? Those paintings are mine," she blurted in her friend's ear.

"What are you talking about, Kayla?" Jessica asked in an urgent undertone.

Kayla grabbed her friend's arm in a vice-like grip and practically dragged her onto her lap. "Those are mine...from Ainsley House. It says they were donated anonymously, but they can only have been stolen to get here. I would never — do you hear — never sell any of my grandmother's paintings."

"Shhh, Kayla, please keep your voice down. People are starting to notice." Jessica frowned and lowered her head a little, as if to hide.

"Don't shhhh me, Jessica Newman. How did your charity come to have my paintings?" Kayla asked.

"I don't know, Kayla. All I know is the staff of Douglas, Moore, and Associates came in to help catalog everything and they brought the paintings and several other items with them," Jessica replied, her tone soothing.

"Well, they're mine. I need to pull them from the auction," Kayla snapped in reply.

"You can't, Kayla. They have been legitimately donated."

As Kayla rose from her seat, Jessica dragged her back down.

"You can't make a scene, Kayla. Remember who's here, and you don't even know how they got them. You'll have to bid on them," Jessica said, her words short and sharp with a sense of urgency.

"Opening bids, Ladies and Gentleman? There we have it—at the back of the room—one thousand dollars. Come on, people. These are superb paintings by an Australian artist. They will provide a fantastic, classy, and elegant talking piece on your lounge room walls. Any advancement on one thousand?"

Kayla stood and proffered her card. "Eleven hundred."

"Beautiful—off to the right. The bid is with you at eleven hundred. From the left, any more on eleven hundred?"

Kayla dropped back into her seat. Her legs were trembling, her throat dry and constricted.

"Twelve hundred."

"Thank you, sir. To my right?" the auctioneer asked looking straight at Kayla.

Kayla waved her number. "Thirteen hundred," she announced.

Then she heard another voice from directly behind her. "Fifteen hundred."

She didn't turn to check. "Sixteen hundred," she said. Her voice wavered. She didn't care how much she had to pay to retrieve the paintings.

The unknown rival behind her bid seventeen hundred and the other eighteen hundred.

She scrutinized the auctioneer and raised her card. "Nineteen hundred."

"The lady in green has bid nineteen hundred. Any advancement, gentlemen?"

Both the others placed bids, and it was now in her court again at twenty-two hundred. She stabbed the air with her card, feeling sick as she did it. "Two thousand three."

"Thank you. Gentlemen in the back?" the auctioneer asked as he indicated Kayla's two rival bidders.

Kayla waited.

"Two thousand four." The man on the back right said.

Now it was back to her. She raised her card. "Two thousand five hundred."

"The bid is with the lady in the green."

The man on the side said firmly, "Two thousand six."

"Any further bids?" asked the auctioneer.

Kayla gripped the card tightly and flashed it over her head. "Two thousand seven."

Silence weighed the room down for a long moment as the auctioneer indicated the two other bidders. "Gentlemen," he asked.

The silence hung heavy. Even the waiters stopped moving in respect of the tension.

"No further bids. The lady in the green has it. First call, second call, and..."

"Three thousand," announced a male voice.

She tried to see who continued to bid, but the crowded room blocked her view.

"Three thousand. Against the lady in the green — any advancement on that, Miss?"

She signaled her new bid by flashing her card. "Three thousand, one hundred," she said, hoping all the time the others would quit bidding.

"Gentleman at the back?" the auctioneer asked. When he was greeted with silence, he surveyed the crowd, paused, then said, "As there are no further bids, we are all done, first call, second call, and third and final call. Sold, to the lady in green. Congratulations, Miss. Please see the cashier after the auction. Thank you, everyone, for your spirited bidding. Now we have lot number fifty-three, a framed, signed AFL Guernsey..."

The auctioneer's voice faded as Kayla covered her face with her hands, fighting to keep tears of shock, and fury from flooding her cheeks.

"I could've lost my grandmother's paintings. Oh Jessica, how could they have got here?" Kayla wailed.

"I'm sorry, Kayla — really I am — that you had to buy your own paintings."

Kayla gave her friend a tight hug. "Don't fret, Jessica, it's not your fault, and the money is going to support a good cause — especially little Robbie."

Jessica nodded.

As Kayla made her way toward the cashier, Wade intercepted her and held out his hand. "Another dance?"

She shook her head.

He continued to smile. "Don't tell me you have to rush off — even Cinderella had until midnight."

"Sorry, Wade. I have to sort something out." She tried to smile, but it was a very insipid effort.

"Hey, Cinderella, you have tears in your eyes." Wade moved closer, a slight frown forming on his forehead.

She pulled away from him and swiped at the moisture lingering on her eyelashes. "I don't," she said.

"Kayla, seriously, can I help?" Wade asked.

"No, Wade. Sorry, but I have to go."

She dashed past him into the cashier's office. While the cashier processed her payment, she tried to peek at the list he was working from, but the name of the donor was blank. "Can I ask you who donated the paintings?"

"I have no details on the donor. He has requested to remain anonymous." The clerk was pleasant but firm in his reply.

She arranged to have the paintings delivered to her flat, and seething with frustration and rage, she retreated to her seat. Back at the table, Kayla stared at her dessert, frustration bubbled up at the multitude of unanswered questions. She just couldn't face it and pushed away from the table.

"I'll see you at home, Jessica."

Jessica grabbed her arm and pulled her back into her seat. "Don't leave, Kayla, I will go and ask Mrs Lindsay-Jones. She will tell me who donated the paintings. She knows all the gossip."

Kayla watched as Jessica made her way across the crowded room to where Mrs Lindsay-Jones sat. Her friend leaned in close and after a few minutes of animated conversation, Jessica placed a polite kiss on the older woman's cheek and headed back.

As Jessica slipped into her seat, she searched the room. "You are not going to like this, sweetie. Apparently the paintings were donated by Faxton

Constructions — run by none other than your gorgeous hunky dancing partner."

Kayla felt sick, her insides sank with an ungainly thud. No. Not the gorgeous sexy man she had just had hurried, but frenzied, sex with. *Oh my God.* She felt a right idiot, but now his identity was revealed, she was not all that shocked. Just furious.

"Are you sure?" she asked.

"No mistake. Mrs Lindsay-Jones says he has been a long-time supporter of the charity. Apparently it is a cause very close to his heart." Jessica seemed disconcerted by her revelation.

"Close to his heart...*really*. That does not cut any ice with me. Dear to his heart or not, he has no right to use my property to show what a wonderful philanthropist he is. Where is he?" Kayla asked as she scanned the room.

Jessica wriggled in her chair. "I saw him go out onto the balcony while you were in the cashier's office," Jessica replied.

"Well, he better have a damn good explanation ready for how he came to be in the possession of two stolen paintings." Kayla's words were barely a cracked whisper as she jumped out of her chair and marched across the room. Without slowing down, she barged through the balcony doors, sending them flying fully open with reckless abandonment. Blinded by the rage and frustration that consumed her, she stormed forward until she unexpectedly crashed hard against an immovable object.

"Oooff!"

She felt the eruption of breath rather than heard the grunt from the broad chest of the man now pressed hard against her breasts. Her clutch purse tumbled to the floor. Winded by the force of their collision, Kayla fought for balance and the mental focus to cope with the sudden halt to her rage-driven charge. One shoe fell off as she skidded and slipped on the polished tiled floor, but she didn't fall, as she was immediately steadied by a strong, supportive grip.

She struggled to regain her balance, acutely aware of how close she was being held by Wade Faxton. His jacket hung open and the warmth of his body radiated through the thin fabric of his shirt—the steady beat of his heart was going about half the pace of the out of control cadence of her own. His warm breath stirred her hair and a shiver of sensation raced across her skin. The hardness of well-toned muscles crushed against the softness of her breasts was both titillating and disturbing at the same time and she struggled for a split second with the instant desire to cuddle closer and the need to push away.

Warily, she locked gazes with his deep set hazel eyes, fringed by long, dark lashes. His eyes now sparkled with amusement, the corners crinkling ever so slightly. The tangy scent of after-shave assailed her senses.

"Oh! I…" she said before she fell silent.

She was still clinging to his neck and he had made no attempt to release her.

"Ah, Cinderella, you have taken pity on Prince Charming and granted him another dance after all," he said. The husky timbre of his voice vibrated through his chest—driven by barely suppressed laughter.

Kayla stiffened and pulled back. He let her go.

She glared up at him in an attempt to regain her composure. His amusement died under the red hot force of her palpable hostility.

"Kayla?" His voice was hesitant, her name rolling off his tongue like honey.

She glared up at him. "Don't you 'Kayla' me, Mr Faxton, of Faxton Constructions. You explain to me right now how you came to be in possession of my property. How you came to donate two of my grandmother's irreplaceable, priceless paintings to a charity auction?"

He cocked his head slightly to the left but continued to stare right back at her. "I donate a lot of things to charity. That is my right to do so," he responded.

"But not stolen property! Not *my* stolen property. Is that why you donated them anonymously—so you could conceal your ill-gotten gains?" she snapped.

He held up his hands as if to fend off her angry tirade. His defensive action simply added fuel to her rage.

"I have no idea what you are talking about, Kayla. I have never stolen anything in my life," he said with just a touch of heat in his tone.

"*Liar!* Those two paintings by Eloise McLeod are mine—have always been mine, and I did not sell them, nor did I give permission for someone else to sell them. How did you get them?" she screeched.

"They came with the house," Wade said calmly.

She grabbed his bicep and tried to shake him. "House? What house? They were hanging in Ainsley House," she yelled at him.

He resisted her manhandling with ease. "Correct, they *were*—along with a number of other extremely good artworks that will also be donated to charity as Ainsley House is soon to be demolished." He spoke slowly now, as if to a child.

"It is *not*. Ainsley House is *mine*. Well, it belongs to the McLeod Family Trust. I think you have made a very serious mistake, Mr Faxton."

"I'm sorry, Kayla, but I have not made a mistake. I took possession of Ainsley House at settlement of my father's estate four weeks ago. It was payment in full of a very large gambling debt. The house is scheduled for demolition within the next two weeks," he announced.

She glowered up at him but really didn't see him. Her mind was turbulent mush as she tried to grab onto one thought that made sense. The one solid thought to bring everything back to normal. "Ainsley House is an artist's retreat, gallery, and museum. It has two managers, and artists and students from around the world come to paint and —"

He cut her words off. "The retreat has been closed since July or August last year. I took vacant possession of the building," he stated calmly.

"But you can't have… Where are Pierre and Abrial?" she shouted at him.

He shrugged "I have possession of the house and who the hell are Pierre and Abrial?"

She froze. The world stopped then spun in and out of focus. She opened her mouth. She felt her throat move, but no sound came out of it. Her knees dissolved. She grabbed the balcony rail for support and finally forced the words out. "No! No! No! Ainsley House is *not* going to be demolished. It's *mine*. It's protected by the family trust."

He stood there shaking his head at her vehement denials, a mild expression of confusion, irritation, and pity shadowing his face. Something inside her snapped — the physical pain of fury out of control. She leaped forward, her hand swung back to deliver a stinging slap — anything to wipe that expression from his rugged features.

He raised his arms and latched onto her bare forearms. "Don't, Kayla. I can see you have received a shock — a terrible shock, apparently, but I do not tolerate violence upon my person. And hysterics and temper tantrums will get you absolutely nowhere."

The roiling rage whooshed away from her and she sagged, her face burning with the heat of embarrassment. "You gangster. You thug," she cursed at him. "You fuck me while you are blithely selling off my property. The apple didn't fall far from the tree, did it?"

His face flushed a deep red. "Damn it, Kayla, our little interlude had nothing to do with it. I had no idea the paintings were yours or that you would have an issue with the house..."

She silenced his excuses with a vicious snarl of words. "You used me," she cried.

"For God's sake, don't go there, Kayla. It wasn't like that at all and you know it," he muttered.

Behind them, the balcony door creaked open.

"Kayla?" Jessica asked tentatively.

At the sound of her friend's voice Kayla turned and fell into her friend's open arms, tears welled up and poured down her cheeks. "Someone has shut the retreat and sold Ainsley House. Only they can't..." she wailed.

From behind them, Wade spoke. "Ladies, this is not the time, nor the place, to get to the bottom of this fiasco, so I would suggest that, Kayla, you attend my offices tomorrow morning. Bring any relevant paperwork and we will have a civilized discussion. Here's my card."

He was almost snarling. Kayla glanced over her shoulder as Jessica took the proffered card, and was shocked to see the deep frown distorting his handsome features and the dark shadows in his eyes that could be mistaken for hurt, if she didn't know better.

She sighed. "I owe you an apology, Wade, but you have given me some unbelievable and horrific information that is intolerable to me personally, and if true, as you say, will have a number of very grim consequences. It must have already had some intolerable outcomes for my friends who manage the retreat, the two elderly caretakers. What has become of them? Why has no one contacted me? I was in Scotland, for God's sake, not Mars." Her voice began to crack as her throat choked up again.

"I have no answers for you, Kayla, but I will accept your apology and be happy to help you sort out the facts."

"I didn't mean what I said Wade, about...about..." She fell silent.

He nodded in acknowledgment of what she was trying to say, but the grimness of his expression didn't soften. She knew he was angry, but so was she, and the sex had nothing to do with it at all.

"Come, sweetie. We will work it all out tomorrow," Jessica said, as she ushered her toward the door.

* * * *

Back at the flat, Kayla tore off her gown and slipped on some shorts and a halter neck top. She wasn't sure where to start, what to look for, who would have answers.

She dialed the main number at Ainsley House. It rang out. She dialed the private number of Pierre De' Longni, Master of Arts, who ran the retreat and gallery for her. Her call was answered by a trite message saying the retreat was closed. She dialed both Pierre's and Abrial's mobiles. They both went to voice mail. She then called the retirement village where her Uncle George had been residing since his health had deteriorated last year. As one of the trustees of the McLeod Family Trust, he should have some answers.

The nurse said she could not put her through to Mr Mitchell and for further information, she would have to contact Mr Mitchell's son, Phillip.

Even though she was loath to call him because of his ongoing antagonism toward her since childhood, she dialed his number because he was the obvious choice.

"Phillip, I have a problem. I need to talk to Uncle George urgently."

"What? Lost your return flight ticket?" he sneered.

"You're such a shit, Phillip. Actually, I am already back," she said.

"You weren't supposed to get back until after New Year," he accused.

She heard surprise and something else in his tone. He didn't seem at all pleased she was back early.

"That's right, but things change. Is it an issue for you?" she asked.

"Why would your early return even be of interest to me, little cousin, let alone an issue?" he snapped.

"Good. Then you won't mind giving me the okay to speak to Uncle George. Some of Eloise's paintings came up at an auction today. I want to know how and why."

"I would have thought you already had enough of the old girl's art work on the walls of that hideous mausoleum you call an artist's retreat," he responded. His voice was hard and contemptuous.

Kayla took a deep breath in an effort to control the urge to scream at him. She hated that he was so scathing about the house. "That is not the point, Phillip. The man responsible for their donation also says he now owns Ainsley House, and he is going to demolish it." She was almost snarling as anxiety sharpened her tone and reduced her patience.

"Oh come on, Kayla, you pull me out of my sickbed because of some rumor. It's locked up safe as Fort Knox," Phillip drawled.

Kayla ignored his dismissive response. "This is much more than a rumor, Phillip. We need to stop them."

"We, Kayla? I seem to remember through my flu fogged brain that Ainsley House is yours — not ours, or mine. Perhaps you don't remember Great Aunt Eloise disinherited me." His tone now was outright burning sarcasm.

"She did *not* disinherit you, Phillip. That is a gross exaggeration. Now, as you are my sole cousin, I think I have the right to your support, regardless of who actually owns Ainsley House. Then again, I could go directly to Uncle George — "

"No, Kayla, I don't want Father disturbed. I am sure we can sort this out without putting any extra pressure on him. He's very unwell. Then again, have you considered it might be your Master of the Arts — Pepé La Pew — who has done the dirty on you? Sold up the paintings and pocketed the money," Phillip mocked her.

She knew immediately he was trying, with a clumsy attempt, to cut through her absolute trust in her managers.

"For God's sake, Phillip, I wish you would not use that term for him. Besides, this is not just about the paintings, it is about the house."

"Never mind about the house. Nothing can happen to the house unless you authorized it... Can you be absolutely certain, little cousin, that your precious manager hasn't sold you out?" Phillip sneered.

"Pierre is dedicated to his craft — "

"Have you spoken to him?" he asked.

"Not yet. He has not answered my calls." Her voice faded, uncertainty draining it of expression.

"Well then, what other explanation do you need?" Phillip sniped.

"I want to speak to Uncle George about it, but the nursing home wouldn't let me, apparently under your instructions." She knew she sounded accusing but then again, perhaps that was how she felt.

"That's right. My father is not well at the moment and does not need people bothering him, including you, especially over a couple of lousy paintings and unfounded rumors," Phillip snarled.

"Fine, be uncooperative, Phillip. I won't disturb your father for now, but I will not allow anyone to demolish Ainsley House either. Do you hear me?"

"Have fun, little cousin." Phillip snorted down the phone.

She heard him chortling in the distance then he was gone.

"And of course you wouldn't offer to help, would you, you lousy bastard..." she muttered as Jessica handed her a fresh coffee.

Jessica frowned. "No help from him?" she asked.

"The thing that does puzzle me though, is that I was away for a mere ten weeks. I don't understand how this has happened without Uncle George or Phillip knowing it was happening—or the other trustee, Frederick Carven. It was a complicated trust. There would have been no loopholes," she muttered, more to herself than her friend.

"Could it happen without them knowing?" Jessica asked.

Kayla sipped her hot coffee. "I wouldn't think so because it is all tied up legally, but Uncle George has been unwell of late. I know Phillip resents me, but surely he would have contacted me if he knew about it."

"Well, there is nothing you can do until you've spoken to Wade Faxton," Jessica said.

Kayla fired up the computer. "Perhaps not, but I can at least get the low down on Wade Faxton before that happens. I know his background and it is not exactly squeaky clean. His father was a high rolling gambler and loan shark to other gamblers. He was always just a touch inside the law," she said. While she waited for her coffee to cool, she typed in 'Faxton Constructions'.

It resulted in several million hits. She sipped her coffee and scrolled through, instantly realizing she needed to narrow the search. She typed in 'Faxton Constructions, South Australia'. There were plenty of articles—many with photos of Wade shown squiring around a bevy of beautiful women with headlines that ranged from *Playboy Faxton* to *Womanizing Executive Director breaks another Heart*. She ignored them and skimmed through until she found one with some historical information.

Wade Faxton is the epitome of the self-made man, rising from an illicit background of gambling and family tragedy to business success. His younger brother died of cancer at the tender age of seven and, unable to cope, his mother took an overdose. His father, stricken with grief, turned to making bigger gambling deals that were closer and closer to the criminal element. Wade has overcome huge odds to make Faxton Constructions one of the biggest, most respected, construction companies in South Australia.

No wonder the Childhood Cancer Foundation is close to his heart. Then she found one tying Wade to Ainsley House.

Faxton Constructions has signed a secret multi-million dollar deal with Seville Investments to build a convention center and multi-story hotel resort on the twenty-acre waterfront site of the recently acquired ...historic building, Ainsley House, and the land adjoining the block. Ainsley House was built by Hamish Campbell in the 1840s as a tribute to his wife, Ainsley Jones. It will be bulldozed to make room for the project, which is expected to bring tourism and jobs to the struggling fishing and farming town. Wade Faxton, Executive Director of the company, said work is expected to begin immediately. The valuable heritage contents and renowned art collection were auctioned.

Her breath caught in her chest as she struggled to fill her lungs, but all she could manage were tight little gasps. She clutched the mouse so tightly her fingers cramped, and the cursor scrolled down the page. The full meaning of the article was all too clear. She shook her head. There had to be a mistake.

"They can't do this! They can't!" she cried.

She printed off the articles and dug out her copies of the will and the trust deed ready for her appointment with Wade. Sleep did not come easily when she finally gave in and went to bed, but it wasn't the house she thought of as she drifted off, but the sex they had shared.

Chapter Two

As she walked briskly to the offices of Faxton Constructions, her heart beat a rapid tattoo above the butterflies that fluttered relentlessly in her stomach, but when she glanced at her reflection in the huge mirrors that lined the staircase, she saw a calm, fresh-faced young woman dressed in an apricot suit that appeared business-like, but feminine. Just the image she wanted. Satisfied with her appearance and her preparation, she turned and continued up the stairs. She did not delude herself that this was going to be a simple exchange of paperwork and apologies.

When she was announced, Wade came out himself to collect her. He wasn't smiling, but that did nothing to take away from his symmetrically pleasing features, or cool the warm liquid melt that began in her nether regions in response to his hand pressed gently on her back to guide her into his huge corner office. She felt distinctly like she was about to enter the lion's den, so she dredged up what resolve she could muster, straightened her back, and marched in front of him into the sunlit room.

She perched primly on the edge of a huge leather chair and waited, without a word, for him to take his place behind the wide expanse of desk. He stood with long legs apart and arms folded across his muscular chest. His stance was harsh and unyielding — there was no sign of reprieve in the jutting jaw. Sparking chips of topaz shattered the deep golden hue of his eyes. All signs of sexual interest in her were absent. He was a different man from the one who had openly flirted with her yesterday on the dance floor and made passionate love to her against the bedroom wall. She mourned the loss of the sensitive, flirty Wade as she squirmed uncomfortably under his penetrating scrutiny.

"Kayla, you made some rather outlandish accusations yesterday about the ownership of Ainsley House," he stated bluntly.

She nodded.

"I am not used to having my integrity questioned or to being publicly reviled in such a manner, but I am a man with a sense of fairness and would wish to understand the reason behind your accusations and to determine the facts. I hope you have brought some evidence to help us do that?" he asked.

"I have brought some legal documents to support my claim," she replied, as she reached into her handbag. She wished he would stop glaring at her so relentlessly.

She regretted her outburst of temper last night and wished she could retract her rash words, but it was too late for that or to undo what her little intimate escapade had done to her confidence. His intent gaze made her acutely aware of the huge advantage he had in this matter, along with his overwhelming male presence. The memory of his cock thrusting into her, the feel of him, the smell, and the unbridled response, was still too fresh in her mind to overlook the uninvited sexual awareness that tingled through her body.

She placed the documents on his desk. "I have a copy of my grandmother's will, which names me as her sole beneficiary. I also have a draft copy of the trust deed, which protects and ties up Ainsley House in the McLeod Family Trust. It dictates it is to be used as an artist's retreat, gallery, and museum dedicated to local artists and craftspeople in perpetuity."

Wade reached for the paperwork then slowly sank into his chair. As he quickly scanned their contents, he ran his hand through his shaggy, collar length locks in an unconscious gesture that tousled them. All he achieved was to make him appear even more rakish and desirable. Kayla felt her clit tingle in response and moisture start to warm her pussy. She tried to ignore her body's reaction and concentrate on the task at hand.

He shuffled the sheets of paper. "These are not signed by all parties and witnesses, which makes them almost worthless," he said, as he laid them on the desk. He picked up the phone.

Kayla sat back in the chair, stunned by Wade's assessment of her evidence. She knew they weren't signed by all parties, but she didn't expect that to render them useless. Moments later a short, thin man with a shiny bald head came in.

Wade made brief introductions. "David, this is Kayla Mackenzie. Kayla, my lawyer, David Richards."

The lawyer nodded acknowledgment of the introduction as he took the papers Wade held out.

"David, could you please go over these and check the authenticity, as you can see they are not signed or stamped, so I guess they are just working copies. And you brought the other documents I requested?" Wade asked.

Wade opened the white folder David handed him. "There are no records on the title to the effect Ainsley House is under any trust," he said bluntly and swung the folder around to face her. "See for yourself."

Kayla's fledgling suspicions burst into full grown fears as she studied the documents. There was more going on here than a simple mistake. "But there must be!" she protested, running her finger down the transfers.

Eloise Ainsley Campbell, Frederick William Carver, George Samuel Mitchell, Hugo Faxton (Deceased Estate), Wade Faxton. The transfers and title appeared totally legitimate, even to her inexperienced eyes.

"It lists Carven and Mitchell, but they were never the owners, just the trustees and executors of the will. They couldn't sell without my permission. My grandmother had her solicitor, Mr Frederick Carver, draw up the papers. He was joint trustee with my Uncle George Mitchell. I am the beneficiary and will take control of the estate when I am twenty-five." Her words spilled over themselves as she tried to piece it altogether. None of it made sense.

"The property wasn't sold to Hugo Faxton, Kayla. It was transferred to him as payment of a large gambling debt. I suggest you pay close attention to the third document contained in the file," David advised.

On David's instructions, she picked up the third document—a single page. It was a letter addressed to Frederick Carven authorizing the transfer of Ainsley House to Hugo Faxton. It was dated the day she had left Australia. At the bottom was her signature. She studied it closely. It appeared genuine, but she knew it was not.

"This is not my signature," she said.

"Sign this," Wade ordered, and slid a blank sheet of paper in front of her.

She glared across at him then without a word, she picked up a pen and signed. The two men put the signatures together and studied them. Then Wade slid both copies across to her. Even she couldn't tell the difference. She knew, though, that the one on the letter was not hers. She regarded the two of them for a long moment.

They both watched her with identical, slightly indulgent, expressions.

"It's *not* my signature," she reiterated.

Wade's eyebrows quirked up and his mouth tightened as he handed all the documents to David Richards. "Copy all our documents and Ms Mackenzie's, so we both have a complete set. We may need them."

"Obviously it seems genuine even to me, but I can assure you, it's not," Kayla repeated.

"Well, regardless of that, Kayla, my inheritance of Ainsley House from my father's estate is legitimate. It has all been dealt with by my lawyer, probate has been granted, and I have a watertight deal with Seville," Wade said.

"So where does Seville Investments come into it?" she asked.

"Seville is an old partner of my father. He now runs a consortium, building resorts and conference centers. He thinks, even now, he should have inherited Ainsley House because the debt was from when he and my father worked together. But the debtor thought differently and signed it over to my father's estate. There is nothing about a trust, and Seville's contract with me is legitimate. Everyone is happy." Wade's gravelly tones tore across her.

"Except me," she snapped. "Who paid their debt with my house?" she demanded to know.

Wade looked at David then back to Kayla. "The debtor did not want to be identified and I haven't insisted on knowing… It's not important."

"It *is* important to me, Wade—very important. Something underhanded is happening and I need to know who is behind it."

"I can get my lawyer to do a little digging if you like," Wade suggested.

She nodded. "Yes please, Wade, I would appreciate that. Do you know anything about the closure of the retreat?" She was struggling to hold back her tears now.

"I don't know anything. The place was empty when I took possession four weeks ago. The retreat had been closed prior to that. I had nothing to do with its closure," he said.

Her confidence faltered. "It can't be closed, just like that! What's happened to Abrial and Pierre, my managers, and the caretakers, Joan and Bill?"

Wade shook his head. "I know nothing of managers or caretakers. I inherited the place, untenanted, unencumbered, and mostly unfurnished," he responded.

"But Pierre would not just walk away—not without contacting me," she said.

"But you were overseas—were you not?" Wade asked.

"Yes, in Scotland, and while mobile phone reception is always a bit dodgy, my email was always up and running, and I checked it every day," Kayla replied.

"I'm sorry, Kayla. I cannot help you with that, but I will have David inquire into the matter of who paid their debt with the house. I will keep you informed, but as far as I am concerned, Ainsley House is mine and the demolition will proceed. If you get more substantial evidence, we will talk again. I'm sorry." He reached out to her. "Kayla, about yesterday…it wasn't meant to be a one-night stand, but I don't suppose in the circumstances, you want to have dinner with me…pick up where we left off?"

An embarrassed flush heated her face as she stared at the outstretched hand, the long fingers curled slightly to show neatly manicured nails. It was a strong hand, but Kayla knew it could just as easily evoke passion as well as pain. Reluctantly she dragged her gaze away and up looked up into his eyes. She dabbed her eyes fighting tears. This was not how it was supposed to turn out.

Angry at her inability to stop the tears, she reached out and picked up the file he had compiled for her then she looked directly at him as she took his proffered hand. "I'm sorry too, Wade, but I don't think it would work out, really. But I didn't mean what I said yesterday…about your background."

He nodded.

"And I don't regret being with you one bit," she said firmly.

She saw the expression on his face mellow at the sight of her tears—or her apology, she didn't know which—but she didn't want him pitying her or underestimating her determination to fight to the bitter end to save Ainsley House. Just because she had sex with him—and wanted to again.

"I understand this is distressing for you," he said quietly. "But I cannot be of any more help unless you find something illegal about the arrangement. I will not be involved in something illegal. I had enough of that as a kid."

She smiled then at his assertion he was on the right side of the law but made no comment, just in case she put her foot in her mouth, again. "I understand that, but know this, Wade. Today is not the end of the matter."

He inclined his head. "Until we meet again then, Kayla."

Dismissed, she had no choice but to leave. Her head was spinning. The file she held in her hand might as well have been a poisonous snake. She wanted to fling it from her. What it contained told her one thing — someone was trying to destroy her beloved Ainsley House, her business, and her credibility. While Wade and Seville seemed obvious candidates for the blame, she could not see how they could have forged her signature. She reluctantly admitted both Pierre and Abrial would have the knowledge and access to set this up, even to producing a credible likeness of her signature, but she couldn't find it in her heart to accuse them. They were so close — they were like family. Better, than real family.

Then there *was* family, her cousin, Phillip. Without even thinking about it, she knew Phillip had the knowledge, the access, and probably the motive. Damn him. He already hated her for dobbing him in after the accident so many years ago, and he had been very bitter when Eloise had only left him the villa in Parkside. He hated Ainsley House for the connection it had to his ruined life and saw it as the cause of his secret drug addiction. Yet she shied away from suspecting Phillip. Despite the ups and downs of their relationship, her cousin and his father were her only living relatives since her grandmother had passed, and she had clung tenuously to that connection. She knew that he had not been impressed with her grandmother's provisions for the old house or Kayla's attachment to it. He was also less than sympathetic to her feelings of guilt about not being there when her grandmother died. She knew he was the most likely suspect for these events. She cursed herself for underestimating his bitterness and overestimating his loyalty to kin.

She was shaking so much by the time she reached the car she could hardly get the keys in the ignition. With the air-conditioner blasting directly on her, she pulled out the file Wade Faxton had given her. She picked up the letter. She stared at the signature, so much like hers and yet, she knew it wasn't. Its very existence became the catalyst for a primeval fear that entrenched its tentacles deep inside, twisting her gut into a tormented knot and tightening her chest. That signature was evidence of just how far her enemy would go to rip Ainsley House out of her possession. Whether Phillip was involved or not, she fretted about what else besides Ainsley House her enemy was determined to take from her, and just how far they would go to achieve their goals.

Back at the flat—and fortified with a coffee—she began to make notes, beginning with the auction of the paintings and moving outwards. She included all parties who might have a stake in this debacle. No, not a debacle—a carefully planned and executed plot to rob her of Ainsley House. She was worried about Joan and Bill, for they had a lifetime job and tenancy of the caretaker's cottage. Wade had told her there had been no caretakers when he took ownership of the property, so where were Joan and Bill? She rang Bill's daughter, who lived in Queensland.

"Why are you ringing me, Kayla? You're the one who sacked them — paid them a lump sum to quit. They were so devastated, they moved up here. Mum died a month ago and Dad has moved into a nursing home."

"But I had nothing to do with it, Susan — "

"Really, Kayla? Well, I hold you responsible for Mum's early demise and my father's decline. I have nothing more to say to you," Susan snapped.

"But..." Kayla stopped speaking because she had already been disconnected.

She dialed the number again, but it rang out.

She threw the phone into her handbag. What was going on? She was being blamed for something she had nothing to do with. She added a couple of names to her notes. Much as she was loath to even consider them, she could not eliminate Pierre and Abrial. She had known them for years and would trust them with her life. Surely they would not even dream of harming her or Ainsley House in this way. She studied the names, letting her scattered thoughts tumble through her mind in the hope some pattern would emerge and give her the answers she so badly wanted without incriminating the ones she loved and trusted.

It didn't happen. None of it made sense. Other than her managers and the unknown debtor, Phillip came up as most obviously, and very starkly, the pivot. Even Wade seemed to be a peripheral player in the plot.

She jumped as an urgent thudding on the front door shattered the silence and still struggling to sort her thoughts, she opened the door. Phillip stood on the step, his usual, not quite genuine, smile on his face.

"I don't think I want to talk to you right now, Phillip," she said.

"Where are your manners, little cousin?" he admonished.

He pushed the door wide as he stepped past, solicitously brushing her cheek with the slightest of kisses.

Kayla waited still holding the door open. "I have things on my mind right now, Phillip. I would prefer you left," she said.

He ignored her. "Why are you home early? Was the trip less than satisfying?" he asked.

"Never mind my trip, Phillip. What about Ainsley House?"

He glared down at her. "Really, little cousin, what about Ainsley house? Your rumors again?" he mocked.

"Oh, this is not a rumor, Phillip. Faxton Constructions plan to tear it down in less than two weeks. Thanks to your generous amount of input and assistance, I have that in hand," she responded, sarcasm making her tone sharp and accusing.

A frown appeared on his high brow, pulling his straight dark eyebrows down to shadow his light brown eyes. "*Really*, Kayla?" he asked.

"Yes, really. Wade Faxton is the most charming man," she announced.

"Unfortunately, it is not Wade Faxton you have to convince, little cousin. It will be his investors, and I can tell you they will not halt the progress of the project for little old you," Phillip sneered.

Kayla shrugged in an attempt to hide her discomfiture at this piece of information.

"What do you know about his investors, Phillip? What do you know about the whole thing?"

He rubbed his hands together as if to warm them. "Absolutely nothing," he said. "But, if it makes you feel better, I will visit my father this afternoon and see what he knows, but I am sure, as trustee, he will have what is best for you. If anything has happened, it is obvious you were not consulted because you were gallivanting around the globe and incommunicado."

She didn't believe him for a second. "I wasn't gallivanting. I was on a study trip and working! I had my phone and email — there is no excuse for him not to have consulted me about something so drastic," she squeaked as tears welled in her eyes.

With the slightest flick of his eyebrows, he made his impatience with her emotional response clear. "I understand your attachment to that house and the memories it holds for you of your grandmother, but don't go getting upset. Come on. Let me deal with this. I am sure my father has all the appropriate paperwork on hand, so don't you go worrying your pretty little head about it right now. Anyway, the house is tied up tight in the trust. I am sure you have nothing to worry about," he said.

How dare he lie to her — patronize her. *How dare he!* Kayla fought the trembling rage that threatened to incapacitate her. "I don't understand how something like this could happen? Uncle George and Frederick Carven were tasked with protecting everything until I turned twenty-five, which is in fifteen months' time, by the way."

"I'm sure there is a simple explanation, Kayla, but if you are suggesting my father would fail in his role of trustee or do something illegal, I suggest you stop right there." He was snarling now.

She glared back at him, resenting the sharpness of his tone. "I am not accusing anyone, Phillip, but something is not right about this," she snapped back at him.

"I don't know what has happened. Stop worrying, Kayla. All we need are the original documents and it can all be sorted out. I am sure Father will be able to explain it all when I see him this afternoon," Phillip said, soothingly.

"I am coming with you," she stated.

Phillip shook his head. "No, Kayla. My father is not a well man and I will not tolerate you upsetting him with your hysterical claims and accusations. Do you understand, Kayla? You are *not* to contact my father about this. I will get his papers sorted, and then we can get together first thing tomorrow morning."

She flounced away, then turned back, not at all pacified. "What if Uncle George doesn't have the signed originals?" she asked.

"Then we'll need to find them," Phillip stated bluntly.

"I have no idea where the signed originals are," she wailed, deliberately. She had a sudden need to deny her knowledge of their whereabouts, wary of giving Phillip any additional information.

"Are you sure? What about the old girl's papers stored in the coach house?" Phillip suggested. His face was slightly misshapen with a sly smile.

She contemplated Phillip's smug expression. It seemed so out of sync with the sharpness of his tone. Kayla couldn't put a finger on it, but a ripple of unease raced through her.

"Maybe," she said, trying to be non-committal. "Now will you please go? I have things to do."

As she shut the door behind him, she breathed deeply with relief. She wasn't a good liar. She knew where the signed originals were and she intended to retrieve them, along with whatever further information she could find.

There was one other option to find answers. The pages of the telephone book crackled sharply as she hastily flicked them over until she found what she needed. With the number in her mind, she shoved the book out of her way—its purpose served—and stabbed the buttons on the unoffending phone. She tapped an impatient rhythm with her foot as she waited for an answer. The receptionist was extremely unhelpful, and said Kayla must refer to his home number. Kayla looked it up then dialed.

"Elizabeth Carven, speaking."

"Can I speak to Mr Frederick Carven, please?" Kayla asked.

"I'm sorry, that is impossible. Who did you say was calling?" Elizabeth Carven asked.

"It's Kayla Mackenzie speaking. They told me at the office Mr Carven wasn't available, but I need to speak to him urgently."

"I'm sorry, you can't speak with Frederick. He passed away nine weeks ago. There was a fire at his office—everything was destroyed. Frederick was working late...he didn't get out." Elizabeth Carven's voice was barely audible.

Although she had rarely had brief dealings with her grandmother's solicitor, a sudden weight of grief and disappointment clenched her stomach. "Oh. I'm truly sorry for your loss, Mrs Carven. I didn't know. Could you please tell me who is dealing with all Mr Carven's work now? It is very important."

"I'm afraid all my husband's clients have been scattered amongst various firms," Elizabeth Carven replied.

"I see. Do you know who is handling the McLeod Family Trust?" Kayla asked.

"McLeod Family Trust? I think you have made a mistake, Ms Mackenzie. My husband never dealt with a McLeod Family Trust." The voice on the phone was breathy and hesitant.

Kayla suspected she was being lied to, but she didn't know why. "Mrs Carven, please, he was my grandmother's solicitor for years…and she was your friend from childhood…"

"I can't help you, Miss Mackenzie. I have nothing more to say. Goodbye," Elizabeth Carven said.

Kayla heard the click as the receiver was quietly laid down. The frustrating whirr of the dial tone filled her ears. Damn her. What was going on? Why did she deny her husband had been a trustee for her grandmother's trust? What was she trying to hide?

A tiny bundle of unease settled in her stomach. Elizabeth Carven's denial had un-nerved her. She was glad when Jessica arrived home for lunch and interrupted her morbid thoughts. Jessica made food then sat quietly opposite Kayla, waiting for her to talk.

Kayla bit into the fresh salad sandwich Jessica had made for her and chewed thoughtfully. "I think a visit to Uncle George is in order. With Frederick Carven dead, there is no-one else who would know the truth," she mused out loud.

"What about Phillip's edict?" Jessica asked.

"I'll ignore it. I'm sure it is just Phillip's over protective instincts coming to the fore. Uncle George has kidney troubles from the paraplegia caused in the accident, and Phillip still carries the guilt from that. Besides, the last thing I want to do is cause Uncle George any distress," Kayla said quietly.

After Jessica left to go back to work, Kayla snatched up her keys and headed across town through the searing heat to the retirement village where George Mitchell resided. She had always felt for Phillip, despite his prickly personality, because he had carried the heavy burden for a long time of his father's disability and the three deaths that night, and his guilt had been accentuated in recent years by his father's rapid decline in health. Not that anything in the past justified what he might now be doing to her, she was not going to let him stop her from talking to his father — either as a trustee, or as her Uncle George. She would protect Ainsley House, come what may.

The retirement home was classy. Inside, quiet elegance seeped from every corner, despite the lockable doors. The receptionist was very pleasant, but unhelpful.

"I'm sorry, Ms Mackenzie. I can't discuss Mr Mitchell, but I can give you his son's details, if that would help," the receptionist said.

"Thanks, but I have Phillip's details," Kayla replied She was sure there was something the receptionist wasn't telling her.

Now completely frustrated, and getting more confused by the minute with this strange turn of events, she returned to her car and sat for a long moment with the motor running, and cold air pumping from the air conditioner. She tried Phillip's mobile again, not even bothering to leave a message when it went to message bank.

She jumped at the sharp tap on her window. An elderly lady stood there, buffeted by the hot wind. Kayla wound the window down.

"I heard you asking after George Mitchell. A lovely man. He was my client for volunteer visiting for more than a year. His son moved him about ten weeks ago. George didn't have any say in it. The son and he had a barney here one morning, and George had a funny turn apparently. I was away. They took him to hospital, and next thing I heard was that he wasn't coming back," the woman said.

"I see. Do you know where they took him?" Kayla asked.

The woman pulled her clothes closer around her and nodded. "They moved him to that new flash place in Lightsview, that new development. I think it is called Weemala Nursing Home."

"Thank you..." Kayla said as she looked at the woman's name tag, "Miriam."

Why would George be moved to a higher dependency facility, and why would Phillip keep that fact from her, unless his health had unexpectedly deteriorated significantly? Perhaps she had underestimated Phillip's desire to protect his father from any unnecessary outside stresses.

* * * *

Nobody queried her at the new home when she asked to visit George Mitchell, but she found it slightly disconcerting to be taken through locked doors and down a long passage to his room.

He was sitting in his wheelchair, facing toward the window. He made no attempt to turn around when the nurse announced her.

"Uncle George," she said.

When he failed to acknowledge her, she almost crept across the room, concerned he was asleep. She slipped into the seat beside him and peered into his face. Her whole body cringed at what she saw, but she could not tear her gaze away from the ravaged man in front of her. He tried to smile and reached out with an unsteady hand to lay it on top of hers.

He tried to speak, half his mouth paralyzed, his face sagging and one eye partly closed. "My dear, my dear Kayla." His words were barely intelligible as he struggled to make the sounds with a mouth that no longer took commands from his brain.

"Oh, Uncle George," she wailed.

He shook his head and his eyes watered. "No matter…me. Must fix Carven's…" His mouth worked as he tried to compose more words.

Kayla's heart clenched with grief for this once intelligent, capable, articulate man who had always treated her with gentle fondness.

"House…mistake…" His hand clenched hers, and she could feel the papery skin tightening against hers as he tried to impart his message. "Phillip…papers…"

She squeezed his hand back. "I know, Uncle George. Phillip came to get your paperwork to sort out the issue with Ainsley House…"

"No! Phillip did…"

"What the hell are you doing here, Kayla?" Phillip yelled. "I told you not to visit, not to upset him. See what you've done. Just look at him."

She had jumped at Phillip's unexpected entrance and furious outburst, but now she turned her attention back to her uncle. He was crying and flapping his hands in her direction, his mouth working, trying to make understandable sounds.

"Not…Carven's fault…" George said, as he pointed a shaky finger in Phillip's direction. "My son…"

As Phillip put his arm around his father's shoulders, the older man tried to shrug him off. With his good hand George pushed at his son's arm. He got more and more agitated.

"No...will not... Kayla...be careful...not..." He continued to shove at Phillip's restraining arms, his damaged mouth working hard to form words as tears poured down his cheeks. "Sorry...I couldn't stop..."

Phillip strode to the door and began yelling. "Nurse...Nurse!"

At Phillip's shout, a heavyset male nurse entered with a syringe in hand. He sank it deftly into the old man's arm. George stared up at her with tears streaming down his face and the shadow of fear in his eyes. He reached out to her with his good hand until it fell limp at the side of the chair under the effect of the drug.

Kayla jumped from her chair and ran out of the room, unable to stand the scene before her a moment longer. In the passage she stopped and leaned her head against the wall, as her stomach churned with grief, and distress balled in her throat threatening to choke her. Hot tears scalded her cheeks.

"Now you see why, little cousin. Why I said no visiting."

She didn't make any attempt to meet his gaze. "You didn't tell me he was that bad... When did he deteriorate so much? Why wasn't I told?" she said, her tone accusing.

"As his health is none of your business, I don't have to tell you, Kayla."

"But he is my uncle *and* my trustee. I am entitled to know," she cried.

"No, Kayla, as long as your trust is managed adequately, you are entitled to nothing. Now he has had to be sedated for his own good, and that is an extra stress on his body. You caused that, Kayla. You also distressed yourself seeing him like that without warning or support."

"I'm sorry, Phillip. I didn't realize."

"Sorry isn't good enough, Kayla. You are just as willful as you were when you dated Peter. It isn't any wonder to me that Peter did what he did or that Great Aunt Eloise tied everything up in trusts until you turn twenty-five. But it seems it should have been later, as you are still acting like an irresponsible teenager — selfish and narcissistic."

"We all have our faults, Phillip. We all make mistakes. Even you!" she said in a subdued shout.

"Don't go there, Kayla..." Phillip warned.

"Why, Phillip? Don't you like being reminded that I am an orphan because of your mistake?" she asked.

They glared at each other with just inches between them. The air around them sizzled with rage, grief, and regret.

As soon as the words left her mouth, Kayla wished them back. Just because she was hurt by what she had seen and shamed by her defiance of her cousin, there was no justification for lashing out with such cruelty. "I'm sorry. I shouldn't have said that."

"Forget it, Kayla. Nothing you can say on that subject can wound me any more than what has been said before," Phillip muttered.

She couldn't meet his gaze, knowing it would be filled now with betrayal because his anger at her had exploded under her accusation and his self-imposed guilt.

"Just stay away from my father. He is a very ill man and he is my responsibility." Phillip advanced on her, his expression hard and unforgiving. "Anything to do with your trust and Ainsley House will need to come through me. Do you understand, Kayla? I am now in *control* of your trust. Behave yourself or I will make things very difficult for you in the next few months."

She nodded, unable to reply to his uncompromising statement. She turned and hurried down the corridor. Her breathing was jerky and her throat tight with unshed tears. The lump in her stomach churned and roiled. She felt so alone. She knew Phillip was justifiably angry with her because of her unannounced visit to his father, but he seemed unnecessarily harsh. She wasn't at all happy with him having control of her trust — she was not even sure if it was legal for him to take over from Uncle George. She was acutely aware she faced two formidable enemies. Either way, she was unlikely to win, but she would not go down without a fight.

She struggled to walk normally as tremors of shock and fear rattled through her body. When she glanced back over her shoulder, Phillip was standing just outside the door glaring in her direction.

When she reached the car, she leaned for a moment with her head on the roof. The confrontation with Uncle George had been traumatic enough without the threats from Phillip, and all the time at the back of her mind was Abrial and Pierre's silence. How had the closure of the retreat been managed without them contacting her? She cradled her head on her arms, closed her eyes, and took a couple of calming breaths.

His touch seared through her. Every nerve jangled. She jerked her head up and jumped sideways. Her hands already up in a defensive gesture as she spun to face him.

"Sorry. I didn't mean to startle you," Wade said.

He stood there smiling, small lines radiating from the corners of his eyes, accentuating the depth of the golden color. Despite the heat, Wade appeared cool and comfortable. Kayla drew in a deep breath. The tousled hair and designer stubble was set off by a crisp white, button-through shirt, open at the neck, and hanging out over a pair of beige cargo shorts. His shapely calves were bare, his feet tucked into a pair of casual loafers.

"It's you," she said, trying to pull together what few remnants of composure she had left.

His lawyer stood a few feet behind him.

"Who were you expecting? You looked petrified," Wade asked.

"My cousin, Phillip. He threatened me, and Uncle George is…" That was all she could get out as the vision of her stroke-ridden uncle snapped her reserves of strength. Hot tears spilled down her cheeks and she was helpless to stop them. She cursed her weakness and wiped them away with sharp swipes, but they wouldn't stop.

"Is that the Phillip Mitchell who works for Neil Moore?" Wade asked.

She nodded.

Wade frowned. "He's your cousin?"

She nodded again.

He turned to his lawyer. "David, I think you should go ahead and try to see George Mitchell. I will look after Ms Mackenzie."

Kayla glanced at David. "No, you can't. Phillip won't let you in there. He just threw me out and warned me to stay away. He's still in there. Uncle George has been sedated because he was so upset by my visit," she said.

Wade looked across at the entrance to the home then back to his lawyer. "Never mind, David. Just take the car back to the office. I am taking Miss Mackenzie home because I don't think she is in any state to drive right now."

"I'll be fine, Wade. Thank you, but I will manage," she said.

He held out his hand. "No you don't, Kayla. Now hand over the keys."

She stared at him, fear nibbling at the edges of her reason. "I can't, Wade."

His smile faded. "Can't what? Trust me or consort with the enemy?"

"Both," she said.

His laughter burst from him in a rich melodic rumble. "Oh, Kayla. I know you feel cornered right now, but even though I own and plan to knock Ainsley House down, I am *not* your enemy."

She glared up at him through tear filled eyes. "Well, if you are not my enemy then why not just abandon your plans to knock my house down?"

He reached out now and took the keys from her numb fingers. "I have a great deal invested in that property and a binding contract to build the convention center. I have friends who have invested in the project. They are big players and have high expectations that I will deliver on time. If I withdraw now, I will damage both my bank balance, I also destroy my reputation—and I do not want Edgar Seville breathing down my neck, looking for his kind of justice," he said.

"So you *are* the enemy. I know this whole deal is not quite legal, but I don't know how or who yet." Her words were meant to be a warning and she was pleased Wade heeded her words.

"No, Kayla. I promise you I will not do anything illegal. I have my lawyer investigating every angle and if the destruction of Ainsley House proves illegal, I *will* halt the project, regardless of the cost to me."

Almost mesmerized by the liquid warmth of his voice, she let him take her arm and guide her to the passenger seat of her car. In the small confines of her hatchback, she was immediately aware of his closeness, his scent, and the warmth radiating from his body, but she was too shaken to really appreciate it. She stared ahead and took deep breaths, trying to recapture her equilibrium before they reached their destination.

There was an awkward pause as they came to a standstill in the driveway and Wade turned the ignition off. They both hesitated in a long silence, filled with expectation, sexual tension, and wanting.

He turned to her. "Kayla, I..." He fell silent and handed over the keys. "I'd better call a taxi," he said as he pulled out his mobile.

She reached across the car and curled her hand around his phone. "Wade, do you want to come inside?" She wanted him and intended to have him, regardless of the huge specter of the demolition that lay between them.

"Yes, Kayla, I do," he said.

He didn't touch her as he followed her to the door and inside the flat, but as soon as the door clicked shut, he latched onto her waist and pulled her hard against him. "This time, Ms Mackenzie, we will do it properly. Now where's the bedroom?"

She giggled and pointed. He swept her into his arms and strode across the living area and into her room. Without ceremony, he dumped her on the unmade bed and began to strip. She draped herself on the mattress and studied him as he removed each item of clothing—the broad chest, prominent pecs, and smooth, flat abdomen, the deep navel, and the trail of hairs that shadowed his skin to the waistband of his trunks and beyond.

Her body hummed in anticipation of his touch. Satin skin against the velvety warmth of his body, sexual sparks firing up red hot embers. She sighed with expectation. He hesitated, both thumbs hooked in the waistband of his underwear. He watched her. She waited for what seemed like an eternity, then when she was almost squirming with need, he moved toward her with slow, lithe movements. The fire in her pussy sparked and sizzled. Wade smiled — a smile that promised more sensual delights to come.

She watched him, barely able to control her breathing. Wade leaned into her. The movement sent his intoxicating aromatic mix of aftershave and raw, vibrant male wafting over her. He kissed her mouth, a slow gliding of a tender caress over her lips. She sank deep into the mattress as with one smooth movement Wade straddled her. She reached for his trunks, but he removed her hand and tucked it under her hip.

"Uh uh uhh," he scolded, in a deep sexy rumble. "Patience, Ms Mackenzie."

She stared up at him, soaking up his aroma.

When she remained passive, he reached forward and began to undo her buttons, one at a time. As each inch of flesh was exposed, he lightly smothered it with kisses. When her bra was fully revealed, he reached under her and with quick precision, unclipped it. With reverent care, he slid it above her breasts and lowered his head. She gasped at the burst of sensation that roared through her body when his mouth encased her nipple and sucked strongly. She moaned and lifted her hips. She could feel his erection, hard and hot, pressing into her abdomen when he leaned forward.

While he continued to suck her other breast, he eased her bra and shirt back until she could slip her arms out. His hair tickled her bare skin then brushed lightly over the swell of her breasts as he layered kiss after kiss down her chest and over the soft curve of her abdomen.

"Wade, please take me. I want you."

He chuckled. "Such impatience, Ms Mackenzie," he said. Now he unclipped her shorts and with dexterous ease, pushed them and her knickers down over her hips. She wriggled them down and kicked them off.

"Mmmmm, very nice," Wade murmured, and eased himself down until he was semi lying between her parted legs.

He pushed her legs farther apart and sank his head into the apex of hot, wet flesh. He ran his tongue around the layers before he sucked on her inner lips. She felt the fiery tingling of arousal flash through her when he slid his tongue up under the hood and flicked it lightly on her clit. Then his tongue was dipping into her, caressing the skin at the entrance. She moaned and whimpered under his thoroughly intimate ministrations. She felt something slip inside her, she guessed two or three fingers. He moved them in and out and turned them clockwise first then back, anticlockwise. Her pussy clenched and spasmed in response. He moved up and over her, but she barely felt the change from his fingers to his cock, as he slipped all the way in. He lay there waiting for a moment before he began to caress her clit to climax. She clamped her legs around his waist and met his thrusts with tilts of her hips.

A trail of tingling pinpricks scattered all around right down to her butt. She clenched her cheeks together and pulled the sensation deep inside, where it burst into a mass of needle sharp points of pleasure. She bucked under its dominating rush through her body, and Wade moved faster, his body sinking deep into hers. He groaned and he exploded inside her at the moment she gave in to her own release, which rushed over her all the way to her head. Every hair stood on end and trembled under the onslaught. Her body bucked and writhed with an agony of pleasure. Slowly the sensation faded, and they collapsed together in a tangled, sweaty heap. The only sound in the room was the rasp of their uneven breathing as they both fought for control.

"Wade, I…"

He put his finger to her lips. "Shhhh, Kayla. Take this for what it is—two people who want each other. We both know the fight for Ainsley House is far from over, and there is no future for us, whoever wins, so let's just enjoy what we have now—a physical relationship with no emotional involvement—and deal with the consequences later."

She nodded. "It just sounds so…I don't know…calculating."

Wade smiled. "It is. I want you and you want me—that's all there is to it."

"I'm not so sure, Wade" she said quietly. "Anyway, Jessica will be home soon. Do you want first shower?"

He lay back and closed his eyes. "You go first. I'm going to grab a cat nap."

He was snoring gently when she returned and he started when she touched his shoulder. "Your turn. Do you want a coffee?"

"Yeah, that would be good," he said, as he disappeared into the bathroom.

She had coffee and lamingtons set out on the breakfast bar when he joined her.

He slid onto the stool opposite her. "Do you want to talk about this morning?" he asked.

The urge was strong, but she shook her head, unable to get past the issue of trust. She felt disorientated by the intimacy of the sex and the divisiveness of their conflicting goal.

"Okay. Well, I will update you on what we have found out. It's not much and probably not in your favor. Firstly, David checked the trust deed. The copy you have given us has not been witnessed, so it won't stand up in court. You will need the original. Unfortunately, the will — while it is a bona-fide copy — doesn't help you much because the trust overrides it."

Kayla felt her stomach sink. Her heart clenched then beat faster.

"Also, it appears that even if you find the original trust deed and it is all signed, because it has never been registered with the appropriate government department it might also struggle to stand up in court."

"So my case is sinking fast then?" she muttered.

He reached out and embraced her trembling hands with his large, warm ones. He leaned closer and she saw flecks of warm golden amber moderate the expression in his eyes.

"I'm sorry. It's not going in your favor at the moment. I have asked David to have an expert analyze that signature though."

He completely enclosed her hands in the warm embrace of his that was both comforting and teasingly disturbing. She wanted to caress the length of his thumb with her own, to feel the strength under hers.

Her mouth was dry as she tried to speak. "I did not expect you to go to that extent for me, Wade. Why have you?" she asked.

He reached out and gently brushed tendrils of hair from her face and tucked them behind her ear. His trailing fingers left a fiery trail over her chilled skin.

"Kayla, I have wanted you since university. I still want you, but it's more than that. It is your passion, your obvious love of that old house… Something in what you have been saying has touched a chord," he said. "And I would not like to see anyone get a bum deal from someone unscrupulous."

Heat slid up her neck and burst onto her cheeks.

He smiled now, and ran his finger over the heated skin and down over her bottom lip.

"Besides, I've done my research—you're a very talented art restoration specialist, an artist in your own right, and a savvy business woman. To be honest, I am surprised the retreat has been closed. It had a gilt edged reputation. You would have no need to lie," he said.

"Thank you." She lowered her head and with concentrated effort attacked the lamington she didn't really want.

"In addition, Kayla, I am a man of integrity. I will not knowingly aid and abet criminal actions." He smiled at her, a wide, genuine smile. "Maybe because of my father or despite him—I am not sure—but I intend to stay on the right side of the law."

"Well, your plans of demolishing Ainsley House will be criminal in more ways than one. Firstly it is my property, but secondly it is a heritage icon in South Australia and also a center for art and culture, especially for local artists," she replied, unable to keep the sense of desperation and anger she felt out of her tone.

His response to the hard edge of her words was mild, but blunt. "Then you have to get proof, Kayla. Solid proof," he stated.

She sighed. "I don't know who is behind all this. I can't rule anyone out—my managers, my cousin, my trustees, you, or your investors. I have been ambushed by an unknown enemy."

He had his head cocked slightly to the side, his expression serious, but expectant, as he waited for her to continue.

"Phillip has been cruel and threatening and tried to prevent me from consulting with Uncle George. Uncle George tried to tell me something before Phillip turned up, but…" Her throat tightened and her voice cracked. She looked up at the man opposite her. "Wade, it was awful. I knew George was unwell, but not to that extent, and he seemed distressed about my cousin's arrival at the home—even frightened of him. I can't help but be suspicious of my own cousin."

"So, if George Mitchell isn't capable of fulfilling his duties as trustee, who has been dealing with the trust?" Wade asked.

"Well, the other trustee is dead—has been for about eight weeks or so, and his wife won't talk to me. Phillip told me he has taken control of my trust fund as proxy for Uncle George."

Wade frowned at that, but made no comment. "And have you tracked down your managers and caretakers yet?"

"I have tracked down my caretakers." Again her voice cracked and betrayed her deep distress. "Apparently the caretakers were driven off with a big payout and moved to Queensland. Joan is dead and Bill is now in a nursing home. Joan's daughter blames me. I have heard nothing of my managers. I have tried ringing Pierre and Abrial every day and sent emails, but nothing has come in response."

"You were close to them?" he asked.

"Yes, they were more like friends than employees. I was going to ask them to become partners in the Retreat, once I had control of the trust."

Wade took hold of her hands again. He squeezed them firmly and fixed her with a stern stare. "Are you sure they wouldn't do the dirty on you? Perhaps they thought they were doing too much for too little…"

"No, I don't believe Pierre would ever betray me…" Her breath caught on a sob, but she squashed it down. "Besides, how would he have got hold of the house? None of it makes sense."

"Had you broached the idea of them being partners?" he asked.

Kayla nodded. "We had discussed it and what it would mean for all of us."

"Well, it doesn't sound likely, but it is still possible they have done the dirty on you. Anyway, I have David digging around, so we'll see what he turns up." Wade glanced at his watch. "I'd better go. I have a meeting in an hour." He put his mug in the sink, gave her a lingering kiss then headed out of the door.

* * * *

Barely half an hour later, Jessica bounced in the door. "Kayla, I have a way you can stop him knocking the house down. You can put a caveat on the property. The boss at work reckons you would have enough evidence with the will and the trust deed. Then Wade will have to go to court before he can demolish the house."

Kayla stared at her friend for a moment then booted up her laptop. Fifteen minutes later, armed with information about caveats from the web, she made a snap decision. She would put a caveat on the house, check the balance of her trust fund, then fly to Port Lincoln to retrieve her grandmother's papers. While she was there, she would track down Pierre and Abrial.

Chapter Three

As soon as Jessica had left for work the next morning, Kayla booked her flight, collected her documents, made an appointment with a JP at the Attorney General's Office, and called Neil Moore before she headed for the city.

"Neil Moore, please?" she asked the receptionist.

When she got Neil on the line, he was puzzled at her call.

"Kayla. Phillip's not here," he said.

"That's okay, it's you I want to speak to," she replied.

She heard Neil clear his throat. "What can I do you for?" he asked.

"Who has been looking after my trust fund since George became incapable?" she demanded to know.

"Why are you asking, Kayla?"

"Just answer the question, Neil."

Neil cleared his throat before he spoke. "Phillip has been doing the leg work since George officially retired six months ago. George has just been overseeing and signing, but I don't understand what you mean by *incapable*," he said.

Kayla heard the rise in his voice and suspected he was a little unnerved by her question. He was, after all, the boss and all responsibility stopped with him.

"So you are not aware that George had a massive stroke ten weeks ago that rendered him unable to talk, partially blind, and definitely unable to sign documents with a legible signature?" she announced bluntly. She was hoping to shock him.

His indrawn breath made a hiss on the line. "No, I was not aware. If this is the case, it has serious ramifications, Kayla. Phillip's taken some leave, so I can't ask him."

"*Really*. Do you have access to my fund balance, Neil?"

"Ummmm. What are you implying, Kayla?" he asked.

"Nothing yet. I just want a balance. Can you get it?" she asked.

"Give me half an hour and I'll get back to you," he said. There was a muffled click as he hung up.

Impatient to put her plan into action, Kayla headed into the city. She collected the appropriate forms at the Land Titles Office and walked in the stifling heat to the Attorney General's Office. Once the Justice of the Peace had determined she had reasonable cause to place the caveat on the property, he assisted her to fill in the form, and made sure she had all the required details and paperwork. With it all completed, she returned to the Land Titles Office.

It took ages to get the caveat lodged and she traveled home feeling edgy about what she had done without warning Wade.

It was nearly six when Neil called back.

"Kayla, I haven't been able to get a balance because the file is password protected and Phillip has changed the password on the internet banking for your main account. Phillip is on leave and he's not answering his phone."

"I want an answer, Neil. Get one of your IT gurus to unprotect the file and work out the passwords," Kayla snapped.

"I can try, Kayla, but wouldn't it be better to wait for Phillip to get back?"

"No. I don't want Phillip to know. Now get me that balance, Neil, or I will be seeking legal advice."

"Keep calm, Kayla. I am sure there is nothing untoward with your balance or the file being protected, more than Phillip being overzealous," Neil responded in a soothing tone.

"Get the balance, Neil." She hung up without waiting for a response from him.

* * * *

The flight to Port Lincoln was turbulent, with silver forks splitting the dark clouds as the flashes of lightning came down through them. It was still and sultry as she headed in along the highway. Boston Bay was an iron-gray reflection of the brooding clouds gathered on the horizon as it laid mirror calm before the storm.

The house gave off a distinctly deserted feel as she drove through the gates and up the unraked gravel drive. She put down her suitcase and fumbled for the keys. The small tingle of unease that had dogged her since the auction became long grasping tentacles of fear that squeezed her stomach, interrupted the rhythm of her heart, and burnt through her chest.

Despite knowing it was closed, she had in her heart not quite accepted that it would really be closed. The life wrenched out from a thriving hub of people and art.

The house was gloomy, exceedingly hot and stuffy, and eerily empty. Silence enveloped her — an echoing silence of an empty building. She turned on the lights and the air-conditioning before she ran up the stairs to Abrial and Pierre's flat. Out of habit she knocked on the door. It swung open. Even though she knew it was pointless, she called their names. "Abrial? Pierre? Where are you?"

Silence. She moved cautiously into the entrance hall. The flat was empty of furniture. Her heart thudded, fear wrapped itself around her like an invisible cloak as she tried to find some sense in what she was confronted with. She tried calling all the numbers again — again to be greeted by the slightly artificial voices from the voice mail of those she sought to find

None of it made sense. Why had Abrial and Pierre just left without contacting her? The answer to her question seemed obvious, but not one she could accept. Even now, with evidence that they had indeed gone, she could not accept that they were behind this terrible situation. She locked the door and sat on the front steps in the ethereal light of the pre-storm gloom. She was hot, sweaty, and trembling with the beginnings of rage and panic. She finally had to accept that the retreat was closed and everyone was gone.

She went through her purse and pulled out a couple of business cards. She dialed the number on one — a previous student.

"Caleb, its Kayla. Do you know what happened here at the retreat? It is all closed up and Pierre and Abrial are gone."

"Don't know much, Kayla. Just that it was open one day, closed the next. I think Pierre and Abrial did a bunk actually. Some bailiff guy let us in to get our work and all the furniture was gone from their flat."

She choked back tears. Her throat closed over and she struggled to draw in air.

"Kayla?"

"Yes, I'm here, Caleb. I just can't believe it. I have to go. Thanks for the information."

She hung up as the tears poured down her cheeks. Their betrayal cut deep. She had often felt alone since her grandmother had died, but nothing like how she felt now that her rock—her one stable place in the ever revolving world of business—was shattered. Her friends were gone and her trust with it. She swiped the tears away and choked down her sobs. She needed to be strong, to get to the bottom of this.

Unshed tears burnt the back of her eyes. Irritated with her weakness, she gathered up her bag and headed into town to the office of the local paper. Perhaps Simon, artist and owner-editor of the local paper, could fill her in.

He wasn't smiling as she was shown into his office, but he indicated the chair in front of his desk. "What brings you here, Kayla? I thought you had cut your ties with Lincoln."

"What do you mean, Simon? Cut my ties?" she asked.

"Well, you shut the retreat, cut poor Abrial and Pierre off at the knees, and shunted poor old Joan and Bill onto the street. What the hell are you up to, Kayla—chasing money like that wily, grasping cousin of yours? I know the property is worth a mint and I heard you had sold it for development, but I never thought I would see the day you would betray your heritage or your grandmother. I would never have thought you so greedy or hungry for money," he said. His words were clipped and sharp — an accusation with no expectation of innocence on her part.

His outright accusations cut deep into her soul.

She stood up and leaned over his desk. "I did *not* shut the retreat or shunt anyone into the street. I would *never* betray my grandmother. I loved her and the house. Now everyone is gone — Joan and Bill to Queensland and Pierre and Abrial have just disappeared. I don't understand, Simon. How this could be happening?" she questioned.

Simon frowned. "What do you mean, you don't know how this could be happening?"

She heard the sarcasm in his tone and resented it deeply, but she had no-one else to turn to who might have some answers.

"Just what I said, Simon. Tuesday, two of Grandma Eloise's paintings came up for auction at a charity function. After I bought them, I confronted the man who donated them — Wade Faxton — and he told me he had inherited Ainsley House..." Now the tears fell and she didn't even try to stop them. She couldn't.

Simon seemed taken aback at her distress. "Oh come on, Kayla. I have a letter signed by you that says you are closing the retreat because it's not financially viable and the land would be better utilized for a development."

Before she could protest, he slapped a file on the desk and removed some papers.

"Here, I have the letter you sent to me so I could put a notice in the paper. Here is the paper with the article I ran." He shoved them across the desk at her.

She stared in horror at the letter and the article. She studied the signature at the bottom of the letter. It was almost an exact copy of hers, but she knew it wasn't. She knew she had not sent this letter.

Kayla tossed the papers onto the desk. She glared up at Simon MacDonald. A sense of injustice and bitterness rose up like bile in her throat.

"Damn lies. For goodness sake, Simon, you could have done me the decency of speaking to me personally and worse still, you should have known I would never ever do or say something like that. You were my father's friend, damn it. Why didn't you contact me? A phone call? An email? Anything, except to believe these lies of me," she cried.

"I sent you several emails, but got no answer. Silence from you only confirmed the letter," he snapped back at her.

"Well, I never got your emails. I knew nothing about this until Tuesday. Nobody can touch Ainsley House. It is locked up in a trust, which will see it go on for perpetuity as an artist's retreat and museum for the people of Port Lincoln. I only have the right of tenancy, not ownership." She stood now, exceedingly pleased to see Simon's mouth gape open. "I don't think we have anything further to discuss. Goodbye, Simon," she said, as she spun on her heel and marched toward the door.

"Kayla. We need to talk about this," Simon called after her.

She heard him as she stormed out of the room but chose to ignore him. To be betrayed in such a manner by someone so close cut her deep, leaving her soul raw and exposed.

She was being framed—manipulated by forces unknown and beyond her control. If she couldn't trust Simon Macdonald... If even he believed she had sold her grandmother and friends out for money, what was left for her?

She tried calling Pierre again, but only his wonderfully French accented voice reached out to her through his voicemail. She disconnected with a click.

She sat in her car in the shade of the Moreton Bay Fig trees and stared unseeing out across the bay, as she tried to make sense of the bizarre nightmare she found herself trapped in. She needed those missing emails, perhaps the answer laid in cyber space. She grabbed up her laptop and marched back across the street to the local computer shop.

He was ready to close as she laid her computer on his counter. "I need to know two things…"

"I was just shutting," he replied.

"Sorry, not until you answer my questions. I will pay for your time. This is your business, is it not?" she asked.

The man nodded.

"Good. What I need to know is if it is possible for someone to hack into my email and divert emails — say, of a certain type — without me being aware of it? And second the question, has it been done to my account and can I retrieve the emails that have been diverted?" She took a breath and waited for his reply.

He gave her the weirdest look of stunned surprise then reached for her computer. He signed into her email when she gave him the necessary access information, pulled up a stool, and stared into her screen. She waited in silence aware of the faint click of the keys as he worked.

Fifteen minutes later he peered over the screen at her.

"To answer your questions — yes, you can hack into an email account without the owner being aware.

Two — yes, your account has been hacked into. Three — certain emails — mostly based on address or subject line — have been diverted to an email address, prince-charming at castle dot com, dot au. Fourth — yes, they can be retrieved. I have done so and placed them in a folder label 'Retrieved'. Is there anything else you would like to know?" he asked, as he closed her laptop.

She opened her purse. "No, thank you. You have been most helpful." She handed him her card. "What is a fair price for your time? One hundred dollars?" she asked.

"That's a bit much, Miss."

"No, it's worth that for answers. Take out one hundred, and we'll call it a deal," she replied.

Unable to cope with any more today, she collected some staples and a takeaway before she returned to Ainsley House. She changed into a thin cheesecloth sun frock and settled on the balcony with her food and her laptop. She gave a sigh of despair. Her world had been turned upside down and she didn't know how to fix it. She rocked gently in her grandmother's chair. She stared out over the ocean and let her thoughts run riot as she tried to work out just how she came to be in this position. There were no obvious answers, but she was determined to find out the truth and who was behind this debacle. She would save her heritage, find her friends and restore her integrity. The stress of the last few days had drained her natural energy, but here on the balcony she felt at home and despite the shuffling of ideas in her mind she gradually relaxed. Her eyelids drooped. She dragged them open.

* * * *

Awareness returned slowly with the feel of Grandma Eloise's chair beneath her. Below her, the azure blue of Boston Bay had faded into lavender, gray and midnight blue. All around, lights twinkled on the sea, creating a picturesque fairyland under the thunderclouds that gathered on the horizon and only the faint glow from distant streetlights broke the impending gloom. The heat was oppressive. Thunder rumbled ominously around the bay and she suddenly felt very lonely — a different kind of loneliness to the one she often felt on her travels — this was deeper, more emotional. Where there should have been a comfortable feeling of belonging — of coming home — instead, every nerve in her body sizzled and jumped in a chaotic sense of uncertainty and fear.

She disposed of her mostly uneaten roll and opened her laptop. Firstly, she opened her internet banking account for the retreat. The balance was zero. An icy flow of disbelief flowed through her. No. How could they? Why *would* they? She had loved Pierre and Abrial like family.

She logged out and accessed the folder of diverted emails. There were five from Bill and her heart lurched at the painful contents. The impassioned pleas from a man suddenly deprived of the second love of his life and his appeal to her as almost a daughter. The last one was short and sharp, filled with broken-hearted bitterness. There were six from Simon — all angry, accusing, and full of recriminations. There were quite a few from past, current and already pre-booked students — mostly angry and frustrated. There were none from Abrial and Pierre. She went through every one again. One of Simon's emails mentioned her friends but all it said was he had seen nothing of Abrial or Pierre since just before the school closed and what had she done to sever that arrangement so thoroughly that they had even left town without a goodbye?

A nagging fear throbbed deeper. Something was very wrong with Abrial and Pierre's absence. She could not—would not—believe that they were in any way responsible for any of this and she was certain they would not have just accepted a letter of closure. What had been done or said to them that they had left without any attempt to even contact her? Surely somehow they would have made contact, even if she was in the wilds of the Scottish highlands.

It was time to explore the rest of the house and see if she could make sense of it all before she turned in. She didn't even realize she was tiptoeing down the stairs until the third from the bottom cracked loudly in protest and she flinched and looked around. She smiled then, despite her current unpleasant situation. How could she have forgotten it? She'd always tried to avoid it during her tempestuous teenage years, to escape her grandmother's wrath when creeping home in the early hours of the morning after a wild night with Peter. Her grandmother had hated Peter with vengeance because he had killed her only two surviving children while driving drunk, the youngest being Kayla's mother.

She switched on the standard lamp and flung open the windows. Not a breath of wind stirred. The air smelled of the sea, and periodic flashes of lightning lit the sky. Kayla turned away and searched the house. The art studio was neat and clean, but unfinished canvases sat on easels and a pile of canvases were stacked against the wall. She instantly recognized Pierre's brush strokes and choice of shades and colors on the larger one. She touched it. The oil paint was long dry. The other painting was an abstract and could have been anyone's. She moved through the gallery, the gift shop and the tea room. All were clean and in order, but deserted. As the tightness in her chest grew, she walked through to the museum. It was a big, airy room facing the sea. She loved this room with its polished wooden floors, huge leather lounges and glass cabinets. The hours she had spent here on rainy days dusting Grandma Eloise's treasures were fond memories she cherished. Her favorite was the doll collection. She curled up on the dusty floorboards and carefully drew the first doll out of the glass-fronted cabinet. With a corner of her dress, she lovingly dusted the porcelain face and fluffed out the antique lace gown. The outside world receded and she was once again a child. Tears fell for what had been and for what she had been lost.

It was an effort, but she pulled herself out of her nostalgic self-pity and replaced the doll before she went to check the office. The filing cabinets still held all the accounts from the retreat, but the desk was starkly clear. She ruffled through the drawers but found nothing unusual. Then she saw it. A large black briefcase concealed behind the filing cabinet. She pulled it out and laid it on the desk. It was locked. She grabbed up the letter opener and with surprising ease, jimmied the locks open. It was jammed full of documents. She picked up the first. The title registered and a shiver raced through her — Faxton Constructions Profit and Loss Statement. She shuffled through the rest of the contents. They all belonged to Faxton Constructions. She sank into the chair. Her hands trembled as she stared at the papers she held. With her mind scrambling to make sense of what she was seeing, she shuffled through the remaining documents. Most of them related to Ainsley House and the planned convention center. She could see from the balances the project was huge. She stared at the blueprints and was stunned by what was planned.

"What the hell are you doing here?"

His roar raced across her nerves, ripping her rudely from her thoughts.

A scream of pure terror tore from her throat as she leaped to her feet and spun around to face the intruder.

Wade Faxton loomed, poised, ready to pounce.

She stood stock still with a sheaf of papers held protectively across her breasts and glared at the man in front of her.

"What are you up to, Kayla Mackenzie? Spying? Trying to find evidence of wrong-doing? How dare you? I thought we had an understanding. Put those papers down and leave," he shouted.

She lifted her chin in a gesture of defiance and glared up at him. "This is *my* house, Wade, regardless of what your papers say. I am *not* leaving," she pronounced loudly.

A hard lump weighed heavy in the pit of her stomach. She was highly aware of her predicament. Her nerves sizzled to critical pitch. He would be perfectly capable of overpowering her if he chose.

"You didn't even tell me you were coming here. Why, Kayla? You sleep with me then don't even bother to tell me you are moving into my house. I thought we had an understanding to work on this situation together." His voice was calm and composed, belying the hard accusing glare that blazed its way over her lightly clad body.

Kayla felt naked—physically and emotionally. This *was* her house and she wished she had worn something more substantial. But then she wasn't expecting company either. "I wasn't spying. I thought it was Pierre's!"

His eyebrows knitted tightly over glittering eyes. His words ground out past straight white teeth, but Kayla noticed his anger was not quite obliterating the sensual fullness of his mouth.

"The first document would have cleared that up. You've been right through them, haven't you? What did you hope to find? Evidence of illegal activity by the gangster's son? Something you can use to bring me down? Well, now you know. I need this development. I need the cash. Payment of my late father's debts has left me skint, okay. If I lose this deal, I lose everything. Happy now that you know my deepest darkest secret?" he snarled.

"Wade, I'm sorry. I know I was snooping, but I must save Ainsley House however I can." She was almost whimpering.

He shook his head. "I thought better of you, Kayla. I never expected you to invade my privacy like you have. I trusted you."

"Ainsley House belongs to the McLeod Family Trust. See these? These are my grandmother's…" She pointed to the paintings. "And these are mine. Do you understand, Wade? They're mine. See here. See my name on the bottom? Kayla Mackenzie. They belong to me, not you. I will use any means possible to get this house back. I warned you. I told you bedding me would not change my mind."

He prowled forward, deliberate footsteps crunching on the floorboards. Kayla glanced briefly outside. Plump heavy raindrops now splattered the windows, their perfect shape distorted beyond recognition on impact. Surely he wasn't going to throw her out in this. She could hear his breathing now, shallow and fast—fueled by anger—and smell his scent, a heady mixture of aftershave and potent male that almost overwhelmed her fear. It beckoned her, trapped her breath in tiny gasps from lungs restricted by apprehension, both of his anger and her response to him.

She drew on the residual strength and anger that remained with her after reading the emails this evening and stood tall and straight. She wasn't going to be bullied.

"Until you prove otherwise, this is *my* house and *you* have no business here," he stated bluntly.

The tiniest flexing of muscles and a tightening of his jaw warned her. She backed away even as he closed his hand over her arm.

"I believe the exit is this way," he growled, and propelled her forward with the weight of his own momentum.

Kayla had no choice but to move in the direction he dictated, her bare feet shuffling on the boards.

Perspiration trickled between her breasts. Her nipples stood out starkly against the thin material. "Don't do this, Wade," she cried.

Overhead, thunder rattled and moaned. Iridescent flashes of lightning formed a kaleidoscope of shadows and eerie electrical light. Despite the heat, Kayla shivered.

"Out!" he shouted, thrusting her across the wide verandah and down the steps.

All around the world vibrated with the brutal force of thunder. Huge drops of rain smacked against her exposed skin. Kayla jumped as a fork of lightning ripped through the darkness, illuminating everything in silvery gray as it grounded itself in the middle of the lawn.

They stared at each other. His eyes appeared to fill with searing chips of dry ice that burnt into her soul. Diamantes of water dripped from his dark hair and ran in silken rivulets down his cheeks, highlighting the beard shadow on his jaw. Kayla stared, fascinated, her fingers twitched with the desire to brush them away. The moisture on her skin sizzled under the palm of his hand and Kayla stirred restlessly against the familiar ache his touch evoked. His grip loosened. Their awareness of each other cocooned them from the tempest of the storm. She swayed closer. A tiny moan forced its way past her lips. The collision with his body heat ignited a heady detonation of need that shattered the spell.

Kayla jerked back and shook the rain from her eyes. "I'm *not* leaving. Do what you want, but I'm sleeping in my grandmother's bed tonight!" she shouted at him.

Another flash of blue fire from the sky dove for the ground. The boom from accompanying thunder burst over their heads. They both crouched.

"Inside, Kayla, before we get hit," he yelled.

They sprinted up the steps and into the house. Wade shut the French doors against the storm before turning to her.

They stared at each other, awareness sizzling between them, smothering the fury and frustration that consumed them both.

"Damn you, Kayla," Wade muttered.

"I'm *not* going away, Wade. I'm sorry you're having financial troubles. I'm sorry I snooped, but I have to know what happened. My managers have disappeared — all their belongings are gone, all the money in the account is gone. It looks bad, but I am struggling to believe they would do this to me or even how they would do this. I loved them like family…better than family."

He frowned now. "It is often those we love most who would, and do, often hurt us the worst. Maybe it is something you have to face," he said.

His words were deceptively quiet. Kayla felt the blood drain from her face.

She shook her head. "I can't…I really…" She fell silent.

With two strides he was next to her. He scooped her up into his arms and lurched up the stairs toward her flat.

"Wade, stop this," she pleaded, acutely aware of what he intended.

"No, damn it, I won't. If sex is all the good there can be between us, then sex there shall be. I'll not continue to bash myself against you until we are both destroyed."

"Stop, Wade. Sex will not make it right. Do you hear me? There is too much between us."

"I don't care," he muttered, as he sat her on the side of the bathtub. "I want you," he stated as he reached in to turn the water on.

Kayla sat where he had put her. She watched him. She wanted him, but her mind was struggling to bridge the chasm between them—the chasm that would ultimately destroy them.

He stripped before reaching out, gripping both arms and lifting her into a standing position. He proceeded to peel her soggy dress and knickers from her body. Her skin tingled with a mixture of desire and cold. Goosebumps rose on her bare skin, every hair stiffened and rose.

"Good grief, Kayla, you're freezing. In, under the shower, now," he ordered.

The water was deliciously warm as it splattered her icy skin. She felt him come in behind her. He brought his body against hers, pressing his hardened cock lightly between her buttocks. She sighed, feeling the anger seep out of her as he caressed her hips, waist, and back, sparking a new kind of tension rushing through her.

He leaned against her, nuzzling her neck and shoulders, as he brought his soaped hands up to cradle her breasts. She moaned faintly and leaned back against him. In a sensual exploration he stroked over her ribs and abdomen before sliding sensuously through the fine hair at the apex of her legs. With long fingers he teased her lips apart and slipped into the hot moistness of her inner flesh. He nibbled at her shoulder as she reached around and cupped his taut buttocks with her hands and drew him closer. He continued to caress her sensitive nub of flesh with one hand and with the other he explored and stimulated her pussy. She moaned again and parted her legs ever so slightly. Wade didn't need any further invitation. With a controlled push, he sank his hard flesh between her legs and into her hot, moist entrance. The sensation was delightful as his long, thick, throbbing rod slid into her body. He moved slowly in and out, all the time playing with her clit. The twin points of sensation heaved and melded into one molten throbbing mass of flesh. She whimpered as he thrust deeper and harder. He tucked his arm around her hips to hold her firmly against his thrusts while she clutched the walls to support her trembling body as her knees threatened to cave in under the raw passionate onslaught of ecstasy that danced through her body like liquid fire. She convulsed around his hard, pulsing flesh as it slid in and out of her. He increased the tempo, as they were catapulted toward climax. Kayla cried out as she was engulfed in a burning swirling tsunami of release. Wade groaned in unison as he pressed hard and deep inside her in response to his own release.

She leaned against the wall, letting the coolness of the tiles soothe her overheated body. Wade pressed against her back. She could feel his chest heaving as he tried to drag enough air into his lungs. The warm water sluiced over them, washing away the heat of their intimacy. They stayed like that, still joined, for quite a while until finally Wade pushed away from her. His now soft shaft slipped out of her, stirring one last wave of pleasure along her nerve endings. She sighed. After Wade turned the water off, he placed a towel over her shoulders. Not bothering with a towel for himself, he picked her up and laid her gently on the bed.

"Get dressed, Kayla. I'll make coffee, or would you rather some wine?"

"I think wine might be the thing," she said.

* * * *

When she came down, he had also changed into fresh clothes. The drapes were pulled now against the fury of the storm and he lounged on the couch, two glasses of red on the coffee table. She sat opposite him, unsure what to say next. She studied the paintings on the wall. Except for the two at auction, the four left here were the most precious to her—two of her mother's, one of hers, and one more of her grandmother's. As she stared at them, a thought flickered at the back of her mind. All the other paintings in the main gallery were gone, but these, one of her grandmother's and one of hers, the most valuable, were left behind. The thought hammered now.

Wade sipped his wine, savored the taste then put his glass down and sat up. "So are you willing to consider your managers as the culprits? Everything points to them, you know."

She picked up her glass and swirled the wine around. She stared into it before she looked up at Wade. "I know the evidence points at them, but…" The thought burst through her vagueness. She surveyed the paintings again. "No, Wade, it doesn't. If Pierre did this, he would have taken these paintings," she said as she waved her glass through the air. "He would never have left the most valuable ones behind."

"Kayla, really…"

She stood her glass down with an impatient slap. "No, Wade, there has to be evidence." She leaped up and began to prowl the building.

He made no attempt to follow her, but she sensed he was watching her closely, while he sipped his wine.

The main gallery was stark and bare. She had already been through the office and there was nothing of use. She opened and shut every cupboard and drawer.

"Let it go, Kayla. You aren't going to find anything. It had all been cleaned out before I came here, except the studio, and all that is left in there was unfinished paintings."

She headed toward the studio. "I can't leave it, Wade," she muttered. "A lot of things are just not adding up."

He followed her, but kept his distance as she started to shuffle through the canvasses. She propped each one back against the other wall, her sense of anguish and frustration growing with each one. Then she saw the gilt edge of a frame standing above the raw unfinished edges. She knew what it was. She hauled the six other canvasses away to reveal her proof.

"I knew it. I knew it. Pierre and Abrial would never, ever have left this behind," she cried.

Wade moved forward and stared at the erotic painting of a couple making love under the moonlight on a tropical beach.

"A painting?" he asked.

Kayla locked gazes with his skeptical one. "Not *just* a painting, Wade, but Pierre's masterpiece, their honeymoon painting. To Abrial and Pierre, it would be like leaving their baby behind."

"Oh come on, Kayla. You can't call that proof." Wade scoffed.

She glared at him. "Yes, I can. I know what this painting meant to them. They may have left and taken all their belongings, but it wasn't willingly."

There was a crash on the front door, the stained glass panels at the side shuddered. "Faxton, open the door. We need to talk," a gravelly voice yelled.

"Damn, it's Seville," Wade muttered. "Best if you are not seen, Kayla, until I find out what he wants." He began to push her toward the stairs to the flats. "Stay upstairs until I call you," he ordered.

"I'm going to bed, Wade, so take as long as you like. I have no desire whatsoever to meet Seville."

He smiled. "Okay. I'll be up soon to share it with you."

She shook her head. "Not tonight, Wade, I need some space right now."

He frowned but didn't comment, as the hammering was repeated.

"Open up, Faxton. I know you're in there," Seville bellowed from outside the house.

She hurried up the stairs, her thoughts tumbling around and around. She was drawn to him like a moth to a flame and the result would be the same—annihilation of them both. Even though they had agreed it would be sex only—no strings—it wasn't that simple. Now she knew Wade was in financial difficulty, it put a different perspective on his insistence that he knock the house down. He was also very angry at her invasion of his privacy and her exposure of his secret money difficulties. It must have been a blow to his pride to admit he was on the edge of being broke if this deal failed. He was fighting for his survival as she was fighting for the survival of her heritage. Neither of them could afford to back down. It would be a fight to the death. And now Seville was there and he sounded angry.

She waited just inside the flat with the door open a crack. She could just hear bits and pieces from below.

"Damn it, Faxton, this was supposed to be a simple deal. Now my brother tells me you have encountered a problem. Want to fill me in?"

"Edgar, I am on it, okay? There seems to be a problem with ownership of the house..."

"What problems? Mitchell assured me it was all above board. The place would have been mine except for the old codger transferring it to your father's estate. Have you talked to Mitchell about it?" Seville asked.

"I've tried, but the old man is pretty sick," Wade replied.

"Nah, not the old bugger. His son, Phillip Mitchell. He's the one you need to speak to," Seville said.

The voices faded a little more and Kayla thought they had either moved to the office or were speaking quietly. Her phone shuddered in her pocket then let out a series of little squeaks. She grabbed it as she pushed the door shut. She hoped it hadn't been heard below. It was Neil.

"Kayla, I've got past the password and have accessed your accounts. I am not sure I understand your balances. The retreat account is empty and there is a small balance of about fifty thousand left in the main account. A couple of large withdrawals have been made recently, but it seems you've been frittering it away fairly quickly. I didn't think you were the frivolous type, Kayla," he said, an edge of censure in his tone.

"I'm not, Neil, and I have *not* authorized any large withdrawals. I have been living on about three thousand a month and the only other expenditures I've had are the flat and my recent trip."

"All the paperwork appears to be here, including signed requests by you for all the withdrawals," he replied.

"Email them to me now — all of it. And Neil, I forbid you to mention anything to Phillip about this. Matter of fact, you are not to mention it to anyone, and Neil, absolutely no withdrawals unless I personally request it."

"But..." Neil protested.

"I'm warning you, Neil. Keep this quiet or it won't look good for your firm," Kayla threatened in the toughest tone she could.

"Kayla, really..."

"No, Neil, if you so much as breathe a word to anyone, I will make it very ugly for your firm. Do you understand?" she asked.

"Okay, Kayla, you have my word."

So, this one call had confirmed Phillip was involved. She trembled as she pushed her phone into her pocket. Her chest burned with the need to expel her rage and grief, but she held it back. If she started hitting something now, she might never stop. Her main and first concern was the original papers. Phillip would need to destroy them to complete his shonky deal with Seville and Wade. Phillip knew they were in the coach house. If Phillip got hold of them, all was lost. She needed to get them, now, but with Seville and Wade downstairs, she was trapped in the main house.

She spun around seeking a means of escape and she realized in her distress tonight she had automatically marched into her old bedroom where they had just had sex. She chuckled to herself for fate had smiled on her. From here she didn't need a front door to get out, as Grandma Eloise had discovered. She would simply go to the coach house, retrieve her grandmother's original copies, and march right in the front door and shove them up Seville's nose. That should shut them *all* up.

The door eased open without a sound and Kayla peered around it. Wade was on the lounge, hunched over a sheaf of papers, the open briefcase by his elbow. Seville and another man she didn't recognize sat opposite him. She closed the door and turned the key slowly until it clicked.

Without pausing to listen for sounds of investigation by Wade, Kayla grabbed the torch that always hung on the back of the door and padded across the room and eased up the sash window. She almost lost her nerve as she peered down, but quickly pushed her fear aside and climbed out onto the sill. She slung the torch around her neck then reached her hands and feet for almost forgotten niches as she swung carefully into the old apple tree. As she climbed over to the next branch, she heard her phone go plop onto the saturated ground below and cursed herself for being so careless. Moments later, a little bruised and scraped, Kayla slid to the ground with a sigh of satisfaction. Just like riding a bike. She hunted around to find her phone. It had disintegrated into three pieces and wouldn't go back together. She shook her head in disbelief as she slipped it back into her bra, to be dealt with later. *Now, to get those papers.*

Keeping to the shadows, Kayla scuttled across the garden. The rain splattered and the wet bushes slapped at her, but she ignored both. There were no sounds of pursuit. She fumbled with her torch. She was drenched and shivering, but the goosebumps that tingled on her skin were not all from the cold.

Her eyes soon became accustomed to the dark, and she didn't need her torch. Her nerves crackled with tension as she crept around the corner of the coach house, past the big double doors that were barred and padlocked as she expected, and moved down the side of the old stone building. The overgrown shrubs caught at her flowing dress, so with an irritated yank she pulled it free, leaving a small triangle of fabric hanging on the branch like a defiant little flag. Kayla paused to listen for a moment then sidled through the shrubbery with infinitely more care this time. At the back of the building, Kayla crouched for a moment and looked over her shoulder. She saw vehicle lights move up the driveway. Another one of Wade's cohorts, she guessed. That should keep him too busy to pursue her if he discovered her absence.

She moved on to the old wooden side door. She felt the chain and padlock and cursed Wade's security precautions. She rattled it in frustration and was shocked when, with a jangle of chain and a creak, the door swung open. Her teeth began to chatter and she felt the tingle of a thousand nerve endings scream in warning, but she had come too far to back out now and leave without her papers. Besides, she might not get another chance.

A cat screeched a battle cry further down the garden and Kayla flinched, but then there was no other sound to be heard. Even the thunder was silent, having expelled all its pent-up energy in a brief tempest as it passed over town.

She stepped down into the coach house, placing one foot after the other, silently, on the cold flagstones. She knew exactly where the papers were, but as she went to pass the trapdoor leading to the cellar, she started. It was propped open. Her heart jumped, stopped, then thudded rapidly. All she wanted to do was turn and run. The door should not be open. It was *never* open. She peered down at the inky blackness of the steep stairwell. In that instant, she heard the slightest scuff behind her. A bright flash of pain burst in her head. A hand on her back pushed. She fell forward. Each step whacked her as she tumbled down. She grabbed for a hand hold, but there were none. She rolled, head over heels, into blackness.

* * * *

When she opened her eyes, the darkness was so total she couldn't even see her hand in front of her face.

Her head pounded and threatened to burst open just behind her left ear. She lay still for a long moment, trying to regulate her breathing. A pervading iciness seeped through her body. Every inch hurt, and the silence was so absolute that it weighed heavy on her. The air was thick and cloying, a foul odor poisoning each breath. Then she heard the whimpering. A pathetic child-like half sob, half scream. She listened intently for a moment before she realized it was her. She clamped her mouth shut. She needed to fight her slide into panic as the darkness and the silence wrapped itself around her.

She hurt and ached in multiple places, but knew she couldn't stay here. Her ankle throbbed with excruciating torture, so she didn't attempt to walk. Instead, she climbed onto her knees, hitched her dress up around her hips, and began crawling slowly across the cold concrete. There was nothing to give her a bearing but moments later, she bumped her throbbing head on a stone wall. She turned right and followed the wall, making her way around piles of debris, loose papers, and boxes. Each movement forward brought a searing burn across her kneecaps where they were torn and bleeding from the fall and crawling on the concrete floor, but that was the least of her worries as every movement brought stabbing agony in her ribcage.

Pain, frustration and fear snapped at the edges of her mind, but when she reached another corner and turned again to the right, she knew the steps could not be far away. Then she touched a cylinder, cold and smooth. She snatched it up and ran her hands over it until she found the small squishy protrusion of the on-off switch. She pressed it and the cellar was suddenly bathed in the golden glow of mellow torchlight. She was barely a meter away from the stairs.

She swung the pale beam around the stark, rubbish strewn place. The moving beam caught something as it passed. A splash of color. She flicked back. She opened her mouth to scream. No sound came out. Her throat worked. The torch clattered to the floor. Her hands shook so violently they could no longer grip. The light flickered then stabilized into a single straight beam. At the crescent end of the yellow glow was a pair of legs encased in boots. Pierre's famous and always out of place cowboy boots. She tried again to scream. The scream in her head would not translate to her voice. She covered her mouth and crunched over in a ball of horrified despair. Her eyes remained dry. Her throat convulsively tried to swallow until finally she had to open her mouth and gasp for air. As she gasped, her scream escaped. It tore at her. It reverberated around the empty space and stabbed back at her.

"Oh God, not Pierre. My dearest Pierre," she cried.

The torch rattled as she reached out and picked it up. She didn't want to look. Her stomach churned at the thought, but she had to know. The golden circle of light shuddered as she directed it to the boots and slowly lifted it. They were both there, barely recognizable. Pierre sat propped up against the wall and Abrial lay with her head in his lap. Kayla's throat constricted as she snapped her mouth shut on a wail of dismay that bubbled up. They had been dead for some time. She whipped the torch beam away and vomited into the darkness. The sickening odor she had encountered was death—her friends' deaths. And it crushed her.

Wave after wave of shock crashed over her. She curled into a tiny ball of misery under its onslaught. Now the sobs came, dragged from her chest by unbearable grief. Tears obliterated her vision. Unaware of time passing, she drowned in her pain — wallowed in it, as she knelt alone on the cold concrete floor. Shudders of cold finally penetrated her grief. Her body ached as she tried to uncurl. Eventually she climbed unsteadily to her feet and staggered to the stairs. She sat for a long time on the bottom step. Someone had hit her and pushed her down the stairs — that person intended the same fate for her as Pierre and Abrial.

Drained of emotion, her tears had finally dried up. She pulled out the remains of her phone and in the wavering torchlight quickly discovered her precious means of communication was beyond repair. Even though it was useless she shoved it back in her bra, before she began the slow climb to the top of the stairs. She wasn't game to stand up in case she fell. Her ankle seared with an agonizing burn and it had begun to swell and she wondered if it was broken. Her head throbbed and each time she moved, there was a sharp wrench in her ribs. One step at a time she climbed, sitting and resting on every third or fourth one to ease the head spins that made the room rock and spiral in and out of focus. Her stomach lurched and her breathing came in short, painful little gasps.

Finally the heavy wooden door loomed above her, and she slid onto the landing with a sigh of relief. She rested for a moment then pushed with both hands, but it would not budge. She shoved it again, this time using her good leg for leverage. Nothing happened.

Panic lurched at her as she pounded and thrust upwards in vain, but the door remained clamped shut.

Terror tightened its hold and dashed away with her sanity. In a frantic rhythm, she began to beat the wooden slats with the handle of her torch.

"Help me! Help! Let me out!" Her frantic cries battered at her after echoing around the enclosed space. "Help me! Let me out!" She yelled until her voice cracked and faded.

Then she sat silent, listening for sounds of possible rescue, but there were none. Gripped by sick fear that someone meant her to die tonight, she tucked her knees up and wrapped her arms around her legs, trying to glean what tiny skerrick of warmth she could from her semi-naked body in its flimsy clothing. Of course there would be no rescue. There had been no rescue for her friends below. How they must have suffered here in the cold and dark, slowly dying of injury and thirst.

Held immobile by her morbid thoughts, she couldn't stop shivering and the thought finally penetrated her mind that she had to get out and get warm or perish here in the darkness. Her torch had dimmed, but she shined the beam around the cellar, carefully avoiding the corner where they lay. By the left hand side of the steps, she saw some tools—rakes and shovels and other gardening implements. She carefully descended the stairs—half sitting, half crouching—and scrabbled through the tools.

"Yes!" She lifted the pinch bar over her head—this should do the job. Her torch flickered, faded, and shone again. Her teeth chattered, and she couldn't stop the trembling shivers rolling through her body. She had to get warm. She eyed the cartons and papers and remembered what old Fred, the homeless man who had taken a shine to her, had told her when he came to the soup kitchen for a hot meal—*to keep warm when you don't have blankets, my beautiful sweet, you use cardboard or newspapers. 'Tis just as good as the best feather and down quilt.*

She chose a largish carton and emptied the contents on the floor then half filled it with the old newspapers scattered around.

By the time she had reached the top landing again, she was bathed in perspiration and gasping for breath, but she was now armed. She settled the carton in the far corner of the landing then attacked the heavy wooden trapdoor above her head with the pinch bar. Her weapon cracked and thudded into the old timber. Splinters and dust showered down on her head until finally, under one last furious swing, a single board cracked and fell away. She shoved the pinch bar through the hole, but it stopped with a jerk and the clang of metal. She pushed, but it would not be moved. She sank to her knees as despair crushed her spirit. Whoever pushed her down the stairs had not intended her to get out, for they had moved something, probably the old metal tool box, onto the trapdoor so it could not be forced open.

She was all too aware of the depth of her predicament. No one actually knew where she was, except her attacker. The house was too far away. Even if Wade Faxton had been listening, he wouldn't have heard her. She was shivering again, so she crawled into her carton and covered herself with the newspapers right up to her neck. She was meant to die tonight. This wasn't just a small routine to scare her off. But Phillip was her cousin. Surely he didn't want her dead.

Terrified of dying in this dark hole in the ground, she resolved if she got out, she would pursue the perpetrators to the ends of the earth to get justice for Pierre and Abrial and to save Ainsley House.

She must have dozed, but something woke her. Then she heard someone call her name.

She roused herself, used the pinch bar to bash on the bottom of the tool box, and screamed. "Help me. I am in the cellar. Help! Help!"

Her voice cracked and died in her parched throat, but she continued to bang with relentless rhythm on the metal.

She heard the voice again, louder now, then the sharp screeching grind of metal scraping. The door crashed open and the bright glare of a torch blinded her.

Fear flashed through her. She couldn't see her rescuer. She brought the pinch bar to shoulder height ready to swing it in case it was her attacker. As the powerful torchlight dispersed the darkness, a menacing silhouette filled the opening.

"Keep away from me," she shouted, as she struggled to extricate herself from the newspapers and stand up.

He moved in closer, his hands reached for the sides of the opening. She swung the pinch bar in an arc that barely missed his face.

"What the hell?" he yelped.

"Back off." She swung the pinch bar again and he did back away. Now she managed to scrabble out of the box, all the time holding the pinch bar in front of her.

"Don't try anything. I'll not let you finish me off!" she cried.

"Finish you off?"

She brandished the pinch bar with one hand as she climbed out of the cellar. She was relieved to see her unidentified companion keep his distance.

A familiar tone finally filtered through her.

"Kayla, its Wade Faxton. Kayla, put the weapon down. I am not here to harm you."

His phone rang. He automatically pulled it out and answered it, even before Kayla could forbid it.

"Yes, in the coach house," he said into the phone.

Her breath choked in her throat. She would never be able to keep more than one at bay.

The side door crashed open, and Simon burst into the coach house. "Kayla, thank goodness you are okay. What happened?"

His words faded to silence as he took in her defensive stance and the pinch bar held out in front of her like a bat.

Simon looked from her to Wade and back again. "Kayla, it's all right. We are here to help you," he said.

"God help me…" The pinch bar slipped from her numb fingers as it finally sank in that she was being rescued.

Numb, Kayla just stared at them, still partially blinded by the beam, tears drying in salty trails on her cheeks. She was too shattered by the betrayal, the cold, and fear, to think clearly.

She pointed down into the cellar. "Pierre and Abrial…down there. Oh God, they are both dead. They meant me to be dead too…down there, with them. Someone is determined to stop me saving Ainsley House, even if it means murdering me," she wailed.

"For goodness sake, woman, no one is trying to murder you," Wade said.

She waved her hands toward the cellar. "They're dead…down there, and someone hit me over the head and pushed me down the stairs. Why are you here,

Simon? Are you in on it too? This plan to take Ainsley House from me?" she cried.

"Kayla, I came to see you. I wasn't happy about the way we parted today. You are family. When I found Wade at the house, we talked a while then realized you were not in the bedroom." Simon gave a tentative smile. "I knew how you got out. Your car was still there, so we've been looking for you — together."

Her knees gave way. She couldn't do this anymore. Violent shivers racked her body. As she plopped onto the tool box, Simon came forward and wrapped his jacket around her. He tucked it in tightly.

"Stay with her, Faxton, I am going into the cellar," he said.

Simon's face was white and grim when he emerged a short time later from the cellar.

"Call the police, Faxton," he ordered as he sat down beside Kayla.

Chapter Four

As the coach house was overrun with police, Wade scooped her up and carried her outside.

"Where are you taking me?" she asked.

She wriggled in his embrace, but he tightened his hold, pressing her hard against his muscular chest.

"I am taking you to the hospital to be examined for injuries. The police will take your statement later."

Her head throbbed and she felt weak and dizzy. "Simon, please, will you come too?"

"You have nothing to fear from me, Kayla," Wade grumbled.

"Maybe not, Wade, but my friends are dead in that cellar and whoever killed them intended me to be dead too. I can't afford to trust anybody right now, least of all the man who has the most to benefit from my removal from the picture."

"Are you sure that's me?" he asked.

She heard the hurt in his tone and shook her head. "No, I am not sure. I am not sure of anything anymore." She sobbed.

The treating doctor determined she had a mild concussion, a sprained ankle, and bruising all over, in addition to the five stitches she needed in her scalp. While Wade discussed her condition with the doctor, she studied him—the tall muscular build, broad shoulders, and long legs—it all combined to hint at coiled energy, latent strength barely kept under control.

Tonight she thought he looked like a privateer, the white shirt hanging out of black trousers, open almost to the waist, the thin gold chain around his neck and his gold earring. When their gazes met she realized he was also studying her. His direct gaze warmed her inside. He moved closer. The tantalizing scent of his aftershave assailed her senses, and she suddenly craved the comforting feel of his arms around her.

"I want to go home please...to Ainsley House," she said.

Simon frowned. "Kayla, Wade Faxton now owns Ainsley House. Despite the legal wrangling, it *is* his."

She observed Wade, surprised afresh by the unusual color of his eyes. She immediately knew that given the right moment she could sink into the richness of their depths and not care if she drowned. Now there was just the faintest of furrows on his forehead. It pulled the straight thick eyebrows into sharp arches. He wasn't smiling.

"So what happens now?" She looked from Wade to Simon. "Am I barred from my own home?" she asked.

"No, Kayla. I have decided because of the confusing circumstances we both find ourselves in that you should maintain your accommodation at Ainsley House," Wade stated bluntly.

"Really?" she asked.

"Yes, really. I think it's the gentlemanly thing to do," he responded.

"Thank you, Wade," she said quietly.

Now he smiled, and it lit up his face. He was suddenly smoking hot, with a kissable mouth and smoldering bedroom eyes. His expression blatantly shouted his desire for her.

Simon moved a step closer, his face grim.

But before he could say or do anything, Wade stepped forward and scooped her off the bed. She stifled a squeak of protest as strong arms supported her, and she came to rest lightly against his muscular chest. He strode down the corridor and out to the car, his breathing barely altering under the extra burden. A young nurse scurried after them with her crutches and her pills. Kayla could feel the ripple of his muscles against her shoulder and side. His embrace was almost a caress as he cradled her in his arms. Unbidden warmth tingled in her pussy at the almost intimate contact.

With infinite care, he sat her in the front seat, and helped put her seat belt on while Simon climbed into the back seat.

He drove carefully and she could feel his eyes on her as each bump rattled her injuries. She tried hard but she was unable to stop a couple of small cries of pain. At last, they pulled up at Ainsley House.

As Simon slipped out of the car, he gave her hand a gentle squeeze. "It will all work out, Kayla," he said. "Before I go, I will give you these to analyze. I actually came to the house tonight to talk to you about the situation and to bring you copies of the documents I have managed to procure that might prove your case. Susan faxed me a copy of the paperwork Joan and Bill were apparently forced to sign and accept. It is signed by you and it is very blunt. I know you did not, would not, ever have written such a letter to anyone, least of all Joan and Bill. It's downright cruel."

"Oh no," she wailed.

"And by the way, I can assure you if you have any concerns that Wade is the person who attacked you, he was with me. So, go back to Ainsley House, get some rest, and tomorrow we will talk some more about all this." Simon patted her shoulder. "We *will* work this out, Kayla."

"Simon, I'm afraid it can't be worked out. I mean... if this person is willing to kill to make it happen, what can we do?" She reached up and rubbed her forehead. "I can't believe Abrial and Pierre are dead." Tears welled up in her eyes so she blinked furiously to stop them falling.

Simon gave her shoulder a sympathetic squeeze. "I know, Kayla. I'll come around later—and Faxton, I am expecting you to take good care of her. With murder on the agenda, it's obvious they will stop at nothing to take Ainsley House from Kayla."

Wade's mouth tightened into a thin line. "The whole scenario stinks and I am not at all happy about being in the middle of it. The thing is, unless Kayla can provide solid proof of ownership, the project will go ahead. I have a binding contract that I will not break unless I have strong justification which stands up in court. Because that is where it will go if the investors get their backs up."

Simon backed away from the car and Wade stepped into the gap right behind him, and although Kayla had crutches and expected to walk inside, he lifted her out of the seat.

"Put me down. I can walk," she protested.

Wade shook his head "I'm going to carry you, Kayla. We don't want you putting any weight on that foot."

Once in the flat, he laid her on the bed in the master bedroom. She was clad in a flimsy blue hospital gown under the white hospital blanket because the police had taken the clothes she was wearing in the cellar for evidence.

"Umm, where are your clothes?

She pointed to the wardrobe. He looked at them and glanced over his shoulder. "These are all you have?"

"Yes, Wade, they are all I've got here."

"I see." He frowned at the implication of her words. Then he ruffled through the drawers she indicated and pulled out some blue pajamas.

"Are these satisfactory?"

"Yes, they will be perfect, thank you."

He handed her the clothes. "Kayla when you're settled, we need to talk — if you feel up to it that is."

"Okay."

He hesitated by the bed and Kayla waited. "Shall I bring us a cuppa and something light to eat while we talk?"

"Yes, that would be lovely."

Their conversation sounded stilted, but Kayla didn't know what else to say or how to deal with the undercurrent of awareness that buzzed underneath the meaningless words. He hesitated at the door.

"It's all right. I can manage." She smiled to soften her words, which had come out more sharply than she intended.

"Oh, it's not that. I was just wondering if you were going to disappear again, like Cinderella vanishing into the night, leaving Prince Charming bereft."

Kayla snickered. She really wanted to laugh, but it hurt too much. "Don't worry. I am in no condition to shimmy down the tree right now. I will be waiting here when you get back."

When he returned, she was already snuggled up under the blankets. He had brought hot Milo and some toasted sandwiches. They ate in silent companionship.

As he moved the tray off the bed, he looked at her intently. "Shall I go first?" he asked.

She nodded.

"I have also been putting some pieces together and I don't like what I'm finding. When you said Phillip Mitchell was...*is* your cousin..."

"He is," she muttered, not wanting to claim too much connection with the man who seemed intent on destroying her.

"I was pretty concerned because it was Phillip Mitchell who suggested I take Ainsley House, when it was offered as payment for the gambling debt. He said I might not get another chance at redeeming that IOU. I told him I didn't care about my father's outstanding IOUs, but Mitchell was quite insistent I take it. When his boss, Neil Moore, and my lawyers agreed with him, I took it, no questions asked."

"He *what*?"

"Phillip suggested I take the offer. When Seville put his deal on the table to include Ainsley House in his project, it seemed the perfect solution to my own troubles. When he insisted I put cash up front to balance the division of profits, I had to dig deep. Anyway, I had a couple of associates who wanted in, but when we failed to reach Seville's target, Phillip intervened. He appeared so keen for it to all happen he even organized an extra investor—a mate of his, a Peter Tenney, to raise the extra funds... Kayla, you have gone as white as a sheet. Are you okay?"

Her gut felt like she had been hit by one of Jeff Fenech's famous right hooks. Nausea washed over her and she cringed under the cold sickness that curled around her heart and soul. She tried to speak, but her mouth just opened and shut. She couldn't force words past the lump of horror clogging her throat.

She could hardly hear him. His voice was just a squeak above the pounding of the blood in her head. The room receded and blurred.

"Kayla?" He was almost shouting at her.

She stared at him uncomprehending. Then his hand was on her head gently pushing it down between her knees and she felt a cold cloth on the back of her neck.

"Don't pass out, Kayla. Deep, steady breathing."

She breathed deeply and the waves of nausea faded. The room stayed still when she sat up. She focused on Wade. "Now it all makes sense. The problem is when Phillip organized the handing over of Ainsley House to you, he didn't plan on my early return. Ainsley House was supposed to be demolished before I got back. I can't believe Phillip hates me that much, I know he was angry about his inheritance, but to feel so much rage he has deliberately set out to destroy the one thing I truly value, Ainsley House. And as for Peter, well I wouldn't have thought he would have money to invest in anything. I didn't even know that Phillip was still friends with him."

He took her hands in his and chafed them, trying to bring a small amount of warmth to them. She didn't pull away.

"So, do you want to start from the beginning? Tell me what you know, because this is obviously more than just a quick money-making scheme going on. This is nasty," he said.

She nodded.

"Do you know what is behind this?" he asked.

"I can make an informed guess. It was such a shock to see those paintings up for sale, but nothing like finding…finding Abrial and Pierre like that…" She looked up at Wade. "Phillip has already cleaned out my trust fund, and that doesn't surprise me, because he always wanted more money than he had, but I wouldn't have thought that anyone would go to such lengths to seek revenge for some childhood slip of the tongue. Especially my only living relative."

"Revenge?" Wade sounded incredulous. "What the hell for?"

"When I was a child, Phillip did a very silly thing. He was supposed to be babysitting me while my parents, grandmother, and his parents went to a wedding. Instead, he locked me in the broom cupboard and went out with two of his mates. They got drunk and were driving. The car they hit was the one driven by my father. My parents and Phillip's mother, Aunt Marion, died, George was left a paraplegic and my grandmother had multiple fractures. One of Phillip's mates died, but before the police arrived at the scene, his other mate, Peter Tenney, the owner of the car, told Phillip to disappear—to go home and pretend he wasn't involved. When the police came to the house and I was still locked in the cupboard, screaming my head off, their story unraveled. I was so scared and angry at Phillip that I told the police he had got drunk and had gone in the car as well, even though he said he hadn't. Later, when they said David was driving, I said it was a lie because David had forgotten to take his glasses, and he was as blind as a bat without them. Both of the boys got into big trouble."

Wade frowned. "How old was Phillip?" he asked.

"Just seventeen. He was given some time in a youth detention facility, and then a good behavior bond. Of course, his record was expunged when he turned eighteen, but Peter was eighteen and went to jail. He went bad—got into the wrong crowd in jail. It was Frederick Carven who prosecuted them and sought compensation for Eloise. Frederick pushed hard for Peter to do time. Grandma Eloise never forgave Phillip and neither did George, not only for the death of his beloved wife but also for his own injuries."

"Must have been hard on Phillip," Wade mused.

"It was. He hated Frederick Carven with a passion, but it is much harder to hate family. He went off the rails—drinking, brawling and breaking the law. Nothing big, just stupid stuff. One day, Uncle George gave him an ultimatum—either straighten up or he would disown him, and blacklist him from being an accountant, which was Phillip's dream. He didn't cope as he struggled to straighten himself out, so he started using drugs—prescription, at first, for depression—then other stuff. He still uses today. I think he expected to get half of the inheritance when Grandma Eloise died, but his share was the house in Parkside. Everything else came to me."

"Did your grandmother leave him out of the will because of what he did? It seems a bit harsh," Wade said quietly.

Kayla shook her head. "Grandma Eloise was not that vindictive. No, Marion was Grandpa's stepdaughter because Grandma Eloise had been married very young and was widowed before she married Grandpa, so Phillip inherited half of what had come directly through Eloise as a McLeod. All the Campbell and Mackenzie money came to me, as the only descendant."

"And Phillip wasn't impressed," Wade said.

"No, he wasn't," Kayla said.

"And Peter Tenney?" he asked.

She shrugged. "When he got out of jail, he was the ultimate bad boy. I was just fifteen and he seduced me with a fast and easy charm and a wild lifestyle. Grandma Eloise nearly went out of her mind. She hated Peter, was scared for me, and that was when she put everything in a trust. Anyway, when I broke it off after I caught him in bed with two of my friends, I discovered I was pregnant. By then, he was back in jail, convicted of statutory rape on charges brought by Carven and Grandma Eloise. Even though she was a staunch Catholic, Grandma Eloise encouraged me to have an abortion. I was just fifteen and scared, hurt, and confused. I never told anyone about the abortion because I was so ashamed. I know it was the right thing, but there will always be a sad spot deep inside me for that unborn child."

"Of course there will be, Kayla." Wade brushed his hand over hers in the briefest of touches. "And what happened to your grandmother?" he asked.

"After I went away to study, she lived here alone. I suppose I got wrapped up in my new life because I didn't come home much and one winter's night she went out into the garden — I will never know why — and fell. She broke her hip and remained lying out in the garden for three days until some local kids taking a short cut found her. She had died alone. I should have been here, but I wasn't, so I want to make this right for her."

He laid his hand over hers this time. "It wasn't your fault, Kayla, even if you had been here, she might still have died," he said.

"Maybe, but I want to make this right. Besides I have a lifetime tenancy on this flat, and all the memorabilia downstairs is mine."

Wade regarded her thoughtfully, a partial smile curving his mouth. "What if I give you all the memorabilia — store it somewhere until you find another place to put it?" he asked.

She began to chuckle now. "Oh Wade, that is so sweet, but it isn't the answer and you know that."

He moved closer to her, holding her gaze with the intensity of the expression in his hazel eyes. "Yes I know, but seriously, if I do demolish the house, do you want the contents?" he repeated.

She leaned upwards and inwards to lay her mouth very lightly on his for the briefest moment before she pulled back and looked into his eyes. "Thank you, Wade, it would please me to at least have the contents, but you know I am not going to let you demolish this house, don't you?"

"There is not much more I can say to that other than I'm sorry, Kayla, but I have seen nothing to collaborate your claim, despite making some investigations myself, so the demolition will go ahead," he said bluntly.

Kayla looked down at her hands clenched in her lap "I know I have not provided proof of my claim, and I want to give you the benefit of the doubt about being involved, but it has taken more than Phillip with his drug addled mind to pull this off," she muttered then she glared up at him. "And you, Wade Faxton, are right in the middle of it. You also have the most to lose."

He nodded. "I have a great deal to lose if this project doesn't go ahead to schedule, and I have some very influential investors who have supported me at their own risk in this project. I cannot afford to disappoint them either..."

"Would they do something criminal to protect that investment?" she asked.

Wade shook his head. "Not Roger and Damien, but I cannot be sure of Seville and Tenney – or your cousin, for that matter."

"Well regardless, Wade, I am going to do all I can to sort this out and get Ainsley House back."

Now he stood, his face grim. "And I, Kayla, will be doing all I can to ensure the project proceeds. If you can prove your claim and the project fails then I will just have to bear the cost," he stated.

She heard to edge in his tone. "Will the cost be so big, Wade?" she asked.

He began to turn away. "Yes, Kayla, both business-wise and personally."

Her eyes drooped and she struggled to keep from dozing. "Is destroying Ainsley House absolutely necessary for your project to succeed, Wade?" she asked, struggling now to form coherent words.

Wade got up from the bed and stood contemplating her for a long moment. "Yes. Now go to sleep, Kayla. We can fight about the house in the morning..."

"But I don't want...to fight with you..." she muttered.

"I know," he said.

He nodded and smiled, but he had already slipped out the door by the time she could find anything suitable to say in her fuddled brain.

* * * *

They came at her from every direction, semi decomposed faces – Abrial's, Pierre's, her grandmother's. Then they changed and it was Phillip and Peter. They pursued her down the passage and in front of her were hundreds of babies' faces. Dead babies. She ran and ran, thrashed and bucked in the encompassing sheets. She sobbed, real tears wetting her cheeks.

"Kayla, wake up. Wake up," Wade said urgently, as he shook her gently.

She fought his restraining hands and slapped at the solid object that pinned her down.

"Kayla, damn it, wake up," he shouted.

The familiarity of his voice finally penetrated her nightmare. It was Wade, not Phillip or Peter. She gasped and fell back on the saturated pillow, tears still filling her burning eyes. Then he was holding her — tightly. The hardness of his muscles molded her feminine curves to their shape as he embraced her. He kissed her hair as he stroked her back.

"Shh, it's okay. It was only a nightmare. You're safe, Kayla. Safe with me," he murmured in her ear.

Enclosed in his embrace, she felt the terror retreat, leaving a burnt out shell of sadness behind — a deep sadness for her lost friends, lost baby, and the loss of the contentment with the world. The roughness of his cheek grazed against hers. She was acutely aware of his naked chest pressed against her breast with just her light, silky pajama top between them. Her nipples tingled, and she felt a stirring of awareness deep inside. His breath was warm and light on her cheek as his hair tumbled over his forehead, and blended with her own bed-tousled tresses. He gently explored her back and shoulders with his fingers. Desire washed over her. She almost purred.

His hands slipped away, and he leaned back from her. She saw the need in his expression, and the dark shadows of his eyes. He handed her a pill and glass of water, but when she lay back down, he didn't leave. Instead he lay down behind her, and with one arm over her waist, he pulled her against the length of his muscular body. Kayla was acutely aware of his arousal.

"Wade?"

"Shh, Kayla. I will stay with you, but I don't think you are up to any more than that tonight," he mumbled.

She didn't argue. She was glad of the company, but it still took a long time to doze off, and it was not just the fear of more nightmares that kept sleep at bay.

She did finally slip into oblivion, dosed on painkillers, but as the sunlight slipped across her bed, she woke. It was a struggle to move. Her ribs ached, but only really hurt if she coughed or moved suddenly, and her ankle wasn't too bad, but everything else screamed in pain at the slightest of movement.

As she eased into a sitting position, there was a light tap at the door.

"Can I come in?" Wade asked.

"Yes, Wade."

He slipped through the partially open door. "I have some ointment and a bottle of bath salts. I thought they might help…oh boy, you're a mess,"

At his startled reaction, she followed the direction of his gaze saw that most of her visible flesh was mottled black and blue. No wonder she was so sore. A shudder rumbled through her. She was lucky to be alive at all.

He helped her climb out of bed, get undressed, and into the deep, hot bath he had run for her. After a long soak in Wade's concoction, she returned to her room, wrapped in a large towel, to find him waiting, a large tube of soothing gel in his hand and a large towel on the bed. He indicated for her to lie on the towel.

She was too sore to argue so she lay face down, the towel draped over her. As Wade lowered himself beside her, she felt the mattress shift under his weight, and the warmth of his muscular thigh pressed against her hip. His touch was warm and gentle and she felt the towel slip down until it only covered her backside. The gel was cool and smooth where Wade spread it with infinite gentleness across her back and shoulders. His large palms felt silky as they slid sensuously across her tortured flesh. His warmth seeped into her body while he caressed the outline of her muscles with the featherlight touch that left a blazing trail of pure erotic fire across her skin. He pressed his thumbs delicately into the hollows at the base of her neck, then slid over the curve of her shoulders, and slipped down either side of her spine. Her body sang with awareness. With a steady rhythm, he used his fingers to soothe the muscles down her side and waist before he moved the towel up to cover her back and left her buttocks exposed. Now he delicately manipulated the flesh across her lower back and hips. She felt a pool of coolness on her left buttock then the warmth of his hands as he moved them down over the curve of her cheek, around her hip, and down to her thigh. She felt the ache of sexual arousal deepen in her lower abdomen and her pussy silently pulsed with the need to be filled. She couldn't hold back a slightly shaky moan.

"Did I hurt you?" he asked. There was concern in his voice.

"Mmmmm…no, not really," she murmured, almost choking on her words.

Immediately she heard a quiet thrum of laughter. He was fully aware of what he was doing to her and not at all repentant. The heat his touch had evoked raced through her veins, stoked to greater heat by the knowledge he knew she was aroused by his ministrations. The slow stroking continued, down her left thigh, one hand on either side almost completely encasing her leg then up the other and back to her buttocks. The tips of his fingers nearly, but not quite, touched her intimately. She wanted to scream with frustration as her body erupted in a volcanic blast. Desperately she wanted him to caress and explore her now wet and throbbing pussy. No matter her current delicate condition, her body wanted so desperately to be loved — to feel his hardness slide into her, to possess her, and drive her to the pinnacle. As she fought with her rampant sexual urges, he suddenly stopped.

"Turn over, Kayla," he said.

She awkwardly rolled onto her back and found he moved the carefully draped towel to cover both her breasts and the apex of her legs.

He held out the tube of gel. "I will let you finish the front while I go organize some brunch."

She stared up at him, disappointed he was not going to continue his gentle massage.

"Don't turn puppy dog eyes on me like that, Ms Mackenzie. You are in no condition to be ravished and that is what will happen if I continue my anointing on the more desirable, tempting side of your deliciously gorgeous body," Wade growled in a husky rumble.

"Wade…"

He put his fingers to her lips. "Shhh. Finish with that gel, get dressed, and come and eat," he said.

She lay there motionless long after he had shut the door. Her body glowed and hummed from his touch, but a chill of cool air and dull aches in every inch of her body were already beginning to quench the flames of desire that still teased her. She quickly finished rubbing the gel on her bruises and dressed.

He had coffee, yogurt, fresh strawberries, and hot buttered toast waiting for her when she hobbled out into the kitchen.

He immediately jumped up and came around to assist her.

"Thank you, Wade. The massage and gel have helped a great deal."

"Good."

As he helped her get settled and laid the crutches against the bench, she could see a barely suppressed smile. He perched on the second stool, his long leg swinging slightly. He reached out with his fingertips and caressed her cheek, teasing every nerve ending into a fiery dance of anticipation. With excruciating slowness, he caressed her chin and she answered the slightest pressure of demand and lifted her eyes to meet his.

"You really believe in what you're doing, don't you?" he questioned, with deceptive calmness.

Kayla nodded, not trusting herself to speak. The husky resonance of his voice called to her. Her heart skipped a beat and a tightness deep inside held her suspended as she realized he was going to kiss her. She knew then she was in trouble. Not only had she opened up her body to this man, but also her heart as well. It wasn't supposed to go like this. They had agreed sex only. No emotional involvement. There could not be any emotional involvement with the house between them.

In a desperate effort to quench the familiar vibrations of need that throbbed inside, she sternly upbraided herself. *This man is the enemy! Be immune to his masculine charisma.* But it was almost impossible and she knew she had lost the battle before it had even begun.

He peered down at her, his eyes still serious, despite the partial smile that now hovered on the full sensual lines of his mouth. He continued to stroke along her jaw with the pad of his thumb, the heat on contact liquefying the hardness of the bone.

"Kayla, I want you, not just to bed, but more. Surely when this is over—"

"I don't think so," she said, cutting off his suggestion of a future. Kayla stared up into his eyes, now unfathomable pools of mysterious shadows, framed by thick dark lashes.

He didn't blink. She saw the passion lurking and was almost overcome with her desire to fan it into a raging inferno. Only the stark thought of this man destroying her beloved home held her back. The scent of his skin enveloped her and suddenly her throat was dry. She swallowed, her heart thudding behind too tight ribs. Her fingers begged to be allowed to touch, to explore the rugged planes, to smooth away the savage angles that drew his face in stark relief. She wanted to feel that heady, enticing magic once again that he had elicited from her willing body every time he touched her.

"Kayla Mackenzie, you are the most bewitching woman," he muttered.

"Wade, I need answers…" Her voice broke, she swallowed and croaked. "Not kisses."

His hand dropped away, his smile faded. "I know," he said as he shook his head and ran his hand through his already tousled mop.

He reached out and with a touch, as intangible as thistle down, he outlined the fullness of her mouth with his thumb. At the lightest of pressure from him she lifted her face to him. As he moved closer, she felt the warmth of his breath dance across her cheek and automatically parted her lips in anticipation.

The shriek of the doorbell shattered the aura that surrounded them. Wade went rigid, gave her a rueful grin, and clattered down the stairs.

He was already opening the envelope couriered from his lawyers as he entered the kitchen and he scanned the document as he perched back on the second kitchen stool.

He glared at her over the document. She shrank back in her chair feeling the heat of fury that radiated from him.

"You've taken out a caveat on the house," he shouted.

"Yes, I did it before I left Adelaide. I could not let you just destroy the house. It's mine. I needed time to sort this out," she yelled back at him.

"Oh Kayla, do you realize that this document will be an open declaration of war as far as your enemies and my investors are concerned. I'd hoped we could resolve this without resorting to a long drawn-out process in the courts."

"Oh, so that is what all this gentleness was about? Seduction? You think if you seduce me, bed me enough times, and perhaps even win my heart, I will just give you Ainsley House?" she screeched.

"No, Kayla, my attempts to romance you are because I desire you as a woman—nothing more," he said calmly.

"Desire me? For how long, Wade? As long as I'm useful?"

"No. I want you—"

"Don't even go there, Wade. Your track record with the ladies is not what it should be, is it?" she said loudly.

"No, it isn't. But I haven't met a woman like you before…" he murmured.

"Haven't had a woman stand between you and a goal before, have you? How far were you prepared to go with the seduction Wade, to get the house? A declaration of love, maybe. Don't try it, Wade. I've been conned by the best of them," she shouted, all her past hurts and future expectations of hurt sharp in her tone.

"Damn you, Kayla, and damn this accursed house. My feelings for you have absolutely nothing to do with it." His words were a deep grumble.

"Funny, but I don't believe you—not for a moment. That a man like you, who can have any woman he wants with a crook of his finger, but vows to never give his heart to any, has suddenly developed such feelings?" she cried.

He shuffled the papers back together and held his hands wide. "I can't explain it," he muttered.

"Exactly. So let's see what happens when the house business is resolved. Let's see then if you still have 'feelings' for me," she challenged.

"You are a hard woman, Kayla Mackenzie. I can tell you right now my 'feelings' will remain and they'll be even stronger then. You'll see," he replied.

"Even if you lose the house?" she asked.

"Yes, even if I lose the house. But I will not let you jeopardize a multimillion dollar project, especially after offering me nothing more than your word. To think I was almost sympathetic to your cause." He threw the caveat documents down on the kitchen bench. "Why the hell didn't you tell me you were going to do it? At least, discuss it with me?" he snapped, his smoldering glare holding her captive.

Her heart thudded against her ribs. He took another step, but stopped just out of reach. Kayla shivered. And the knowledge that her reaction was not all caused by apprehension irked her. She met his direct stare, determined not to back down or crumble in the face of his intimidation. The rise and fall of his chest showed his agitated breathing matched her own.

"It seemed, at the time, the best way I could stop you destroying Ainsley House until I worked out what the hell was going on. I did it before I knew other forces were involved, before I knew my friends had been murdered, and Phillip had cleaned out my trust account. Besides, I was afraid you would talk me out of it," she blurted out. She reached out to him in an impassioned plea for understanding and perhaps forgiveness.

His fists clenched and unclenched at his sides. "For God's sake, Kayla, when news of this gets out, we could both be in the firing line and without proof, you don't stand a chance. The Supreme Court will turn this over in an instant. Everything must be in writing. I'm sorry." His words were almost a feline growl.

"I will save Ainsley House," she cried.

He stiffened and lunged toward her, but stopped before he touched her. She flinched, but stood her ground.

"Not without proof…in black and white," he stated.

"Well you have already seen that someone is trying very hard to stop me producing that proof. Murder even. Surely that, in itself, should ring alarm bells!"

Wade backed away. "This whole damn thing is ringing alarm bells," he shouted. "But I don't know what you expect me to do?"

She glared up at him. "Well, maybe you should take a closer look."

"Yes, maybe I should," he replied as he turned away.

The door of the flat crashed shut behind him.

Chapter Five

After Wade's angry exit, Kayla had spent most of the morning making a statement to the police about her fall down the cellar and all the peripheral events. She suspected Wade was downstairs trying to minimize the damage her caveat had caused. She felt guilty now that she had not discussed it with him, but things had changed since then. The stakes now were far higher than just the demolition of Ainsley House.

When the police left, she lay on the bed. To her surprise, she slept heavily, waking hours later when the cool sea breeze fluttered across her skin. It was four thirty and she made a snap decision. She called a cab and just fifteen minutes later, hobbled into the Port Lincoln office of Carven, Thomas and Smith.

She asked to speak to Mr Thomas Senior and, almost immediately, she was ushered into his large, corner office.

"Miss Mackenzie, sit. Goodness me, what have you been doing to yourself?" Mr Thomas asked.

"I was attacked and pushed down some stairs, Mr Thomas."

The lawyer tut tutted. "Oh dear, very nasty," he said. "Now, what can I do for you, my dear?"

"I need to see my grandmother's old file. Eloise Campbell was one of Frederick Carven's clients for many years."

"Oh I see. Unfortunately we don't allow people to look at old files—confidentiality issues, you know." The lawyer frowned and moved uncomfortably in his seat.

"Please, Mr Thomas. Something has come up regarding some property, and the original documents have been stolen. I need something to prove there was a trust and that the property is to come into my care when I am twenty-five. Both the trustees are now out of the picture and I need to find out what contingencies are in place to either replace them or extinguish the trust. I can't just wait until I am twenty-five, in fifteen months' time, because the house may be destroyed before then." She moved forward in her seat as she held his gaze with a pleading one of her own.

"I see…and what would that property be?" the elderly lawyer asked.

"Ainsley House."

"Well…let me just check in the summary of our archived files."

Even though his actions appeared to acquiesce to her request, the tone of his voice became cold and tight the moment she mentioned Ainsley House. She waited while the elderly lawyer clicked though some files on his computer.

Mr Thomas looked across the desk at her, his face blank of expression. "I'm sorry, my dear. We don't seem to have anything on Eloise Campbell or Ainsley

House. Are you sure you have the correct lawyers?" he asked.

"Yes, Mr Thomas, there is no mistake. Frederick Carven was her lawyer for many years. There has to be a file on my grandmother," Kayla assured him.

"I'm sorry, Miss Mackenzie. There is nothing. Now, it is five and we are closing. Can you show yourself out? I have a couple of things to finish."

He stared intently at her, his expression shuttered and grim. She was in no doubt she was being dismissed.

With awkward movements, Kayla stood, and gathered up her crutches and bag. She didn't believe the old man for one moment, and she was damn well going to prove it. Once out in the corridor, she turned left instead of right, took two steps, and opened the door on her left. She struggled with the ten steps, but at last she was in the basement archive room where she had spent hours filing for the firm as a teenager.

It was almost six by the time the last car left, and only now was she game to start hunting through the cabinets that lined the room. She covered up the window, turned on the light, and began.

She found the cabinet showing the year of her grandmother's death. She worked through the old files. Every now and again she came across one that contained papers with burnt edges and she suspected she was on the right track. At last she found a file labeled *Eloise Campbell nee McLeod*. It was thick and most of the papers had burnt edges. Some were mere scraps of singed paper.

She sat on the floor and opened the file. With meticulous care, she worked through the papers, one sheet at a time.

Many of the documents dated back to before Kayla's birth and she read them carefully, along with anything related to her parents' deaths. She couldn't see anything that appeared to be the trust deed or the will. She wondered what had happened to the final typed and signed copies, as she shuffled through the musty papers struggling to read the spidery hand that crawled across the pages in faded blue ink. Then she found a clue—faded and partly burned—but it was definitely the rough notes on Grandma Eloise's will and how the trust would work. It was dated and had a note that confirmed the document should be ready to sign a fortnight later. She scanned the scratchy handwriting for details that might be useful. An amendment was outlined on a separate sheet of paper, including a contingency if both trustees became incapacitated or deceased before the beneficiary reached the age of twenty-five. As long as she was over twenty one it was noted that the trustees' control would lapse and Kayla would have sole control of Ainsley House and her funds. This information had not been in her copy of the trust deed. Not sure quite what it meant in regards to Uncle George, but knowing it was important to think it through, she slipped it into her pocket and continued to look.

The door crashed open. Cold fear gripped Kayla.

"Police. Come out from behind those cabinets," a gruff voice ordered.

The powerful torchlight dispersed the gloom as two burly coppers filled the doorway.

Numb, Kayla just stared at them, too shocked to respond to their request.

"Stand up. You'll have to accompany us to the station, Miss."

Despite her protestations, she was bundled firmly into the back seat of the police car. Nobody spoke on the short journey through the almost deserted streets and Kayla pulled herself into the tiniest ball in the corner of the car. She felt defeated, humiliated, and afraid. She had never been on the wrong side of the law before.

At least they hadn't handcuffed her, and at the station she was quietly escorted to an interview room where she was left with a very quiet, young, female constable. After what seemed like an eternity, a sergeant joined them.

"Sergeant, I would like to explain…" she began.

"And so you should, young lady. Last night we rescued you from a cellar containing two deceased and tonight we have apprehended you for a break and enter." He fixed her with a steely gaze. "Were you at the office of Carven, Thomas, and Smith this afternoon?"

"Yes," she whispered.

"For what purpose?" the Sergeant asked.

Kayla squirmed in her seat. "To retrieve some documents from my grandmother's old files," she said.

"So when you couldn't get them this afternoon, you went back tonight to finish the job?"

Kayla looked down at her hands again, tears threatening to spill over making her vision wobble and blur. "Not exactly. I didn't leave. I was hiding in the basement."

"Ms Mackenzie, someone tried to break in last night and set the alarm off. They made a mess, but apparently took nothing. Do you know anything about this?"

Kayla flinched, dread gnawing at her insides. "No, Sergeant. As you already know, I was in the cellar. Someone tried to murder me and I found the bodies of my friends. I would suspect the two incidents are related."

"And why do you think that, Miss?"

She leaned toward him. "I think they are connected because whoever attacked me last night was searching in my late grandmother's filing cabinets, I suspect for papers proving ownership of Ainsley House. They would have been searching for the same papers at the lawyer's office—the same papers I was also trying to find. Don't you see, Sergeant, this is all a conspiracy to deprive me of my property."

"And who do you think is behind this so called *conspiracy*?"

"I'm not sure, Sergeant, but I suspect my cousin, Phillip Mitchell, has something to do with it—and Edgar Seville or even Wade Faxton."

"Really. So you think Wade Faxton might be behind this?"

She heard the skepticism in his tone.

Kayla shrugged. "Maybe."

The sergeant went on preparing her statement. When she had read it through, he shook his head then sat back and observed her for a while before he spoke. "So what do you expect me to do now, young lady? You're injured and last night you were under Wade Faxton's care. Does this mean I shouldn't call him to retrieve you? Do you consider your life in danger from Mr Faxton?"

Kayla gazed up at him. Tears welled up in her eyes. "I don't know. I just don't know anymore."

The sergeant stood up and left the room. Kayla was alone.

She was so tired. She crossed her arms on the tabletop and laid her head on them to wait out the uncertainty. What now? She just wanted to lie down and sleep—hopefully to wake up on the other side of this nightmare.

A good half-hour later the sergeant returned. Behind him, Wade filled the doorway with his ominous presence, his face a dark, shuttered mask. He turned a furious glare on her but he said nothing.

The sergeant handed her the statement. "Just sign this and you're free to go, Ms Mackenzie—for now—but don't leave town without notifying us. We may have further questions about this matter."

Kayla nodded as she watched Wade out of the corner of her eye. He hovered in the doorway—a volcano on the verge of a fatal eruption. Kayla felt very, very small and vulnerable.

"Shall we go?" His voice was hard and clipped.

Kayla's skin crawled with nervous awareness of a raging anger held carefully in check.

She followed him to the car. The westerly wind now whipped at her bare arms as she struggled to handle her crutches on the uneven surface of the car park. By the time she managed to get into the car, she was shivering from the cold and trembling inwardly in anticipation of his wrath.

"Why this debacle?" His question was a searing blaze of fury as it lashed across the space between them.

"I need to find the papers, Wade. I have to…and I thought the lawyer might have a copy," she squeezed out between chattering teeth.

His lifted his eyebrows slightly. "Well, why not just ask for them?" His words slammed at her.

"I did ask! Mr Thomas was evasive right from the start. I am sure he knows something, but he wouldn't tell me and then I couldn't find the documents."

His savage frown obliterated the faint shadow of confusion from his face as he spat out the question. "Are you always this impetuous, Kayla Mackenzie? Do you ever really think things through before you go rushing in where angels would fear to tread?"

He didn't repeat the question when she stayed silent. Obviously he hadn't expected an answer. Without asking her how she felt, he threw a jacket from the back seat into her lap. She pulled it on with a muttered 'thank you' then glared out of the windscreen as she hunched back down in her seat, too angry to speak. They completed the remainder of the journey to Ainsley House in silence. Kayla stewed, acrimonious words brimming. He was the one who had demanded proof and when she went to find it, he had the nerve to be upset. At least he hadn't left her the tender mercies of a police cell.

The door had barely thudded shut behind them when he turned on her.

"Of all the stupid stunts to pull. You can barely walk, you are bruised all over because someone tried to kill you last night, and still...you go off on some wild goose chase and damn near get yourself arrested," he yelled.

"Someone has to look after my interests, Wade! Are *you* going to? Is Phillip? Or my incapacitated uncle? No. Someone burgled the lawyer's office last night and I would say they took the papers. I know it wasn't you, but that does not mean you're innocent," she shouted back at him.

"Yes, so it seems. The sergeant said you still suspected me. Damn it, Kayla, I can't do this anymore. Can't you just let it go?"

"I went to find proof — signed copies of the originals should have been in her files. I understand you want proof in writing and that is fair enough. The other night I was trying to get proof and got pushed into the cellar for my trouble. Now, the lawyer's office is broken into one night, and I come along the next and get the blame, but still no papers. There are a number of people, including you, Wade Faxton, who are going to benefit, big time, if this project goes ahead, and it is those people who have murdered, lied, and committed theft to see it does. Even the lawyers are lying and I don't know why. I have little or no ammunition — I had to try every option to fight back," she cried.

He moved out of the shadows and Kayla could see his face clearly for the first time. Involuntarily she recoiled from the naked danger there. His eyes were two burning embers in a face contorted with rage. Very slowly he advanced, like a tiger on the prowl. Kayla backed away, acutely aware she had gone too far by openly implicating him in the plot.

Every muscle in his lean body strained as if held in check by some invisible force. His hands clenched and unclenched at his sides as he drew closer. He stopped, inches from Kayla. Her breath came in burning little gasps. Hypnotized by his wrath, she stared up at the very lips that had forced a sensual response from hers the instant they touched. Now, they curled into a contemptuous sneer and when he spoke, his voice dripped ice. He made no attempt to touch her.

"No one! Do you hear? *No one* questions my integrity!"

Kayla shook her head defiantly. "You're as guilty as those who have murdered to make this happen. Do you hear me, Wade? You're just as guilty."

Her words died in her constricted throat as he moved closer and ground out each word. "No one accuses me..."

She took a step back, not sure whether to flee or stand and fight. Her foot caught in the hall rug, sending her tumbling back against the hall table. It rocked, totally unbalanced her, and she crumpled into an inelegant heap on the floorboards. As she tried to get her body to react, to scramble away from him, she looked up, expecting the worst, but instead she saw his expression had paled and softened. His own fury must have shocked him, for suddenly his shoulders slumped and a brooding resignation filled his troubled eyes.

His voice was subdued now, almost incredulous. "You carry out a burglary to get evidence — something, anything to give credence to your claim — then accuse me. Childish tactics won't make it the truth, no matter how much you want it!"

"It *is* the truth," she yelled at him.

He shook his head. "Not without proof. To ask for proof is a reasonable request." He molded his mouth into a sour grimace, but his eyes held a resolute light. "Go to bed, Kayla," he ordered, as he held out his hand to help her up. She stared at it and her uncertainty and fear must have shown on her face.

"Don't be so frightened, please. You have nothing to fear from me," he said in a resigned tone.

She took his hand and he pulled her up from the floor. He steered her in the direction of the stairs and handed her the crutches.

"Go to bed," he instructed, as he gave her a gentle push to set her feet in motion.

He waited in the hall, watching as she climbed slowly.

When she reached the landing, she swung around to face him. "Wade...despite everything, I don't want to believe you are involved in this campaign to stop me saving the house..."

As she fell silent, he turned and walked into the lounge. Reluctantly, she retreated across the landing and stumbled to bed. Damn the man. How had he got under her skin so badly? She had fended off plenty of ardent males since Peter, but none had even got close to touching her heart and soul the way Wade Faxton had. It rankled that she would have to destroy him to save Ainsley House, but save it she would, even if it was the last thing she did.

Grandma Eloise would definitely not approve of the way she had handled this whole affair. For the first time in her life, since Peter, she had let her heart rule her head, but Wade made it impossible to make cool, detached judgments.

Silently she cursed him and the undeniable power he held over her. She hated what he was going to do, but she couldn't hate him, not with the memory of his searching lips, caressing hands, and hot, passionate lovemaking. A tiny knot glowed in the pit of her stomach at the thought of his touch, but ruthlessly she stamped it down. Stubbornly, she refused to delve too deeply into the mixed emotions that surrounded her relationship with the vexing Wade Faxton, but she vowed to go on fighting him until the bulldozers hit the house.

Her thoughts pounded back and forth until, finally overtaken by total exhaustion, her mind refused to form further coherent ideas so she took a painkiller, pounded the pillows into shape, and tried to sleep.

* * * *

Muted dawn light filtered through the net curtains and Kayla groaned as she extricated herself from the rumpled sheets and pushed back the tangled strands of hair. Her eyes burned and her head ached. Deep sleep had been elusive. There were no signs of movement outside her door, but she couldn't relax. There was too much to think about. Last night's fiasco seemed almost as distant as an unpleasant nightmare — such savage exchanges. Woefully she sighed, cursed her failure to get any relevant papers, and her need to fight with the man in the next room.

A light tap on the door startled her.

"Kayla, are you awake?"

The handle rattled, and fueled by last night's anger and the unwanted thought he was implicated, somehow, in the plot, she piled out of the big bed and wrenched the door open.

"What now! Haven't we tormented each other enough?" she shouted, very ready to fight back if he intended to continue the conflict from last night.

But no, he was smiling. He appeared so young and alive, but she wasn't foolish enough to think he was harmless.

"Good morning, Kayla. Will you to join me for breakfast?" he asked amiably. "And I'd also like to apologize for being so uncivilized yesterday. I don't usually give into displays of temper like that."

"Really, Wade?" Her heart jumped a little before it settled into a slightly off beat rhythm.

He was so cute, oozing charm and apologizing. Maybe last night's scene hadn't been a total disaster after all.

"We need to talk rationally about the situation we find ourselves in," he said firmly.

"Talk...*rationally*?" Her temper zoomed to white hot in a millisecond. "You're going to knock this down, probably around my ears, despite every sign pointing to the fact it is illegal, and you want to talk *rationally*?"

A wry expression moderated the accompanying flicker of anger in his eyes. "Temper, temper," he admonished. "Never in my life have I had to deal with such a persistently prickly female. Come and eat. Maybe with a full stomach you'll be more tractable," he said.

As she opened her mouth to protest, he continued.

"I'm willing to admit that perhaps I've been a little hasty in dismissing your claims. I have discussed your caveat with a couple of my investors and they are not happy about any delay it might cause, but while Robert and Damien are sympathetic to your declaration of ownership, unless you find your documents quickly, the court will overturn your petition and then the date for demolition will proceed soon after. It is currently in the hands of my legal advisers and they are working overtime to sort it out, as the whole project has a deadline of twelve months. My investors are expecting their returns by then."

"Phillip is expecting... Sorry. I would say he is desperate for his returns by then," she snapped.

"Why Phillip Mitchell, in particular?" Wade asked.

Kayla stood straighter and lifted her chin. "Oh, my darling cousin has been propping up his extravagant lifestyle and drug habit with my trust fund balance. I would say he intended to reap the benefits and replace the funds so he stayed out of prison. But I think this thing has got out of hand. I think he's got greedy and intends to take all my money, as well as destroy Ainsley House. He intends to destroy me too."

Wade sighed. "It definitely seems that way, but enough of that for the moment. Breakfast with me in half an hour—croissants with jam or hot toast and coffee?"

After he had left for the kitchen with her preferences, she found herself hurrying ever so slightly. She tried to ignore the fact that she was on dangerous ground with him.

* * * *

The French doors to the balcony had been flung wide open. The air was cool and crisp. The westerly change had dropped the temperature and, typical of Port Lincoln, it would now stay pleasantly cool for a few days. Below them, the magpies called above the shush of breeze through the gums. They hopped across the lawn before flying up and perching on the balustrade in cheeky anticipation of a tasty morsel. The sunlight streamed in the open doorway and danced across the tiles. Seated opposite Wade on the sunlit balcony, Kayla wanted nothing more than to relax and enjoy the beautiful morning and his company, but the memory of last night loomed between them and Kayla cursed the situation that had brought them to this point. He was making pointless small talk about nothing in particular and she was responding with stilted, polite words. She knew that something had to be said, the air cleared. Kayla fought the urge to laugh. Nobody would believe his briefest touch could send liquid fire through her that obliterated rational thought by racing through her veins or that a wrong word could have her overcome by rage. Her body, even now, trembled with anticipation of his touch, skin against skin and the feel of him sinking his hard cock into her throbbing pussy.

She shook the sense of unreality aside. There were things to be said. She clenched her hands into fists and stared steadily at Wade, her breathing light and shallow. "Wade, I'm grateful that you came so promptly last night," she said.

He nodded and grinned, his eyes crinkling up at the edges and the dimple forming in the velvety smoothness of newly shaven skin. The fresh tang of aftershave, soap, and freshly brewed coffee was a heady mixture that almost hijacked Kayla's thoughts.

Wade frowned. "I know you think I am being a bastard for not halting the demolition of the house, but you have to understand, I am locked into a binding contract that must be fulfilled unless proof of its illegality is justification for breaking it. I'm as trapped in this as you are."

"And without those papers, I have no chance of stopping it, do I?"

"No."

She pulled out the scrunched up paper she had taken from the file at the lawyer's office. "I found this in the file last night. I know it is not proof, but at least it does outline the conditions of the trust and trustees, including contingency plans if the trustees are incapacitated."

Wade took the scrap from her trembling fingers and smoothed it out on the bench. As he read it, the frown furrowing his forehead grew deeper by the minute. "And both trustees are incapacitated?"

"Yes both trustees are in fact incapacitated so, as I am over twenty-one, I can — and intend — to take control of my fund now — or what is left of it. I am not sure how, but I have a meeting on Skype with my lawyer this morning."

He reached for her. Kayla guessed his intentions and tried to snatch it away, but already he was encasing hers hand in a tender grip.

"Kayla…"

She shook her head, trying in vain to pull away, but he held her firmly. She didn't want to hear what he had to say — something that shouldn't, couldn't, be said. Not now, maybe not ever.

"Listen to me, Kayla. Despite my project, you can't deny the attraction between us." He rubbed his thumb smoothly across her knuckles, cradling her palm with his fingers. With the curved firmness of the pad he lightly traced the edge of each nail as though he was mapping them for future reference. With infinite slowness, he turned her hand over and lifted it to his lips.

Kayla sat motionless, her gaze trapped by the deliberate motion of his action — unable to react, to pull away. Her breathing was a mere whisper in her throat, her body so leaden with desire she let him kiss her. Each feather-light kiss across her palm deepened the spell, dismantled her certainty, and melted her resolve.

"You are an intoxicating woman and I want you in my life, regardless of the future," he murmured.

His voice was a gravelly purr that rumbled across her skin, his gaze full of promise and sincerity. She was drowning in his magnetism. She gasped and struggled to rise above the intoxicating spell he was weaving.

"Stop, Wade. Don't do this," she pleaded.

He pulled away, but she could see he wasn't happy. "I'll be back as soon as I can. I'll leave my chauffeur, Billy, here to watch over you," he said as he headed for the door.

She didn't know what to think of Wade any more, but he was right. She couldn't deny the attraction between them. She sat for a long time after he'd left, her chaotic thoughts tumbling around in her head. She was fast running out of options on how to stop the planned demolition of Ainsley House. She poured herself another coffee and picked at a croissant as she mused on what could have been.

* * * *

With frustrating slowness, she hobbled downstairs and out into the rose arbor where she sat, letting the warmth of the sun ease her aching body. Her mind raced from thought to thought. She didn't know how long she had been sitting there, but she heard voices, and thinking it might be Wade returning, she reached for her crutches. She was still struggling to rise when an elderly couple came around the corner. Wade's chauffeur, Billy, appeared from nowhere and came to stand just in front of her, but slightly to the side. He was ready for an attack, but was trying not to make it look like it.

"Hello. I think we might be trespassing, but we came to have a tour though the gallery and Ainsley House. It is such a beautiful, old colonial home and I believe it houses some of the best local artwork," the woman said.

Kayla's face flushed with a trace of anger and regret as she sank back down on the bench seat. "I'm sorry, the house is currently closed," she said as politely as she could.

The gentleman glanced over his shoulder at the house. "Such a shame," he said. "I believe it's going to be demolished."

Kayla nodded.

The woman adjusted her hat and handbag. "Well it should be stopped. Surely public opinion would be against the town heritage being destroyed by an outsider?" she muttered.

Kayla smiled. "I don't think they've been consulted," she replied.

The woman almost bristled. "Well, someone should ask them!" she snapped.

Kayla stood now, and leaned on her crutches. "Yes, maybe they should be asked, and I am the one that should be asking. Thank you. You've given me an idea. If you will excuse me, I have a phone call to make."

Startled at her sudden dismissal, the couple stared at her for moment then turned and walked toward the gate.

Kayla cursed her injuries as she hobbled inside. It was time to call in a few favors and to test how the community really felt about Ainsley House. She rang the *Port Lincoln Times* office and asked to speak to Simon McDonald.

Before she could speak, Simon jumped in.

"Kayla, is everything okay?"

"No, Simon, things are not okay, and I am beginning to think they never will be again. I need a favor," she replied.

"Anything you want, Kayla," Simon promised.

"I need some help to stop the illegal demolition of the house. I know Phillip is behind it — Phillip and that

Seville guy—and I need to stop it. I want the townspeople to protest the demolition of the town's heritage icon," she announced grandly.

"I'm glad you'll set the record straight because most people here think you have sold out the town's heritage—and your own grandmother—for money."

"I want to place an editorial and an ad for a public demonstration to be held, if you can, for tomorrow's edition of the paper."

"Hmmmm. I think we can swing it because we don't go to print until late tonight. I may be able to move a few things around to make the space. When can we get together to talk?" Simon asked.

Kayla stared out of the window at the restless sea for a moment. "Well, I'm at Ainsley House now," she said. "I'm not going anywhere."

"Okay, I will be with you in an hour, with a photographer," Simon said firmly.

She smiled. "Thanks, Simon. I was hoping you would help."

By lunch time she had her article and photos—all for the front page—and also a full page ad, at half the cost. She could easily imagine, and fear, Wade's reaction to her plans and the high level of exposure, but the theft of her papers had left her with little choice, but to use more drastic means.

She knew she had already lost her heart to Wade but given their conflict, she knew it would bring her nothing but heartache. Even if he believed he was infatuated with her right now, even if his feelings had nothing to do with the house, as he claimed, Kayla did not want to become another notch in his belt. If she ever fell in love again, she wanted it to be the forever kind. And there could never be forever between her and Wade with such differences between them. After the paper came out, that gap would widen into an unbridgeable chasm. She should never have let her heart out of its cage. She should never have made love to Wade in the first place, but somehow she couldn't find it in her to regret it.

Wade had not returned by the time she crawled into bed. Billy bedded down on the couch still clothed in his uniform. Despite her unease, she slept soundly.

* * * *

Kayla was glad Wade had already left when she woke. She didn't want his reaction to spoil her anticipation of the early edition release. Simon had one copy delivered to her just before it went on sale. The article was fantastic. It tugged at the heartstrings and the ad was in color, big and bold. No one who read the paper could miss it, and it had the Ainsley House phone number in large print.

Within half an hour of the paper hitting the stands, the phone began to ring and didn't stop—people she hadn't spoken to in years, those she had never spoken to, and outsiders as well. All promised to support her and pledged to be on the front lawn of Ainsley House at ten on Monday morning to protest the project that would destroy one of their favorite heritage icons.

Her heart pounded as she realized the swell of support was for her. But she worried each time she picked up the phone that it would be Wade.

Then he was there, looming large and very angry in the doorway to the flat.

"What the hell have you done *now*?" Do you realize what you have set in motion? For God's sake, Kayla, why do you do these things?" he shouted.

She quailed under his overwhelming presence. "Because no one is really listening to me — even you. This way I am speaking louder. It is not just my voice. Maybe then you will hear me."

"Damn it, Kayla, I *was* trying to hear you, but you had nothing to back yourself up with. This is a multimillion dollar project with several large investors. We can't stop it on a whim. If you want to stop it, you have to provide proof," he snarled.

She stood now, so she didn't feel so vulnerable and submissive to his dominant presence. "I've tried Wade. Believe me, I've tried. How do you think I feel when the only family I have is the one trying to destroy me? He knows how much I love this place, how much it means to me. It is the one thing he could destroy that is certain to hurt me. He may even be the very one who tried to kill me the other night. I could have broken my neck falling or died of hypothermia or worse still, died a long, slow death of starvation in that dark hole just like Pierre and Abrial. If you hadn't found me — " Sobs threatened to choke her.

He stepped forward and put strong arms around her and pulled her hard against his chest. "Kayla, Kayla. What am I to do with you? I want to love you and hold you, but you won't let me. You don't believe me. I *am* trying to help you, but you continue to fight me and can't provide me with the one thing I must have. He lowered his head and kissed her face, her eyes, her nose, and her lips. "Kayla, my little witch, I am fighting for my life here, for the survival of my company, my financial future, and my reputation. Yet, I want to throw it all away when I am near you. When I'm holding you in my arms, when I feel your heart beating rapidly with fear, all I want to do is hold you, to protect you, and make you mine in a way I never have before with any other woman, but you are my nemesis." He groaned.

"Oh, Wade, I'm sorry, but I am also fighting for the survival of my heritage, my rights, and my reputation."

He kissed her with explorative demanding kisses. She curled her hands up around his neck and pressed herself against him. The regret would come later, but for now, she just let herself sink into the sensations that sizzled between them.

Then he put her from him. "Kayla, we both have to do what we have to — fight to the bitter end. One will win and we will both lose. I fear there will be no room in this bitter battle to salvage what we feel for each other. Too much will have come to pass."

Tears welled up as the coldness of the truth wrapped itself around her. Once this was over, there would be nothing left of the love they had between them. For now, it was too new, too tender, and too uncertain to survive the bitter battle ahead and the hurt of the loser would snuff out anything that remained.

She tore herself from his embrace and fled as fast as she could to her room, suddenly overwhelmed by the need to be alone — alone to mourn the death of love.

"Kayla."

She ignored his impassioned plea, shutting the door, even as he followed her. He didn't knock, and she was glad, for she was beyond facing him right now.

* * * *

It was a long night — a long night of waiting, of wondering. She heard small sounds of movement and knew Wade was pacing the flat — that he was as unsettled and tormented as she. But she couldn't face him, so she stayed hidden in her room

Around three a.m., Wade knocked on the door. "Kayla, I know you're awake. Please come out."

"I can't, Wade. I can't be near you like this," she whimpered.

"Hiding away will not make your feelings, or mine, go away. Is it so bad if we share a brief moment of love—for us—before that love is annihilated? Come, Kayla. Let me hold you. Let me love you," he pleaded.

The desire for him and the angst tore at her, almost rending her heart in two. She sat on the edge of the bed in the darkness, torn by indecision, and acutely aware of Wade waiting outside her door for her acquiesce. Waiting for her to grant him the smallest of gifts—a few moments of her time and her love.

"Kayla?" he pleaded. "Please come to me."

She hesitated for a long moment, but it was impossible to turn away from what they had. Even if it had to end at sunrise, it was worth having. She opened the door.

He was standing outside dressed in just a pair of long shorts, his expression pensive, his strong jaw darkened with new beard growth.

She looked up into his eyes. They were shadowed, almost rusty brown with unacknowledged emotion and desire. He smiled and it creased his cheeks into dimples and lifted the fullness of his mouth into a deep curve.

"Thank you for coming to me, Kayla."

She shook her head. "Then why do I get the distinct feeling I've made a terrible mistake?" she asked.

"Mistake or not, Kayla, it's all we have for now and perhaps forever," he muttered. "Tonight is ours and ours alone."

With athletic ease, he scooped her up and carried her into his bedroom where he laid her among the crumpled sheets. It took only a moment for him to slip his shorts off. She gazed at his muscular body, a matching fire igniting in her belly as his cock hardened and rose slowly under her scrutiny. Their gazes locked. He hesitated. She could still say no. He was giving her the chance to turn away from creating searing wounds on her soul and in her heart that might never heal. But it was too late for that because the wounds were already there. They cut deep and ached abominably.

She beckoned him with one crooked finger as she moved across the bed to make room for him. She watched him approach—every hard muscle moved in synchronized unison. Her body craved his touch, even as she fought back tears, knowing this was all they had.

As he lay down beside her, she eased her body next to his, warm, bare flesh pressed against warm, bare flesh. He cradled her face with one hand, stroking her cheek with his thumb as he explored her lips with his. She caressed the molded flesh of his chest and abdomen, teaching her to remember every inch of his magnificent torso and the strong muscular curve of his back before she trailed them up into his hair to curve around the silkiness of the tousled strands. Her fingers tingled as they mapped his body. Her heart clenched in distress.

With a barely discernible shift of position, Wade began to kiss her neck and shoulders. The exciting interplay between featherlight kisses and tiny nibbling bites made her body sing its own song of desire. Her pussy burned with need, the tender inside flesh melting into liquid fire. He cupped her buttocks, easing her closer. His stiffened flesh pressed demandingly against her mound. She reached down, clasped it, and moved her hand languidly up and down the hard, hot length. He moaned and eased her back onto the bed, sliding his hands with tantalizing slowness over the swell of her breasts. For a moment, he teased her nipple then glided on down over her ribs, past the flatness of her stomach, to between her legs.

She moaned with unrestrained pleasure and eased her hips toward his hand. God, she so wanted him. He dipped his hand between the hot wet lips of flesh that protected her pussy. As his finger slid over her clit, she flinched as lightening blasts of pleasure flashed through her body. She clenched her muscles to capture the thrill of her orgasm before she relaxed and let it flow through her. With an easy familiarity, he played with her layers of flesh, caressing them, teasing each curve before rubbing it with his fingers.

She gasped as he explored the depths of her pussy with his long fingers. She tightened her grip more firmly over his throbbing shaft. She felt the moisture on the tip and slid her thumb through it. He took a deep breath and pushed his cock hard against her hand as he plundered her mouth, filling it with the tensile fullness of his tongue. She sucked reveling in the taste of him, mellow and rich—the exact panacea to fuel her desire. As he released her mouth, he pushed her back on the bed.

She wanted him so badly. "Take me, Wade. Love me."

He eased over her and settled between her legs, the head of his penis just caressing her entrance. He held himself above her, his golden eyes dark with passion. "Show me the way, my love," he murmured.

Kayla reached down and grasped his hot rod of flesh and guided it into the throbbing wetness. He buried himself with exquisite slowness into her, deep and gentle. He paused a moment, letting her feel the fullness and appreciate the strength of his desire as it delved into her pulsing depths.

She squeezed her internal muscles to caress his flesh. He groaned and began to whip in and out with long, even stokes. Slow strokes. As he sank into her, he leaned down and kissed her mouth with quick firm kisses. Her body began to quiver with the slow build-up of tingling and throbbing that promised a fiery rush of release. He moved fast and deep then slow and shallowly, the variation of rhythm stoking the fire inside her. She met his thrusts with small hip lifts. The bursts of passion so intense she was unable to stop small whimpers from escaping her lips as her body shuddered with exploding fissions of delight. She arched and threw her head back onto the pillows. As the roar of release surged through her, she lifted herself to meet his downward movement. Her legs shook with the intensity of her climax, her hair tingled, and she gasped for air. He moved faster inside her, almost savage little pokes. She cried out, sweat poured from her skin as she clawed his back with her nails. He sank his cock deep and took command of her mouth, smothering her cries of ecstasy with a guttural groan of his own release. Kayla floated beyond reality, as the pulsing shudder of the joint implosion thudded with exquisite pleasure behind her breast and between her legs.

Wade relaxed as her cries faded to tiny moans, letting his weight rest on her for a moment before he rolled onto his side and pulled her with him, his shaft still imbedded in her body. When her tears began to fall, he wiped them away with the palm of his hand.

"Don't cry, Kayla. This is not the end for us," he whispered.

Despite his assurances, she couldn't stop the tears from slipping down her cheeks, because in her heart, she didn't believe him.

* * * *

It was almost dawn when Kayla finally pulled free of his embrace and retreated to her room to grieve her sacrifice and her loss. It was sometime later, but finally she drifted into an exhausted sleep.

When she did wake, just after noon, Wade had already left the house. There was no note or indication of his whereabouts. She had barely gulped down a light brunch when Simon arrived to take her to his office where they and a few fiery young reporters spent the rest of the day making placards for the protest. It was fun and rousing, working together, but after a shared slap up feast of crumbed chicken and chips and Simon returned her to the flat, she began to feel a real sense of despondency. Despite the protest being at her instigation, she felt weighed down by what she had started.

Billy was slumped on the lounge, engrossed in a novel, and he just shook his head when she asked about Wade's whereabouts. She hobbled upstairs and fell into bed. It was past midnight when she heard him return.

* * * *

She was up when Wade came out of his room, dressed in his suit and tie—every inch the rich powerful Executive Director of a multi-million dollar company and very ready to do battle.

"David and the other investors will be here in about an hour. We'll use the second flat as an office and conference room. I would suggest you stay out of sight, as I expect there will be some unpleasant fallout. I don't want you subject to any abuse or to be at risk." He gave her a hard, direct look. There was no smile to ease his expression. "Promise me you will take care of yourself today," he demanded.

She nodded. "You don't think anyone will try to hurt me at a public rally, do you?" she asked, feeling just a little afraid of what she had set in motion.

He shrugged. "I don't know, just be careful. Remember Kayla, it is not me you are fighting anymore. It is someone else—someone with a darker agenda than mine," he warned.

Then he was gone.

Kayla felt bereft at his sudden departure. There had been no lingering kiss, and no hesitation on his part. It was as if their passion in the darkness of the long night had never been. It was even harder knowing Wade was just across the corridor, ensconced in the second flat with David. She had plenty of time before she had to be outside, empty time to fill with unpleasant thoughts. An hour later, Simon arrived. He went across and had a quiet word with Wade about expectations. As he returned, Kayla peeped out the window and was delighted to see a stream of cars and people pouring through the gates of Ainsley House. As they gathered, she estimated about three hundred people had arrived and were now milling on the parched lawn below the second flat balcony. Many waved placards and some were chanting "no demolition" and "leave Ainsley House alone".

A cheer rose as she appeared around the side of the building and hobbled forward on her crutches. A large group of people crowded around her — old family friends and old schoolmates, all congratulating her on taking a stand.

"We thought you had sold out, Kayla. We are so glad you didn't," her old headmaster, Mr Smith said.

More people poured through the gates easily filling every available inch of space in front of the house. The police had mobilized and now stood silently to the side, but showed no interest in interfering.

Kayla focused on the upper verandah of the house as the crowd shouted loudly. Finally Wade, David Richards, and several other grim looking men appeared at the balustrade studied them, wondering which one was the killer. Just behind them, she saw a movement and realized Phillip and another man she didn't recognize were standing in the back corner, nearly hidden by the billowing curtains and the others on the balcony.

She saw Wade observing the crowd and suddenly she was staring straight into his eyes. It was too far away to read his expression, but his stare never left her face. More people crowded around. Now there were at least five hundred supporters yelling and brandishing hand written signs screaming for Wade to speak — to explain himself.

As Wade stepped forward, the portable microphone in hand, Kayla saw Phillip slip back into the room behind him.

The crowd surged forward. Wade stepped up to the balustrade, introduced himself, and acknowledged

Kayla and the issues between them about the house. Then he began to outline his plans.

Kayla remained at the rear of the crowd and away a bit, afraid she would be toppled over by the milling angry people. Her arm was suddenly caught in a vice-like grip. She was being shaken. Her head snapped back and forth and one of her crutches slid from under her arm.

"I told you, little cousin, to leave Ainsley House alone. This is bigger than you," Phillip growled in her ear.

"Let go of me, Phillip," she cried.

Suddenly Simon was beside her. "Yes, Phillip, let go of her or I'll knock you flat," he threatened in a deep growl.

He ignored her desperate request and Simon's threat. "Look what you've done—opened up a can of worms." He shook her again. "Do you think the likes of them on the landing are going to care? They will stop you, and they won't care how they do it either. I don't care how they do it. I want Ainsley House demolished." He snarled, his face drawn up into an ugly mask of hate.

Simon grabbed Phillip's arms and forced him to release his grip on Kayla. He pulled him away and held him at bay with a palm on his chest.

She turned to face Phillip. "Why?"

Phillip shoved Simon's hand aside and lunged at Kayla. "Because it represents all the misery in my life—all the hurt and the wrongs done to me by my very own family. It represents my mistake. That one damn mistake. I will never be free while that house stands," he shouted right into her face.

"Oh, Phillip."

Simon dragged him away again and he appeared to calm. Phillip tried to shrug Simon aside but Simon kept a grip on his arms. Phillip ripped one free and pointed at Kayla.

"Walk away, little cousin. Walk away, before you come to a nasty end," he said loudly.

"Really, so are they mafia or something? Did you murder Pierre and Abrial? Did *you* try to murder me or did they?" He glared at her. "I will not tolerate you getting in the way. You should have stayed in Scotland. Next time they will succeed, little cousin. Are you willing to pay with your life for that monstrosity?" he asked.

"Why didn't you tell me Uncle George was so ill? That changes everything," she cried as she tried to pull away from him.

"Even if my father was dead, it changes nothing, because it's too late to be stopped now," He snarled.

"It does, Phillip, because if your father is incapable or dead, I'm now in control of my own trust and it is *not* too late," she announced.

His face blanched.

She felt satisfaction that she had rattled his aggressive confidence. "I know what you have done, Phillip," she said.

"You know *nothing*, little cousin. You're just guessing," he retorted, almost spitting the words in her face.

"I know you've embezzled my trust funds. What was it? Gambling, drugs, fancy living, or prostitutes? Do they have some hold over you Phillip, or are you just a thieving bastard? Whatever it is, it stops right here." Kayla pointed an index finger right at her cousin's face.

Phillip barked a vicious laugh. "Too late, little cousin, you can't stop this now, even if you have Wade Faxton eating out of your hand. Wade Faxton has too much to lose. He will follow orders because he is beholden to those investors if he wants to survive. Do you understand, little cousin? This thing is out of Faxton's control and too big for you to prevent. Just accept it and go home." He sneered. He smashed his fist into Simon's face and lunged forward as the older man fell. With brutal strength he pushed Kayla in the chest.

"No, Phillip." She screamed, as her second crutch popped out from under her arm and she began to fall. At her cry, those in the back row of the crowd turned. Three burly men rushed to her aid, but it was too late. She hit the dry lawn with a thud, re-twisted her injured ankle, and wrenched her shoulder.

"Ouch! You bastard."

She glowered up at Phillip and saw rapid fury and a touch of madness in his eyes. In that moment, she saw him swing his foot back as if he was going to kick her. The men promptly jumped him and wrestled him to the ground. Seconds later, two police constables arrived.

"Mr Faxton says you need some assistance, Miss," the blond one said.

Kayla nodded as Simon helped her to her feet and handed her the crutches.

"Mr Faxton?" she asked a little confused.

"Yes, Miss, he knew this person was coming to confront you so he called us to intervene. Unfortunately, we didn't get here in time. We'll take him away, Miss. Do you wish to press charges?" the taller of the officers asked.

Kayla glanced up at the balcony. The one person still there was Wade. She nodded acknowledgment to him then she glanced at Simon.

"You should," he said.

"Yes, Officer, I do," she said.

"Okay, we will lock him up for the time being and get some statements."

Phillip was whisked away and while the crowd dispersed everyone involved in the incident gathered inside at the drawing tables. The constables took statements from each witness.

Kayla told the full story from the beginning and the police took it all down.

"So, Miss Mackenzie, you believe your cousin, Phillip, has something to do with the other incidents?" the tall officer asked.

"Yes, I do."

"We will question him about it, but I am sure he will make bail. Where can we contact you if we need to?"

"I am staying here at Ainsley House," she replied noticing for the first time Wade was standing behind the constable.

The expression on his face was unreadable. "Are you okay, Kayla?" he asked.

She nodded. "A few more bruises, but nothing drastic."

"So are you up to joining me at a meeting of the investors?" Without waiting for her reply he turned to Simon. "I think we need to put everything out in the open and work out just what is going on here. We need to know just who is behind the unfortunate incidents that have happened. I intend to start with Phillip Mitchell. I'm happy to leave him in the cells, but his mate, Peter, has gone to bail him out. I want Kayla to speak with my investors first, then I will have them removed from the house. My young chauffeur is going to be stationed outside the front door to ensure Kayla's safety until I have completed my business in town and hopefully get to the bottom of this mess."

With that, he scooped Kayla up into his arms and leaving Simon, unbidden, to bring the crutches, he walked into the reception area, and up the stairs.

He paused on the landing. "Do you wish to come with us, Simon?" Wade asked. "You're welcome to stay with Kayla until I get back, if you have concerns for her safety."

Simon shook his head. "No, Faxton. I'm satisfied you will take care of her, but if you don't, I will see you're dealt with appropriately," he warned.

"Fair enough," Wade replied, as he set Kayla down.

When Simon left, Wade pulled her hard against him. "Kayla, what am I to do with you? I am not allowed to love you, I don't hate you, and for some reason, I can't even seem to protect you."

She reached up and ran her hand down the smooth skin of his cheek. "Oh, Wade," she murmured.

She sensed the tension that buzzed around him like a malevolent aura.

"Are you sure you're okay? I can take you to the hospital if you need?" he asked.

She shook her head, her breathing already made uneven by his nearness.

Wade was studying her closely and she sensed he wanted to say something but didn't know how.

Staring directly into his eyes she said, "Shall I say it for you and put you out of your misery? You told me so. You told me I was leaving myself open to trouble by taking this fight public."

"No, Kayla, you don't have to say it for me, because that is not what I was going to say."

"Really."

He leaned closer now, his eyes dark and shadowed with warring emotions. "Your little rally today stirred up uneasiness in a couple of my investors. They have started to ask questions and they don't like the idea of the town being so against the project. Peter was furious and wanted to know why I hadn't shut you up, and Mitchell? Well, he almost had an apoplexy at the sight of such a big crowd."

"I bet he did. That was why he came after me. But what has Peter Tenney got to do with all this? He is just a small time criminal," she said.

"Your cousin recruited Tenney as an investor, along with a bloke called Rossi, after Seville made the offer available to me, but I am not sure what Tenney's place is in all this."

Kayla shrugged. "He would be happy to help Phillip with his plot because he doesn't have any love for my family, but where does Seville fit in and who traded Ainsley House for an IOU in the first place? The two people who had control were Frederick Carven and George Mitchell, and personally I don't believe either of them would have had such a gambling debt or exchanged my property for such a debt. I mean…they were both honest men — friends for years. Their obvious vices were they loved to get together with their cronies for a few too many good malt whiskies, top quality cigars, and an odd game of poker."

"Well, the four — Tenney, Seville, Rossi and Mitchell — are coming for a discussion tonight with my friends and fellow investors, Roger Tobin and Damien Clavell. They are asking the hard questions and I am not sure of the outcome, but I would expect I will take some of the heat," Wade said. He didn't sound angry, just tired and a little resigned.

"I'm sorry, Wade—for all this—but I cannot let this house be destroyed. Never mind that it is mine. It's my heritage."

He leaned forward and placed a gentle kiss on her lips to silence her. "We will sort this out, Kayla. Something is going on, but I am not sure what. I don't want to lose my reputation or my company, but I will not go ahead if it is not legal."

As he opened the door to the flat, she heard angry male voices. Wade scooped her up and marched directly into the lounge room.

Three imposing males were hunched over a table full of plans and building specifications. One of them—tall, lean and swarthy—held the floor simply by the force of his anger. His dark eyes flickered with angry lights. His high forehead below his receding hairline was crinkled in deep furrows. His voice was a harsh bark as a tirade of words spewed forth, each one tainted by a heavy accent.

"This project will *not* be stopped by anyone, especially not some little upstart of a woman. I have invested a significant sum in this project. If this resistance does not stop, I will withdraw my funds and the adjoining land." He glared up at Wade then and stabbed the air with his finger. "Then where will you be, Wade? I gave you preference over another on Phillip Mitchell's advice and you were so keen, you didn't stop to evaluate whether you could even bring this thing to fruition. So both of you have a great deal to answer for," he bellowed.

Wade carefully deposited Kayla in a chair then turned to face his accuser. "Seville, I assure you that you will not be out of pocket, regardless of the project's success or failure. I admit to the one-upmanship, but it was not done recklessly. You will recover all your investments, even if I have to sell everything I own—and then some."

Seville sneered. "It just might come to that if you don't sort this interfering female out, once and for all."

Fury flared and although Kayla felt intimidated by this forceful man, she wasn't about to let his comments go unchallenged.

"Mr Seville," she said loudly. "I'm that interfering female, and I have a right to interfere. This house is mine—held in trust for me. I want to know how Wade came to be in possession of it."

Seville glared at her. She felt like a rabbit, hypnotized in the brightness of car headlights. "Are you questioning my integrity?" he demanded to know.

"Yes, Mr Seville, I am. Ainsley House was held in trust for me with two trustees, Frederick Carven and George Mitchell. They had no reason or mandate to sell it, so how did it get used to cover an IOU for gambling. Whose gambling?" she asked.

She could see Wade watching them. His face was shadowed with concern. She chose to ignore his facial expressions telling her to back off.

"The payment of the IOU was a legitimate business deal, but it should have come to me instead of Wade," Seville said.

"Really, Mr Seville. Then if I am to believe you, both the trustees, Carven and Mitchell, have committed a felony, and if my beloved cousin, Phillip, recommended the property to Wade, then he has also committed a felony," she announced.

Seville's face darkened. She saw real rage in the angular lines of his thin, bony face.

"You are very quick to make accusations, missy," he said. "I know nothing of either Frederick Carven or

George Mitchell, your so-called trustees," Seville growled.

"Really. Then it comes back to whose debt it was? Who signed it over to Wade's father's estate?" she snapped.

"It was a legitimate IOU, missy."

"That is not what I asked, Mr Seville. I intend to get to the bottom of this little debacle. You will all" — she glanced around at Wade and the other two investors — "eventually be subpoenaed to court. All financial records will be examined. All transactions revealed. The Supreme Court will find the truth and I will not remove the caveat or shut up about it until the truth is uncovered."

"I wouldn't if I were you, young lady. Do you know who you are taking on here?"

Kayla tried not to flinch at the threat. "Mr Seville, I don't care who I am taking on, because I have the truth on my side," she declared.

The door flung open and Phillip burst in, followed closely by a short, rotund man, in his mid-thirties, with a short, blond, spiky hair cut. Instant recognition slapped at her. Peter Tenney, a much older, more arrogant and very angry version, but there was no mistaking his identity.

"What's *she* doing here?" Phillip pointed to Kayla, but asked the question of Wade.

Wade stepped sideways and rested his hand on her shoulder. Kayla was extremely grateful for the comforting warmth, because she couldn't stop herself from trembling.

"I invited Kayla here to talk to Seville, Roger, and Damien to see if we can come up with a workable solution for this house business."

"Damn you, Kayla. I told you to leave it alone. See the mess you've caused," Phillip growled at her.

"Me, Phillip? I think the responsibility for this mess lies with others — you for a start, or perhaps even the late, unlamented Frederick Carven, your father, or Mr Seville. Something is very wrong with this scenario — very wrong. You *know*, Phillip, damn you. You know the house is protected by a trust — a gift to the town," she said firmly.

"Shut up, Kayla. You are ranting about things you know little about. You're making yourself look like a raving lunatic." He was yelling now, his fine-boned, angular face red, the veins standing out in his neck as he ran his hand through his short, blunt haircut. His eyes were dark with anger.

"No, Phillip, you're the one who is the lunatic," she replied.

He lunged at her, but Wade was already there between them. His right fist was clenched and raised, ready to strike. Phillip immediately backed off.

"Pick on someone your own size, Mitchell," Wade said very quietly.

Phillip shot a savage look at Wade but took two steps back.

Wade let his fist drop to his side, but continued to glare at Phillip. "Gentlemen, and Kayla, all this angst is not finding a solution. First and foremost, I will not be involved in anything illegal, but I have also made a significant commitment of my resources to this project, so it is my best interest that it goes ahead."

"Who said there was anything illegal?" Phillip asked.

"Phillip, you know that this whole debacle is illegal," Kayla shouted. "You know what Grandma Eloise wanted. You know — "

"You can't prove anything, Kayla..."

"No, I can't, but only because you stole my paperwork and tried to kill me."

Phillip stepped forward again. "Rubbish," he yelled.

Now Wade moved toward Phillip. "What do you know, Mitchell, of Kayla's claims?"

"Huh? Kayla's claim is just a figment of her guilty conscience. You know she left her grandmother to die alone—injured and dying for days because Kayla was so busy with her grand life in the city," Phillip sneered.

"I know what happened," Wade responded calmly. "But does her claim about the house have substance or not?"

"Nothing she can prove." He snarled. Phillip glared at Kayla, almost daring her to challenge him. "So let that be an end of it," he muttered.

"I might not be able to prove it, Phillip, but that does not mean it isn't true. You're a liar and an embezzler—maybe even a murderer. All my trust funds are gone—stolen by you. You're a greedy bastard, forging signatures and falsifying records, but you know what, Phillip? I don't give a damn about the money. You're welcome to it. It is Ainsley House I want."

"Well you can't have it," Phillip replied, as he advanced toward her, his face distorted into a grotesque mask of fury that even Kayla reeled back from.

Phillip waved his fist at Kayla. "Do you hear me? You can't have it. It must be destroyed. Then I will be free."

Wade was there between them again, pressing hard against Phillip's chest. "Enough, Mitchell." The muscles clenched in Wade's arm as he held Phillip back.

Phillip jerked away, spun on his heel, and stalked out of the room. "Peter, Seville," he snapped. Both men moved toward him as Phillip took a parting shot at Wade.

"Faxton, you're a fool, thinking below the belt, not above, but know this—either you sort her out or I will," Phillip warned. "This project *will* go ahead."

Then the door swung shut behind the three. Damien and Roger stared after them in shocked silence until the noise of the three angry men's retreat fell silent then they turned to Wade.

Roger stepped forward, an apologetic expression marring his handsome face. "Look, Wade, we want this project to go ahead, but neither of us is prepared to work with bottom feeders. The mere mention of murder...well, we're both seriously thinking of pulling the plug. We know it will leave you in a hole, financially, and we regret that, but neither of us want to be compromised."

"I know, Roger. I don't want to be compromised either. Will you give me some time to get to the bottom of the issue? Your funds are not at risk. I am the one who will be out of pocket. You can afford to delay your decision for a short while. Surely Roger, Damien...surely we have enough history for you to give me time," Wade asked.

Roger nodded. "Neither of us has the desire to bring you down, Wade. We know things will get hard. We will give you until the original demolition date then re-assess it."

Roger held out his hand and Wade took it in a double handed grasp and shook. Damien followed suit.

"Ms Mackenzie, you have definitely been a fly in the ointment, but if what you say has more than a grain of truth then it needs to be brought to light," Roger said.

"Thank you, gentlemen," she replied.

Wade gestured toward the door. "Why don't you two go have a leisurely dinner and I will meet you in the hotel boardroom promptly at seven." He turned to Kayla. "Kayla, I will leave Billy to keep you company and provide some security while I am gone."

She nodded. As the two investors left, Wade insisted on carrying her across the landing to the flat and installing her on the couch before he ordered in pizza for them all. Moments later, he came back with a couple of painkillers and some anti-inflammatory cream. He sat beside her while she took the pills.

"Now, off with your shirt," he said. "I'm going to rub this cream into your shoulder to help with the new bruising and soreness."

She undid her shirt and slipped it off her shoulders.

"Damn that man. I should give him a good right hook." Wade cursed under his breath. "You have an awful bruise that covers most of your shoulder," he growled as he gently applied the cream.

Kayla peeped over her shoulder and could see the beginning of the bruise in the dip by her neck. She could just see Wade's strong fingers as he scooped up some cream, but could not stop the flinch as they touched her skin.

"Cold?" he asked.

"Yes."

"They say cold hands, warm heart," he said.

She sensed more than heard him chuckle at his own words as he gently massaged the cream into her shoulder, the palms of his hands sliding over her skin, making all her nerve endings dance with awareness.

The warmth that radiated from his hands melted the gel and stoked her desire.

He lifted her hair away from her back and draped it over her shoulder, letting his fingers trail through its length. He moved closer. She stayed still, waiting for his seduction to begin. He began to kiss her, just brief touches on the nape of her neck. His scent swirled around her, sparking multiple fires of desire through her body. She sighed and lifted her face up to him just a little. At her blatant invitation, his kisses became firmer and trailed over her uninjured shoulder and down her arm. Just as she was sinking under his spell, he pulled away and laid both hands on her shoulders.

His breathing was ragged and fast and he moved restlessly on the lounge. "I have to go, Cinderella, before I take you to my bed and miss this meeting altogether. There is a heat pad in your bed, if it helps, use it. Young Billy will stay here until I get back. Will you be all right?" he asked.

She nodded, already feeling the chill creep through her body from the places he had touched. She didn't watch him leave, but the quiet click of the door told her he was gone. The flat felt empty and desolate so she curled up in bed. It had been such an emotionally draining day she barely lay her head down and she was asleep.

Chapter Six

She awoke with a start in the darkness to the jangle of the landline. She snatched the phone up, thinking it was Wade.

"If you want your partner alive, you better come get him. He's in the cabin of the cruiser, Lady Louisa, worse for wear. I'll be watching, so don't call anyone, otherwise he'll be dead before you can reach him. You hear me?"

"Who is this?" she asked.

"Never mind. Go to berth seventy-six at the marina. Lady Louisa. No cops or he's dead," the voice mumbled.

"All right. No police. I'll come alone," she said.

The phone clicked as it was disconnected. She flew out of bed. "Ouch, ouch." Her shoulder clenched and froze, and her ankle burned with pain as her foot touched the floor. She grabbed up her trackies, pulled a sweatshirt over her T-shirt, and slipped her feet into her thongs. With impatient caution, she hobbled down the stairs with her crutches under her arm.

Billy was snoring gently in the recliner by the front door.

"Billy, wake up."

He snuffled and pulled away from her hand.

"Billy, wake up. Wade's in trouble."

Billy opened his eyes. They were red and unfocused. "What's your problem, Miss Mackenzie?" he mumbled.

"I just had a phone call—someone saying Wade is on some boat."

Billy shook his head. "Nah, someone is playing a joke on you. Best stay here, Miss. Wait for Wade to come back."

"But Billy, it's three a.m. He should've been back ages ago."

Billy stirred on the couch, but made no attempt to rise. "He's probably still in the meeting. They had lots to work out after today," he mumbled.

Frustrated with her stand-in bodyguard's off-hand response, she reached out and shook him by the shoulder. "Billy, have you been drinking?"she snapped.

His words were slurred, ever so slightly. He turned beetroot red and dropped his gaze to the floor. "Err, I sort of had a couple of glasses of the wine that came with the pizza," he muttered.

"What wine, Billy? Wade did not order wine."

"Well, there was a bottle." He leaned over and almost fell out of the chair as he tried to retrieve the bottle. It was a mini bottle and it was empty. He would have had two glasses, at the most.

"Damn it, Billy, you drank the whole bottle." She knew her tone was accusing, but she couldn't help it. She was angry and frightened now. Where had the wine come from?

"No, Miss, just a couple glasses, but I feel really sick." Billy's words were garbled and he struggled to keep his eyes open.

"Billy…"

But the young lad was already snoring, his head slumped back on the headrest.

"Damn, damn, damn. So much for security and being chauffeured," she grumbled to herself, as she opened her handbag and pulled out the keys to her rental car. Unfortunately, it was still parked behind the house. Using her crutches, she hobbled to the back door, negotiated the steps with a series of swinging hops, climbed into the driver's seat, and took off in a shower of gravel, forever grateful she had chosen an automatic vehicle.

The thought of Wade lying on some boat—drunk, drugged or beaten—terrified her. She braked and sat for a moment just inside the gates. Was this a mistake? Was this some trick? Should she call the cops? But what if it wasn't and Wade was dying? Obviously he hadn't got himself onto the boat. Her heart clenched painfully behind her breast. Maybe he was already dead. She already knew these people would go that far.

She accelerated out the gates and down the road. She wasn't prepared to take the risk. Despite their differences about the house and her doubts about his long term potential, she loved Wade. If anything happened to him, she would just curl up and die inside.

She hurtled through the dark streets but slowed at the new development. She wasn't overly familiar with the marina layout, as most of it had gone up after she'd left. She hoped there would be signs to guide her.

The marina was deserted except for the fishing boats that loomed up, like silent statues in the darkness, and the only noise was the rhythmical lap of the water against the rocks and hulls. There was barely any movement in the water of the marina channels. The huge moon was reflected in the water, its surface like a mirror. She drove slowly past each of the berths cursing the lack of light, and fighting the panic tightening her chest.

At first, all she saw was fishing boats, but at last she found herself examining cruisers and yachts. Moments later her headlights caught the creamy white hull of a sleek vessel with Lady Louisa emblazoned on the bow. She parked the car as close as possible then, keeping her left foot off the ground as much as she could, she limped over to the boat. It lay still, silent and dark. She wasn't sure how she was going to manage getting aboard with her injured ankle, but quickly discovered a couple of milk crates near the adjacent mooring. She heaved her crutches onto the boat then with careful slowness, she climbed up, hauled herself over the side, and fell. She landed heavily on her knees.

"Ouch," she cried out at the searing pain that shot through her.

In the darkness, she scrabbled around to retrieve her crutches, and once on her feet, hobbled toward the cabin. It was dark and silent. There was no sign of life.

"Wade? Are you here, Wade?" she asked in a frantic whisper.

Then in the weak glow of the moon, she saw him lying on the cabin floor. He wasn't moving.

"Wade," she screamed, and almost fell down the stairs in her haste to get to him.

Hanging onto one crutch, she leaned down and grabbed his shoulders. His coat came away easily and lightly. She threw it aside and dropped cautiously to her knees, immediately checking for a pulse. It was faint and fast.

She turned at an undefined scuffling noise and found a silhouetted figure blocking the doorway. In the silvery light of the moon, she could just make out the gun pointed at her.

"Give us ya phone," the silhouette demanded.

She hesitated, saw the gun wave a little, and decided she was not ready to be shot.

"Chuck it on the floor," the unknown person ordered.

"I don't have one," she muttered.

"Rubbish. Everyone has a damn phone," he responded, as he leaped at her and rammed the muzzle of the gun into her back. His rough hands patted and groped her body, searching for the phone she didn't have. Obviously satisfied after his rough exploration, the figure removed the gun. As she heard him back away, she spun around, but before she could focus on her captor, the cabin door slammed shut and the key turned.

The engine rumbled and feet thudded on the deck as the boat moved slowly away from the dock. As soon as it was out of the channel, it picked up speed quickly, leaving the marina behind as it sliced through the dark surface of the sea.

She pushed herself up and pounded on the door. "Let me out, you bastard. What game are you playing at? Let me out," she yelled.

"Shut up in there or I'll feed ya to the sharks."

She didn't recognize the voice. It was rough and had the slightest of accents. The boat began to bounce up and down as it left the shelter of the inlet. She steadied herself and peered out the small oblong window. In the distance, she could just make out the dense blackness of Boston Island.

She returned to kneel beside Wade. She lifted his head a little and patted his face sharply.

"Wade! Wade, wake up!" she said.

There was no response.

She felt his head for injuries, but there were none that she could feel. She undid the duct tape tying his hands and feet then slipped a cushion from the wooden seats under his head. His breathing was slow and shallow, and his shirt hung open, all the buttons either undone or ripped off.

She crawled back to the seats — which were actually hidden lockers — and scrabbled around inside. The first two were empty. In the third, she found fishing gear and a plastic waterproof torch. In the fourth, she found a small portable barbecue, cooking utensils, and a plastic picnic set, including wine glasses and an esky. In the very bow of the boat was another small door. She opened it and found bottled water and a plastic box. She ruffled through it and was delighted to find chocolate bars and other packets she couldn't identify in the darkness. She pulled the box out and discovered the cupboard went right back. She lay on her stomach and fished around in the dark. When she had dragged the contents out, she had a blanket, two dusty looking life jackets, and a couple of battered boogie boards.

She guessed her kidnapper had removed the lifejackets the boat was required to carry, and the flares, but had missed these discarded ones. Well, old ones were better than nothing. She hoped they would still inflate if required. It was a struggle to put one on

Wade. She dragged him into a sitting position and leaned his head against her shoulder. He smelled vaguely of aftershave and wine. While she had him sitting, she also managed to drag his coat back on. She was glad it was a casual, leather bomber style that had plenty of room to conceal the life jacket underneath. Then she lowered him back so his head was resting on the cushion, did up the buttons of his shirt and the studs on his jacket, and finally, wrapped him in the rather dank smelling blanket.

She pulled out a couple of bottles of water from the adjacent locker and drank thirstily before she tore off the tail of his shirt and drenched it in water. As she bathed his face and neck, he moaned and moved his head away from her ministrations but did not regain consciousness. His hair was a tousled, lanky mess that she brushed tenderly off his pale face.

"Oh, Wade," she murmured as she leaned closer and kissed him on the mouth.

His lips were dry and hot. Still he didn't respond. Frustration and fear prickled at her as she dragged off her sweatshirt and pulled on the second life jacket, tied it securely then pulled her sweatshirt back on.

She knelt beside him and took the lid off the second bottle. She splashed water on his face. He spluttered and tried to evade her efforts.

"Wade, wake up. Please open your eyes. Tell me you're okay," she pleaded.

She slapped his cheeks with quick sharp blows and applied more water. Now he swung his head away and brought one arm up to fight her off.

She grasped his shoulders and shook him. His head lolled backwards onto the cushion as she slapped him again. Without warning, he brought his hand up again and caught her in the side of the face with a thump.

"Ouch." Tears sprung into her eyes and her nose watered. She grabbed his hand to stop him hitting her again. "Wade, wake up," she cried.

But he remained under the grip of whatever he had taken or been given. She huddled beside him, cold now and very glad she had pulled on her sweatshirt.

When she peeped out of the small narrow window again she saw the island looming up, but the boat showed no signs of slowing as it headed out of the bay into the waters of Spencer Gulf.

Panic nipped at her now. If not to Boston Island, where? Were they going to dump them at sea? She was not a strong swimmer and if Wade was still unconscious, he had no chance of survival. There was no way she would be able to hold him up in the water, especially if the life jackets failed to work. Being able to swim could also be a moot point anyway because the ocean around her home town was famed for its great white sharks.

Tears of self-pity welled up. Damn it, that old house was not worth this. Not worth losing her life over. Deep inside, a red hot anger burned. How dare someone mess with her like this? Despite the fact that both she and the man she loved were in danger she vowed right then if she survived, she was going to make them pay.

The bounce of the boat was more pronounced now. The moon had sunk into the ocean. All around the vast emptiness of the sea cocooned them, and there was only the roar of the engine and the thump of the bow, as it punched through the sea, to break the absolute silence. Her stomach curled into a hard, tight knot, and she struggled to hold back the sobs that held her chest in a vice. She felt so alone and helpless.

They had long left Boston Island behind, but Kayla could not make out where they were through the small window. All she could see was enveloping darkness where the horizon melted into the blackness of the sea. Desperation gripped her. She needed Wade conscious to face whatever their unknown captor had in mind for them, especially if it was being thrown overboard. She leaned down and ruthlessly began exploring the fullness of his bottom lip. She demanded a response and moments later, she got one. His mouth puckered, and his lips parted under her bold exploration. He slid his arm around her waist and he pulled her closer. Then without her even realizing it, he had command of her lips.

It lasted for just a sliver of time before he pulled away.

"Wade, we're in trouble," she wailed.

At the same moment, the realization must have hit him that something was out of place. Perhaps the movement of the boat registered through the fogginess of his drugged brain.

"What... Where are we?" he asked.

"We're on a boat, somewhere outside the bay," she replied.

Now he gently put her from him and tried to sit up. "Oh bloody hell, my head feels like it's about to split in two," he moaned.

Kayla held out a bottle of water. "Here. Drink this. It might help. I think you've been drugged. A man called and told me to come and collect you. No police or you would die before I could save you."

"What man?" Wade looked around as if he would see someone.

She shook her head. "I don't know."

He frowned and inspected her visually. "Are you all right, Kayla? Why didn't Billy bring you?"

She shrugged. "I'm fine but scared. Billy didn't bring me because he was drunk."

"Billy, drunk! On what? The kid never drinks more than a stubby of beer or a glass of red, occasionally."

"Well a small bottle of red came with the pizza. He drank it and was totally incoherent."

"Drugged maybe?" Wade suggested.

Kayla nodded. "It's possible, and what about you?"

"I remember discussing the house with Mitchell, Tenney, Roger, and Damien. Seville didn't turn up. Mitchell was pretty aggressive about moving forward demanding the demolition proceed as soon as possible. He completely dismissed your claim as nonsense."

"He would. Phillip is behind it all—Phillip, and perhaps Seville. I don't know where Peter Tenney fits in."

Wade grimaced. "Well, someone at that meeting drugged me and tricked you here for the purpose of no good."

He reached out and trailed his hand down her cheek with a lingering touch as tears welled in her eyes.

"Phillip is the only family I have," she murmured.

He very gently pulled her toward him and kissed her lightly on the mouth.

"Just like Cinderella and the ugly stepsisters. Don't worry. Kayla. We'll survive this."

"But..."

"Shhh..." He hissed with a sharp urgent sound.

The engine had died with a noisy splutter, and an enveloping silence descended. She peered out the tiny porthole but could see nothing—no moon, no stars, and no lights to indicate where they were. She could hear the waves slapping against the hull and a louder sound of a powerful engine coming closer, then voices. She kneeled on the bench seat and peered out. She heard Phillip's voice clearly across the water and the slightly accented one that had lured her down to the boat.

"Pull alongside. Hold it steady." The accented voice drifted through the still sea air.

"Yeah, you don't want to go falling in now, do you? We put plenty of berley out. Sea must be seething with toothy predators by now." Phillip's voice was distorted by a sharp edge of mockery.

Kayla pressed her face up to the glass. She could just make out Phillip, Peter, and another man.

She bashed on the glass with her open hand. "Phillip! Please, Phillip, don't leave us here. I think Wade is dying. Don't leave me alone, Phillip," she cried.

He looked directly at her, but she couldn't discern his expression. He watched her for a long moment, but made no attempt to change her situation.

"Phillip, you can't do this. I don't understand why you are doing this. I'm your cousin, please don't do this," she screamed with pretended hysteria in an attempt to touch his conscience.

He leaped onto the deck of the Lady Louisa and leaned right up to her window. His face was a twisted mask of hatred and anger. "You don't understand, little cousin. Of course, you don't! Little rich kid, never denied anything. Little rich kid who couldn't keep her mouth shut. You cost me a year of my life for tattling, almost cost me my chosen career. You made everyone hate me. You and that accursed lawyer. Well, he got his. I'll never forget the expression on his face when Hugo laid out his winning hand and Carven realized he had just forfeited Ainsley House. He had no right to. Of course, it was supposed to go to Rossi. It doesn't matter, though, because the result is the same. A bit more work but...and dear Father...so horrified. He refused to sign the documents then went and had a stroke when I signed in his stead, right under his nose. Poor old bastards, they both knew they had been swindled by the smoothest cheat in poker history, but there was nothing they could do."

"Enough of the bragging, Mitchell. Time is wasting. Come on. Get your leg over. No time to wait—it will be getting light soon." Peter Tenney's rasping voice was easily identifiable.

He seemed to be the one giving the orders and that puzzled Kayla. She couldn't imagine Phillip taking orders from Peter and it was Phillip who wanted Ainsley House destroyed, not Peter.

But Phillip wasn't quite finished with his boasting. "See, little cousin, with you dead—tragic accident at sea—I inherit it all. Ainsley House will be gone. Your trust fund and the other properties you don't even know about will all be mine!" he screamed in her direction.

His maniacal laugh reverberated along her spine as he turned away and jumped lightly over the rail to the deck of the cruiser.

The engine of the other boat roared and she heard it punch into the swell as it moved away at speed. Their vessel rocked precariously in the wake then settled to a slow rock from side to side.

She peered out of the small porthole to see the large, white cabin cruiser speeding away from them in a swirl of frothy water. As the sound of the engine faded, all she could hear was the slap of the waves against the hull. She turned to find Wade already struggling to climb to his feet. She helped him and together they weaved drunkenly across the rocking cabin to the door. Wade picked up the small fire extinguisher and belted the lock. It sprang apart on the second blow. The door flew open on a lurch of the boat and Kayla sprawled out and landed with a splash in ankle deep water.

Wade was right behind her and he lifted her to her feet. "Are you hurt?" he asked.

"No, but I am very wet. Should there be so much water in the bottom of the boat?" she asked, knowing full well it was way too much.

"Hell, no. We're in trouble, Kayla. Hand me that torch, please. I need to see if we have a bilge pump and get it going. In the meantime, can you use something to bail out some of the slop. In these seas, if we wallow too deep, we will have the swell breaking over the sides."

"Are we going to sink?" she asked.

"I hope not, but just in case, can you swim?" he demanded to know.

She nodded. "I'm not a very strong swimmer, but I can keep my head above water and our life jackets will help." She lifted her sweatshirt.

"Right," he said. "Start bailing."

As she bailed with a small plastic bucket Wade disappeared to the back of the boat. He wasn't gone long and Kayla had not made any inroads into the water sloshing in the bottom of the boat. In fact, it was getting deeper.

"The bilge pump is not working," Wade muttered.

"Why is the boat leaking, Wade? We're sinking, aren't we?" she said.

"Yes," Wade replied. He gazed out toward the horizon then around the boat. "There are lots of reasons why a boat will take on water like this, but one of the more common ones is a missing drain plug," he said.

"They're not just scaring us off are they, Wade. They don't intend us to survive this, do they?" Her voice wavered as she verbalized her fears.

Wade's expression was grim. "Unfortunately no, but they've gone to a lot of trouble to make it seem like an accident. If they didn't want to keep their hands clean, they would have just shot us or thrown us overboard. At least this way we have a chance of survival."

"So what do we do about a missing drain plug?" she asked.

"We need to find it, a replacement or a substitute, and then swim under the back of the boat and block the hole."

"What does it look like?"

"It's a small plug about two centimeters across with a little sort of handle. It looks a bit like one of those tops that screw into a bottle of soft drink after you open it."

"Okay, I'll have a look."

Wade pushed his hair back off his forehead. It was furrowed with deep grooves. "I'll check the motor, but I suspect it has an empty tank."

The water was now almost knee deep and the boat was wallowing in the smooth, long swell. Kayla struggled to keep her panic at bay, especially when Wade was unable to start the motor.

She had found nothing in the cabin which now had a shallow tide of water creeping over the floor. As she returned to the deck, she almost lost her balance and landed heavily against the side of the boat. Her keys tumbled out of her pocket and slid below the water. As she snatched them up, her key ring ornament tangled between her fingers. "Wade, what about this?" she asked holding it up.

He took the keys from her and examined the miniature champagne bucket with a bottle poking out of the ice. "You know, this just might do the job, especially if I wrap a piece of my leather jacket around it so it fits tight. Hopefully it will hold with the pressure of the water against it."

Using her nail clippers as scissors he tore open the lining of his jacket then broke the stitching. After much tugging he managed to pry a smallish piece free.

The deck was now rising and falling in a slow rock back and forth and together they walked unsteadily to the side of the boat. The sea was almost black and she could smell the salt tang. There was nothing but ocean as far as she could see in the blackness of the pre-dawn.

She peered over the side then back at Wade. He was already stripping and moments later, he stood in front of her clad in nothing but his short black trunks.

"Okay, I'm going to drop into the water and duck under. Don't panic. I will need a bit of time below to determine if this thing will do the job."

She nodded.

"And keep an eye out for sharks," he said.

"Sharks! Maybe you shouldn't go in. Is there any way you can fit it from on the boat," she croaked.

He shook his head. "No, Kayla." Then he slipped over the side and ducked under the pewter shimmer on the surface of the sea.

Kayla scanned the ocean, but could see no landmarks, even as the sky was lightening, slowly turning shades of gray, lavender, and orange.

She peered down into the depths, trying to see if Wade was making progress. Fear clamped around her chest and she could hardly breathe with the pent up tension. She had lived in Port Lincoln most of her life. She had known people that had been taken by sharks. She had seen the results and there were plenty of documentaries of the vicious attacks by the predators of the sea. She didn't know how she would deal with it or what she would do if one appeared while Wade was in the water. She paced back and forth along the stern of the boat willing him to surface.

Almost beside herself, she clutched the gunwale and peered down, just as Wade popped to the surface, spitting out water and raking his hair out of his eyes.

"It's done, Kayla. Won't hold one hundred percent, but it will at least give us some time to either drift with the currents or be rescued. There should be plenty of vessels out in the gulf on a beautiful day like today."

She helped him scramble back aboard and immediately he gained his balance he hauled her into his wet, salty embrace. She slipped her arms around his neck and pulled his face down and took firm, but tender control of his mouth. She could taste the salt of the ocean on his lips and feel the coolness of the single drops of water that fell silently from his hair onto her face. She looked for a brief second into his golden eyes before she shut hers, suddenly afraid to let him see the full extent of her terror at the thought of losing him. She savored the moment as their lips clung with silent desperation, their bodies pressed so close they molded to each other. His hard masculine angles the perfect foil for her femininity. With her fingers entangled in his wet hair, she held him in her protective aura for a long moment. Then, as if by some silent signal, they both pulled away, both of them afraid to release the emotion that sizzled between them.

Moments later, he had put his shirt back on and taken up a position on the port side, bailing with a similar bucket to hers. They bailed in silence for a long time. The water barely showed any reduction in level, but for now, they didn't appear to be sinking any deeper.

With the dawn, the wind dropped out. The boat lay still in the flat silver of the sea. Off to the right, a thick sea fog drifted in. Soon they were cocooned in a silent gray world of damp mist and calmness. The sky and the sea blended into one.

Even the slop of the sea on the hull was silenced. It was unnerving, eerie. Kayla sat in the stern of the boat and peered through the enveloping fog. Then she heard a strange noise—a rhythmic clack, clack. She turned just in time to see four black and white cormorants lift from the water, fly in formation across the bow of the boat, and disappear into the mist. Moments later, she heard a splash in the sea. A few feet off to the right, a seal lazily surfaced, studied the surroundings briefly before diving back under the iron gray satin of the sea.

Wade came to sit beside her. He slipped his arm around her shoulders and pulled her gently to him. She cuddled into his chest. "I think Phillip has gone mad," she said, almost choking on the last word.

"I think you might be right, Kayla. I'm sorry for that and also for taking your house. I knew Seville had a reputation and I took a chance I normally wouldn't have, but if I had known the truth about the machinations going on behind the deal, I would never have got involved..."

He fell silent. Kayla clenched her hands tightly in her lap, not sure what to say. She could hear the gentle flow of his breath in and out and feel the rise and fall of his hard, muscular chest under her cheek. She moved her head slightly and felt the nub of his nipple against her face, so she pressed it more firmly against the warmth of his skin and felt his breathing quicken and the nipple become hard and erect. He placed kisses on her hair as he tightened his grip around her and drew her closer.

"Wade, I don't want to fight you anymore, but I will not let those bastards take away what is mine. Phillip is *not* going to win."

She felt, rather than heard him chuckle. "I don't think either of us has any say in the house right now, but if I did, I would refuse to accept it."

She eased away from him and peered up at him. "What about your company, Wade?"

"That is not important enough, either." He looked intently into her eyes. "You are what is important. You and surviving this to bring those bastards to justice."

"Are we going to make it, Wade? I mean we're just sitting here, drifting to who knows where in a sinking boat."

He kissed the tip of her nose lightly. "Well, I don't think we are moving much at the moment. It is hard to tell with this fog obliterating everything, but I think we need to bail some more. The water is still rising slowly."

They bailed steadily. Finally the sun broke through the fog, a shaft of golden light bursting straight from the delicate curve of a rainbow. The sun reflected relentless up off the water, and bore straight down on them from the clear blue sky. They bailed then rested in the shade, all the time they both scanned the horizon for any sign of land or another vessel. Around noon, Kayla broke out the water and chocolate bars. After eating a meager ration, she lay down on the blanket, her head on Wade's lap.

He lightly stroked her hair with his hand vaguely tucking some loose strands behind her ear. "Get some rest, Kayla. I will keep watch for rescue."

She closed her eyes, but in what seemed a sliver of time, she was being shaken by an urgent grip on her shoulder.

"Wake up, Kayla. I see land."

She ripped through the curtain of sleep that held her inert and pushed herself up.

Wade gripped her shoulders and pointed. "Look," he said.

A small patch of darker gray just becoming visible in the endless blue surrounding them. "What is it?" she asked.

Wade shrugged. "I don't know." Together they watched the tiny splotch as it moved slowly along the horizon. They were moving, not toward the island, but past it. Wade got back to bailing as the water level was getting a bit high again. The sea was choppy now, pushed by a strengthening south westerly wind that had picked up as the fog faded. The stranded half-filled boat wallowed in the slop.

Then she saw it. "Wade, stop. See out there. Isn't that another one?"

She pointed and Wade quickly picked up the new speck on the horizon.

He turned and peered off to the other side. "Look Kayla, see that smudge on the horizon, I think it might be the mainland."

She sighed. "So close, yet so far."

The wind was coming from almost directly behind them.

"We're still in the gulf, aren't we?" she asked.

He pulled her into his arms. "Yes, my love, we are. I think we might be near the islands that make up the Sir Joseph Banks Group. With that many islands so close together, we are sure to pass one close enough to swim to land, and there are always boats in this area to pick us up." He hugged her. "Besides, people will start searching for us soon. Weren't you meeting Simon for lunch today? When you don't turn up, surely he would immediately try to find you."

"Yes, and if he can't find me, the next person he is going to look for is you." She almost giggled at the irony of it all.

Wade's laughter barked out of his chest. "Yes, to have me hung, drawn, and quartered, for failing to protect you. He will probably do that anyway when we get back."

"It's all right, my dear. His bark is worse than his bite," she said. "It's getting late. What if we miss the islands in the dark, Wade? The sun is almost below the horizon."

"Well, one of us will have to stay awake and bail, because we seem to be taking more water on and whoever is awake will have to listen for the sound of water breaking on the shore."

"Well, I'll take the first shift because I slept all afternoon."

Wade grinned and placed a hard fast kiss on her lips. "I was hoping you would say that. I have a thumping headache and I am so tired I could go to sleep standing up."

Wade curled up on top of one of the lockers — one of the few dry places — and was asleep in seconds. Kayla sat for a long moment watching him. The wind was stronger now and the boat rocked precariously in the swell. She took off her sweatshirt and ignoring the chill of the wind, she began to bail. When her arms ached, she stopped, nibbled a small piece of chocolate, and scanned the sea for signs of land.

She felt helpless, small and insignificant in the huge rolling anonymity of the ocean. Even though Wade was just a few feet away, she missed his companionship, his warmth, and the sound of his voice. She missed having him to share the fear with. Afraid to let herself sink into self-pity and a terrifying paralysis, she began to bail again. Her arms were aching, but it wasn't until she could feel his gaze on her that she paused and stood up. She was numb with cold and dripping with water. Patches of her skin were chafed by the constant rubbing in the saltwater. She pulled on her sweatshirt as Wade beckoned her over.

He lifted the blanket. "Climb in and I'll warm you up before I take my turn. No sign of land?" he asked.

She snuggled in beside him and he pulled her hard against his chest and wrapped his arm around her waist.

"No, nothing. Do you think we missed them?" she asked.

"I hope not, but it's always possible," he replied.

As he held her close, he nuzzled her neck, nibbling and biting lightly. He slid his hands under her top and cupped her breasts, gently caressing her nipples. The fire ignited deep inside as her nipples strained to meet his caress and she felt the hardness of his arousal against her back. She pressed back against him, her desire as strong as his. Then he pulled away. "I want you Kayla, but not like this, not here with our future in doubt. Besides, I need to bail or we will have a dunking."

She watched him bail for quite a while until the warmth of the blanket replaced the warmth of desire and she slept.

* * * *

"Wake up, Kayla. We've found land."

The south westerly was whipping the ocean up into constantly moving peaks and troughs of cold, dark water. The boat rocked crazily, totally at the mercy of the waves and the wind. As her eyes adjusted to the darkness, she could just determine a darker, more solid blob, off to her right, trimmed with a moving line of white that danced between the moving navy of the sea and the solid unmoving blackness of the land. Behind the island, she could see the sky was beginning to lighten. At a guess, they were on the south western side of an island. The wind was driving their boat toward it—that and possibly an incoming tide flowing up the gulf.

"Where do you think we are, Wade?"

He hugged her tightly to his side. "I'm not sure. There are lots of islands out here. I just hope it is one we can land on."

"Wade, I can see a small beach there. Do you think the boat will wash ashore?" she asked.

He studied the coastline for a moment then studied the water. "It's hard to tell, because our movement depends on the wind, tide and undercurrents. If we get to the cove, we will be fine, but we might end up on that rocky point and we'll have to swim for it."

"Oh," she said.

He cupped her face with his hands as he gazed intently into her eyes. "As long as you can dog paddle, the life jacket will keep you afloat." He kissed the tip of her nose. "And I'll be there, right beside you."

She smiled, but knew it was a pathetic effort.

"Besides, Kayla, I was the swim team captain at school and university. Together, we will be all right," he said.

The boat heaved up and down. Some of the waves sloshed over the sides. It got worse as they drifted closer to shore. A turbulent swell broke on the rocks, throwing up water and froth. To the right the low, jagged shoreline sloped into a sandy cove where the waves rolled in and smashed themselves on the beach. She wouldn't have a chance if she was washed ashore on the point and she would probably be struggling anyway.

They sat side by side. Wade held her close as they watched the shore come closer. It was scarily obvious that they were not heading directly toward the sandy cove, but more toward the rocky point jutting out into deep water.

"Wade?"

"Mmmmm."

"I don't want to lose you, Wade...to the sea or the house."

His embrace tightened as he kissed her hair in light butterfly kisses.

Her chest was tight with anxiety and it was difficult to breathe.

"I know, my little Cinderella. One can't help hoping for a fairy tale ending — the happily ever after."

"You really want the happily ever after, Wade?" she asked.

"I'd better, because I've already lost my heart to you, Cinderella."

She snuggled closer, soaking up this precious nearness as best she could. Being wrapped in the warm cocoon of Wade's embrace did nothing to ease her trepidation of what was to come as they sat together watching the rocks of the wild coast draw nearer. Kayla was acutely aware of the increased rock and pitch of the boat in the turbulence of the restless sea as it battled under the opposing forces of the tide, wind, and rocky seabed.

Without warning, Wade pushed her off his lap. "Time to get ready, Kayla."

She sat there looking at him. "Get ready?"

"Yes, now. I give us about an hour and we will need to jump overboard. The boat is drifting into those rocks, and we need to be gone before she gets into the surf. Now go get those boogie boards, the water, chocolates, and the little blue esky. Where did you put those crutches?"

She pointed to where she had stuffed them in the cabin.

"Thank goodness, all they had left were these old, wooden ones. Those new metal ones would have been useless. Now, fishing line," he said purposefully.

He tied the fishing line to one of the crutches then looked up at her. "Can I have your clothes?"

"What?"

"Strip to your underthings. You can't swim in those sweats. They'll drag you to the bottom real quick," Wade warned.

Kayla stared in horror at the broiling waves crashing on the shore then glanced back at Wade as she removed her sweatshirt and slipped off her trackies. Wade barely spared her near naked body a glance as he strapped her clothes to the crutches with fishing line.

Then he stood and stripped to his trunks, all six foot three of lean muscle braced against the rise and fall of the deck. He slipped his wallet into his trunks then attached his clothes to one of the boogie boards. He then placed all the snacks in the esky and using the duct tape that had bound his hands and feet to seal it closed. He attached the torch to the esky with a long piece of fishing line. Then he collected the empty bottles and half-filled each with water from the new bottles. These he tied together in sets of three, attaching some to the boogie board and some to the other crutch. Others, he just left loose.

"Do you think it will work?" she asked.

He laughed, a sharp bark tinged with anger and frustration. "I hope so, Kayla. It's the best chance we have of getting to shore if we swim light. I am hoping these other bits wash up on the point or beach, because by nightfall we might need the warmer clothes and water is essential.

The low cliffs loomed nearer. The sea threw itself onto the shore, spray flying up from the edges of foam. The ocean thudded and boomed as it pounded on the rocks. The boat rocked perilously. Wade pulled her roughly against his chest, taking possession of her mouth with his, as they savored each other with tongues entwined, as if for the last time. There was nothing left to be said so they just stood and watched as the boat drifted toward the rocks.

He put her from him. "Kayla, we have to go now, before we get into the heavy turbulence by the rocks." He pointed to the sandy beach at the right of them. "Swim for that, my love. Swim hard and fast."

"Wade?"

"Go now, before it's too late. I'll be right with you."
He helped her onto the edge of the boat, her bare feet
dangling in the icy water. He handed her the boogie
board. She stared in horror at the sloppy surface and
the dark unknown depths.

She began to tremble. "I can't, Wade. I can't," she
wailed.

He held her waist in a tight grip as she perched on
the edge. He leaned closer. "You can and you will.
Now go!"

She dropped into the sea. It closed over her head.
The cold clamped around her lungs. She sank, frozen,
unable to initiate kicking. The salt water rushed up
her nose. She gulped for air and promptly filled her
mouth with water. Then she surfaced, coughing and
spluttering, as she gasped air. She clutched the old
boogie in an iron grip. She was already some distance
from the boat.

"Go, Kayla. Swim for the shore."

She heard him yell, but couldn't see him through
salt-filled eyes. She kicked and kicked, pushing the
boogie board out in front of her like a kid's swim aid.
The life vest was holding her up, despite its age and
decrepit state. She swam. She was scared. So afraid of
what she couldn't see beneath the surface. Desperately
she wanted to find Wade, but she knew it would be
hopeless in the swell of the sea, so she swam on. The
water pulled at her then thrust her away. It tugged at
her legs and splashed in her face. She was tiring
rapidly, her kicking down to a clumsy scissor kick.
Then Wade was beside her.

"Swim, Kayla. Not far now. Kick your legs," he
spluttered through the waves.

She obeyed. It was impossible to keep her face above
the splash of salt water so she clamped her mouth

shut and tried to breathe in the troughs. All the time, she was afraid of what was in the water below her. She knew this area was riddled with sharks, and the man on the boat had said they had tipped berley in the water. She tried to look around, but couldn't without sinking.

"Swim, Kayla. Keep going. The break will pick you up soon and help you get to the shore," Wade yelled.

She turned her head and saw him. He was breast stroking a little to the left of her, his collar length hair plastered to his skull, water glistened on his face. He gave her a quick grin that ended suddenly with a mouthful of seawater.

"Keep swimming. I am going over there to retrieve that bundle. I'll be right behind you," he shouted.

She wanted to cry out. To stop him from leaving her…to stop him from taking a detour, which meant he was in the water longer than he needed to be, but he was already swimming strongly away from her. All she could see was his head as it bobbed up and down in the swell.

Then she was lifted and swept forward into the shallow water. She kicked out, was sucked down, and tumbled over. As she surfaced, she felt the seabed solidly beneath her feet. She pushed off and was swept through the break into the froth and bubble of the waves racing up the beach. She staggered and struggled to find purchase on the sandy bottom with shaky legs then she was staggering, half bent over, up the beach, out of reach of the sea.

She turned and searched the water for Wade. A large crack startled her and she turned in time to see the Lady Louisa fly up and nose dive into the rocks. Waves swept up and pushed the broken hull farther up the granite shore before it was ripped back down into the turbulent surf. With a screech, a crash, and a spine tingling groan, the cruiser split down the middle and fell back into the sea. Moments later, chunks of fiberglass hull, struts, and flotsam popped back to the surface and were thrown carelessly up onto the low cliff. She peered back to find Wade.

He was swimming from dark water to light with the crutch in tow. A shadow appeared in the water, just on the edge of the seaweed line behind Wade, heading along the coast. Her heart jumped and her stomach somersaulted. She couldn't make out the silhouette. It could have been a shark, seal, or dolphin. They all frequented these waters.

"Wade, swim faster. You have something in the water with you," she screamed.

With one hurried glance behind him he turned and struck out with increased force. She snatched up a piece of drift wood and waded out up to her knees as she saw the shadow turn. It slid through the water toward them, but instead of attacking, it swept past and circled behind her. She felt the swirl of water pass her legs and looked down into the dead, expressionless eyes.

She poked it with the driftwood, right in the eye. The shark pulled away and circled in a wide arc. Then it torpedoed through the water directly at them. She saw the mouth yawn and line upon line of razor sharp teeth. Suddenly Wade found his feet. She grabbed his arm to help him through the break onto dry land. The gray fin sliced through the water where they'd been standing then turned and headed out to sea.

Wade gasped in deep breaths of air. His face was white and even as he slipped his arm around her waist, she could feel his body tremble with shock.

He pulled her hard against him, seeking her mouth as he cradled her head with his hand tangled in her wet, salty hair. He captured her lips, as she turned up to him. She tasted the salt then the mellow richness of his essence overwhelmed its sharp bite on her mouth and she let herself sink deeply into him. Savoring his touch, his mouth commanding hers, and his hard body pressed tightly against hers, they stood braced together for a long time.

"My God, Kayla. I love you so much," he mumbled against her mouth.

"Oh Wade, I thought you were going to die. I was so scared," she croaked out of a constricted throat.

He laughed—a genuine deep throated chuckle. "You were scared, Cinderella? How do you think your Prince Charming was feeling with that mouth full of teeth snapping at his butt?"

Kayla couldn't quite find the humor to match his, but gave a wan smile.

"Anyway, let's get organized. We need shelter from the sun and this blasted wind, especially before it gets dark. And we need to look for the other stuff. I hope it has washed up."

He kissed her lightly on the mouth. "You go that way and I will head up toward the point."

Part of her was reluctant to be parted from him—to lose that touch—but she knew she was being silly, so obediently she turned away and, using just one crutch to help her, she walked along the shore to the south.

They met back in the middle of the beach. Wade was struggling under a huge, jagged edged piece of fiberglass which he propped up against the rocks and immediately created a cool blotch of shade on the burning sand. Kayla had the second bundle of clothes.

She opened up both bundles and spread them out on neighboring rocks to dry in the sun.

He handed her his wet shirt. "Put it on, Cinderella. Not quite the ball gown you deserve, but it will keep you from burning."

"And what about you?" she asked.

He laughed. "My skin is darker than yours. I'll survive. Come on, let's head up to the point and see if we can find the water bottles or the food."

He curled his arm around her shoulders as they moved slowly up the beach. He had shortened his long stride to keep pace with her hobbling steps and they had moved down to the waterline to escape the burning heat of the sun blasted sand.

Chapter Seven

Ahead, debris was spread right across the jagged rocks — all that was left of the Lady Louisa.

Wade helped her up the first rocks then, once she was seated, he began to search, while all the time watching for the freak wave that might come higher than the rest. Wade found most of the bottles of water and the esky, undamaged, wedged between the rocks.

On the way back, Wade gathered some wood, such as it was, from the shrubby coastal vegetation and Kayla retrieved four large pieces of driftwood and tucked them under one arm. Between them, they broke off bits of dry twigs and snapped branches into smaller pieces. They built a small structure. Wade added some dried grass then pulled his watch from his wrist. He tapped it against a rock then deftly removed the largest piece of glass.

He held the glass over the grass and faced it to catch the full blast of the sun. He got a small gray puff, but no flame. Kayla leaned forward and energetically blew on the grass as it smoldered. Kayla coughed as she puffed. Then the flame flared and they had fire. As it grew stronger, Wade threw some grizzled leaves on then more small twigs and branches. The fire began to smoke, but the wind was whipping it away as fast as it rose from the flames.

They sat shoulder to shoulder and munched on the chocolate bars that had survived the dunking inside the esky. They drank sips of water and watched the sun sink into the sea in a blaze of golden light.

"We weren't meant to survive this, were we?" she asked again.

He shook his head. "Probably not, but we will. The fire will keep us warm tonight, but tomorrow, from first light, we will make it smoke. There are always plenty of boats in this area—fishermen, fishing charters and yachts—either passing or seeking shelter."

As darkness descended Wade pulled her down beside him, seeking her mouth with his. She gave herself to his embrace, feeling his heart beat in the same uneven rhythm as hers. She needed to be held and loved. She felt the abrasiveness of his stubble caress her face and tasted salt on his mouth as he explored hers. She parted her lips to invite him in and he thrust his tongue into her mouth and caressed hers. She met it eagerly, falling under the spell of his touch, his taste, and his desire which was blatantly obvious against her thigh through the thin material of his trunks. He drew away from her a little and she could see his hair tousled and riotous, silhouetted by the night sky.

"I want you, Kayla—to hold you, to love you, and to make you mine. Damn the company and damn your house."

His words sliced through her passion and she pulled away. She looked up at the darkness of his face and tried to interpret his expression.

"I want you, Kayla. I want you like I have never ever wanted a woman before. I always thought love was a trap, a chain that bound your heart and then broke it when the other person stopped loving you or died. But now I don't care. I think I understand what real love is, for the first time," he said.

"Oh Wade, I want you to, but you can't just dismiss the issue between us because of our situation. When we are rescued, it will all come back to haunt us."

He stared blindly out over the sea. "I know, Kayla, but you know what? I don't give a damn. We could have died today — both of us — and for what? A few dollars, my reputation, and a house. I love you. I want you, and even if the future is against us, I would rather have loved you so completely for a short time than to never have held you so close."

He turned and flicked the torch on. She could read his expression now. The anguish in his eyes was shadowed with the remnants of his passion. He seemed older tonight. The last few days had taken their toll. Gone was the arrogance, the determination, the insatiable drive to achieve. Now, she saw a vulnerable, chastened Wade — a man with a need to be loved. Her need rose to meet his. He was right. They could have died out there today, never having given their shared love a chance to grow and been strong enough to withstand their differences.

Suddenly, nothing seemed more important than Wade's love. She leaned forward and kissed him lightly on the mouth. He stayed still as she explored nibbling at his bottom lip then kissing him and without warning he responded to her tentative touch by covering her mouth with his. He moved his lips over her skin, hard and fast then slow and lingeringly.

She reached up and linked her arms around his neck and as she lay back, she pulled him with her. "I want you, Wade. Make love to me."

He slipped his hand under the shirt she still wore and caressed her midsection then lifted the salt encrusted material up and Kayla slithered out of it. He lowered his head and placed small deliberate kisses on the swell of her breast above the flimsy lace of her bra, up her neck, and over her shoulders then back to her face. As he laid his mouth on hers, he tucked his hand under her, and she felt the hook on her bra release. He lifted the bra away from her breasts and trailed a finger down from her chin to her cleavage before he cupped one breast in his large hand and teased the nipple with his thumb. When it was erect, he dropped his head and took the little nub in his mouth. Firstly, sucking on it then nibbling with the lightest touch. She ran her fingers through his hair, almost cradling his head at her breast. Then she trailed her hands over his shoulders and down the hard muscles of his back until she reached the waist band of his trunks. She eased them down and he assisted with his free hand until he had wriggled free of the clinging fabric. His wallet fell free and he reached for it to retrieve a small foil packet from inside. Unhampered now, she ran her hands up over his hips and abdomen and cupped his buttocks. His cock was hard and throbbing between them, and she cupped his balls and caressed them before she slid her hand up his shaft.

He brushed his hand down over her body and almost immediately it was under her knickers, seeking and finding her clit. Without hesitation, she opened herself to his caresses. She sighed as he caressed the sensitive flesh. His touch was exquisitely gentle, as he explored her flesh and found the entrance to her pussy. With a tantalizing movement, he circled the edge of her opening, igniting a fiery need in her. With a mere flick of the wrist, he disposed of her knickers and they were both naked, the golden light of the fire dancing on bare skin. He took hold of her mouth and kissed her deeply, probing with his tongue into her mouth even as he moved his fingers inside her, continuing to stroke her clit with his thumb. She was on fire, she wanted him so badly. She fondled his body down over his chest and lower still until she found his erect penis once more. She curled her hand around his shaft and caressed him slowly as she proficiently unrolled the condom onto his penis. He moaned.

"I want you, Kayla," he said.

"Take me, Wade," she urged. While she retained her grip on his cock, she eased her other hand around to his buttocks and urged him closer, at the same time adjusting her hips to give him access. He moved until he was lying with half his weight on her as he alternated between kissing her open mouth and sucking her erect nipples.

She lifted her hips to meet him as he thrust downwards. Her breath caught in her lungs as he entered her with one energetic thrust until he was deep inside. She pulled his head down and kissed him hard on the mouth. "Love me, Wade," she murmured.

He began to thrust, teasingly at first, then faster and harder. Her body trembled with the sensation, a pulsing need building from deep inside her pussy before spreading throughout her body. Every nerve sang in time to his thrusts. Forcefully she arched her hips to meet him and everything faded away except the feel of him filling her body. Her legs started to shake. She moaned as she wrapped her arms around his back, raking long fingernails down the exposed flesh to tease the tenseness in the muscles. She moaned again as her body responded, the pressure building, the tingle spreading from her pelvis to all over her body. She shut her eyes, arched her back and cried out as her climax shattered through her. Wade thrust faster and deeper urging her on until moments later he groaned above her and pinned her to the sand with the force of his thrust. She felt his cock undulate rhythmically as he reached his release. Together they were swept on a forceful wave of sensation crashing over the edge into totally sexual satiation. Spent, Kayla relaxed onto the sand and Wade slipped from her as he pulled her close against his chest and entwined his long muscular legs between hers.

He kissed her on the face, her mouth, her eyes, and her forehead. "Oh Kayla, my love," he murmured.

She snuggled closer to him and he enclosed her protectively in his embrace.

"I never want to be parted from you. Damn the company, the project, and the consequences," he muttered.

She touched his face, almost absently stroking the stubbled chin. "Wade, I don't think we can stop it. Phillip and his cronies have already killed to achieve their goal and we were supposed to die. Unless the police can catch them and convict them, we'll both be in danger until that damn house is demolished."

"Kayla, to be honest I don't think the house is going to be enough. I think they want you dead."

Kayla shook her head slightly. "But why? I know Phillip wants revenge, but to want me dead is a bit much, surely. I was young at the time of the accident.

And Tenney? I think he just enjoys being evil. Besides, Phillip already has my trust fund balance. Phillip hinted at more property, but I know nothing about any others."

Slowly Wade pulled away from her and rose up onto his elbow so he could peer into her face. "Kayla, who gets your inheritance if you die?" he asked.

"Phillip does," she said.

"He has a lot to gain, but are you sure Phillip is behind this? To me, it seemed as if Tenney and the other bloke on the boat were running the show. Could Peter Tenney control Phillip through his drug habit?"

"Maybe, but why would Peter do something like this? I mean, what does he have to gain? Phillip gets the money, not Tenney. You're suggesting Tenney is the one who wants my money?"

"Yes. Could he still hold a grudge against you about the baby?"

"But that doesn't make sense, Wade. He was put in jail for statutory rape because I was only fifteen. Carven and my grandmother brought the charges, not me. I never told him about the baby or the abortion. Grandma Eloise was the only other person who knew and I was long gone by the time he was released."

"Did he ever contact you?"

She shook her head. "He disappeared after he was released. Obviously he has kept in contact with Phillip. Maybe he thought helping Phillip was getting some payback for himself."

"I think there is more to this than Phillip's desire to destroy the house," Wade said with firm determination.

"Maybe there is. Remember, Phillip hinted there was property I didn't even know about. I can understand if Peter and Phillip both wanted revenge on Carven, but me, I am not sure. I guess Phillip always had my demise on the agenda. He is such a tortured soul. I am sure now I was meant to die that night in the cellar. They weren't just after the papers."

"But how did they know you'd be there?"

"Phillip knew I would look for the papers. He suggested they might be in the coach house. With me out of the way, Ainsley House goes. They get their investment back and Phillip inherits. Think about it, Wade. No-one knew you were in town. If you and I had not had that confrontation, what would the chances have been of me being found?"

"Oh, hell. None, I would say."

"Phillip must hate me so much to go to all this trouble," she cried.

She pulled out of Wade's embrace, reached for her clothes, and slipped them on, suddenly chilled all the way to her core. Wade followed suit then cuddled her close as they tried to sleep.

As she lay in the warmth and security of his embrace, comforted by the gentle sounds of his gentle snoring and the swish of the water on the shore. She tried to analyze each incident. Her thoughts were jumbled and she tried to straighten them out, but lulled by the timeless rhythm of the sea and the after sex glow that still hummed in her body, she drifted into sleep.

* * * *

His lips trailing over her neck and ear were the first sensation she was aware of. She stretched and purred with contentment. He had already slipped his hand under her top and was playing idly with her nipples as he nuzzled into the curve of her neck. She uncurled her body to press it back against his, instantly aware of his arousal. She turned to face him, pushing him back onto the sand. He lay back and watched her as with a quick tug, she ripped off her top and her pants. Naked, she leaned over him, letting her breasts sway just above his face. As he reached for them, she swung her leg over his hips and straddled him. Even with his trunks between them, she could feel the swell of his appendage pressing hard between her legs. She threw her head back and laughed as he reached up to play with the fullness of her breasts and she wriggled teasingly right on his erection.

Now Wade reached down and slid his hand between them to caress her intimately.

"Mmmmmm, the fresh sea air has made you wanton, Cinderella," he mumbled.

Again she laughed lightly, squeezing her fingers past his to undo his trousers and push them down over his hips, his trunks quickly following. Kayla knelt up to accommodate the long, hard length of his cock. She guided him to her hot, wet flesh before easing herself down to let him sink deep into her. She leaned forward and ran her hands over his chest, tangling her fingers in the light sprinkling of hairs before she moved even lower to nibble at his nipples. All the time, she felt the pressure of his hardness filling her completely as he gave little thrusts inside her.

He watched her while he twiddled lightly with her clit, intensifying the sensation of his thrusts. As the tingling vibrations from her inner core blasted along every nerve ending, she lifted away from him, before pressing down to meet his upward thrust. Their lovemaking totally in unison with each other and the wash of the tidal swell on the sand. Her body felt electrified as the throbs of passion grew and pooled where they were intimately joined. Frissons of awareness buzzed along her legs and centered in her pelvis. Her pussy throbbed and pulsed as wave after wave crashed over her. The turbulence of her release rocked her with shuddering undulations. Fervent heat burned a fiery path like molten lava. Wade groaned and thrust deep as her climax spun out of control and carried her over the precipice in a riptide of desire that crashed on the other side in unison with Wade.

He groaned and gasped for air with his laboring lungs. She leaned onto him, kissing him all over his chest and face. He encircled her with his arms and pulled her closer as he sought her mouth. Then he rolled her to his side and cuddled her. They lay for a long time cocooned in the amorous cloud of sated sexual desire.

She was almost dozing when he hugged her closer for a moment before putting her from him.

"Time to have something to eat then we must get this fire smoking. There are sure to be boats around," he said as he sat up.

Kayla stretched luxuriously, reluctant to be pulled back into the real world—the world where she and Wade were at loggerheads over the house—the world where someone was trying to murder her for her inheritance.

Once he was dressed, he held out his hand to her. "Come on, lazy bones. Up and at 'em," he said.

She groaned, but let him pull her to her feet. "There is no escaping this, is there?"

He shook his head. "No, Kayla. We have to see this out to the bitter end. I want so badly for what we share now, here at this moment, to survive the storm ahead, but I can't guarantee that. So shall we get this fire going, get rescued, and finish it one way or another? Let's get this over with as quickly as possible with the least amount of damage."

She nodded as she blinked her tears away and turned to walk up the beach.

Together they gathered more scrub and bits of driftwood to stoke the fire, which had faded right down to glowing embers.

It took a short moment for the new wood to catch and flare and Wade laid a small branch over the flames to make it smoke. Now that the wind had dropped out, the smoke rose almost straight up, thick and gray. For a while they sat, side by side, ate chocolate bars and drank a small amount of water, each of them absorbed in their own thoughts.

All of a sudden Wade sprang up. "Come Kayla, let's have a swim," he shouted, tearing the melancholy silence between them to shreds.

She lifted her gaze up to him, her mind struggling to comprehend. "Swim? There are sharks out there, Wade — in case you've forgotten."

"Oh, I haven't forgotten," he said with a shudder. "I wasn't planning to go out past my knees. Just a quick dip to freshen up. You watch while I dunk, then I'll watch while you take your turn."

She jumped up, stripped, and naked they ambled together down the sand and waded up to their knees into the sea. Kayla scanned the water. There was no sign of anything but crystal clear ocean and creamy white sand. Wade dipped under then jumped up and splashed her. She screamed as the chilly water splattered her sun-warmed skin.

"Come on, under you go. It's lovely," Wade urged, as he shook the salty drops from his hair.

As he stood up and scanned the open ocean, she held her nose and ducked under.

She jumped back up immediately. "It's freezing," she screamed.

Wade laughed, his dimples deep in the dark stubble sprouting on his strong, angular jaw. His hair hung in disarray, and his golden eyes flashed with amusement and mischievousness. He began to stride toward her through the waves, scooping water in his hands and throwing it in her direction as he came.

"No, you don't, Wade Faxton," she yelled and turned to flee, but hampered by her injuries there was no chance of escape.

But he grabbed her waist and tackled her into the tumbling break at the shore edge. She squealed as she slipped beneath the chilly waves. Wade was kneeling beside her when she emerged from the foam. He cupped her face in his hands, leaned down, captured, and proceeded to devour her mouth. She tasted salt on salt, chocolate, and Wade's distinct flavor. It was drugging her, intoxicating her, and she willingly drowned in his nearness. He broke free and rose to his feet, lifting her out of the sea as he did. With athletic ease he loped up the beach with her cradled against his chest and after one last hard kiss, he set her down on her feet.

He flicked her bottom ever so lightly. "Now get dressed, Cinderella, in case we get company."

She glanced around at the mess of clothes and sand. "I will, if I can find my missing items," she said with a mock glare in his direction.

He laughed. "Well, as long as you have enough to be respectable, because if we are still here by the time the sun sets, I am already planning to take them off again," he warned.

"Wade Faxton, you're incorrigible." She examined his lean length, immediately noticing he was semi aroused by her close proximity and nakedness. His cock stiffened and started to rise under her close scrutiny. She looked up to meet his gaze. "And you're worried about *me* being respectable," she teased.

He laughed. "Well, maybe I should put it to good use and be damned to being respectable," he threatened with mock ferociousness.

"Oh, no, you don't, Wade Faxton," she squealed. "Its broad daylight and a boat could come round that point at any time."

"Yep." He made to step toward her.

Her body already hummed with desire, but she grabbed her clothes off the sand and retreated out of his reach. He watched her dress, not turning away until she was completely covered. With little else to do, they sat together under the shelter as the day warmed, taking turns to tend the fire or nap. They swapped childhood stories, nibbled sparingly at the chocolate bars, and sipped the water.

Late in the afternoon Kayla slipped out of his arms and leaving him snoring gently, she limped down to the beach. To fill in time, she gathered some wood together and just above high tide mark, spelled out HELP in the sand with rocks and branches.

The sun was low in the sky and the south westerly had picked up again. Wade still dozed, so Kayla added more wood to the fire and more green stuff. As a fresh dark plume of smoke poured into the sky, she heard it—the even chop, chop of a helicopter. She shaded her eyes and scanned the bleached blue of the burning summer sky. At first she saw nothing then off to the west she saw a speck that rapidly got bigger—the chop, chop now a distinct throb in the air.

"Help is coming, Wade. Help is coming," she yelled.

She planted a smacking kiss on his mouth then hand in hand they stood waving and yelling in unison, "We're here! We're here!"

The helicopter had turned and was coming directly toward them.

She could make out the colors now — green, blue, and yellow with a huge logo of a bird on the side and emblazoned with the words, 'Faxton Constructions'. A man was leaning out of the open side door and waving. They had been seen. Kayla's chest tightened with choking sobs of relief. They were saved. The chopper was loud now as it landed on the stubbly vegetation, just above the beach. Within moments of touching down, an older man piled out, quickly followed by a younger one.

"Boss," the older man greeted Wade.

"You took your time, Ryan."

The older man laughed. "If it wasn't for Miss Mackenzie's editor friend, we wouldn't even know you were missing, boss, let alone be out here looking for you."

"That's right, boss. Your chauffeur said Miss Mackenzie had gone to a boat so when we saw the smoke signals and help sign we assumed it was you. You've heard often enough that management is always the last to be missed when they go AWOL," the younger man said, grinning from ear to ear.

"Enough out of you, young Silverton. I guess you've arrived with the heavy equipment," Wade said.

"Yep, the wrecking ball, bulldozer, and a backhoe, all primed and ready for action on your orders," Silverton replied with a mock salute.

Wade cleared his throat. "Yes…well, Toby, you might be having some down time on that. We have a few crossed wires to untangle first."

"Well in that case, I'll dig out my fishing gear. Couldn't find a better place to have downtime," Toby Silverton said.

Just fifteen minutes later, they were loaded on the helicopter. It was a short flight to the airport then they were whisked to Ainsley House. Two detectives were already at the house and pounced on them as they arrived.

* * * *

It was almost midnight by the time they had made full statements, been updated on the investigation into the fate of Pierre and Abrial, and grilled about the possible whereabouts of Tenney, Phillip, Seville, and the second man on the boat the one with the accent.

The whole boat thing had frightened Kayla more than she was prepared to admit and she was scared of what would happen next. She was so glad to be home, but she was finding it hard to settle and became uneasy when Wade left her for a moment to give Billy instructions about the car for the next day.

"Come on, Cinderella. I don't know about you, but I think we both need a hot shower and a good night's rest. So are we sleeping in your bed or mine?" Wade asked.

She poked her tongue out at him. "Well, I thought you would sleep in yours, and me in mine, seeing they are both made up."

"Really? Is that what you really want, Ms Mackenzie?" He stalked toward her. "I sort of had other ideas."

"Did you, Mr Faxton?" she asked in a sassy tone and repeated her cheeky gesture with her tongue.

"I did," he replied as he lunged, grabbed her around the waist and pulled her hard against him.

She slowly curled her arms around his neck and pulled his face down to hers. She kissed him, a demanding, possessive kiss. He responded immediately, kissing her back hard, probing deeply with his tongue into the secret recesses of her mouth as he pulled her hips into firm contact with his groin. The hardness of his cock left her in no doubt he wanted her.

He swept her up, carried her into the bathroom, and set her gently on the edge of the bathtub. She watched him as he turned the water on in the shower and stripped naked. He took the two steps it needed to bring him in front of her. She was very aware of his erect appendage embedding itself in the cleavage between her breasts. She hunched her shoulders to enclose his hot rod in a tender embrace. He pushed against her and the moisture from the tip wet her skin. Wade took her hands and pulled her to her feet. With infinite gentleness he removed her clothing and when she was naked, he lifted her into the shower. The hot water sluiced over them both. Wade caressed her breasts as he pressed up behind her, his hard penis dipping between her buttocks. Kayla propped herself against the tiled wall and pushed her derriere out toward Wade. He moved forward and kissed his way down from her shoulders to her buttocks. He slid his hand sensuously across her wet flesh and in between her legs. With deft fingers he easily found her clit and with exquisite slowness, he caressed it up and down. She moaned as the ache of arousal throbbed and radiated out from the sensitive nub of flesh. He moved closer until every inch of him was in contact with her. With his other hand he reached around her hips, delved between her lips, and slipped into her pussy. She pushed against his invasion reveling in the feel of his fingers wriggling within her muscular resistance. She pulled her pussy tight against his movement and she whimpered as the sensation sharpened and spread. Wade nuzzled her neck, nibbling at her drenched flesh. She moaned. When he let his hands drop away she felt the thrust of his swollen flesh push between her buttocks and slide easily into her sopping pussy. She pushed against his thrust, creating a flare of heat that spread rapidly out of control through her limbs. Wade pulled her back closer to him each time he thrust. Her knees began to tremble as molten desire exploded deep inside and washed in crashing breakers through her body. She whimpered and moaned with each shudder that rolled over her. Wade sank deep inside her, paused just for a moment then he thrust again and again, reigniting the shudders of passion in her. She moaned and cried out as passion imploded and her second climax sucked the strength from her bones. She would at that moment have sunk to the floor if Wade was not supporting her with the weight of his body. She stilled, absorbing his thrusts, and the gentler shudders that followed her release. He groaned then and stilled. Together they sagged against the tiled wall. Wade heaved a sigh of satisfaction, turned the water off and swept her into his arms. She grabbed a towel from the rack and when Wade laid her on the bed, he took it from her and toweled her dry. Feeling cold she slipped beneath the covers but watched him closely until, he dried himself, discarded the towel, and climbed in beside her. He bundled her into his arms, pulled up the quilt, and turned out the light.

"Sleep, Cinderella, for you are safe again in your castle." He nuzzled her neck for a moment then stilled.

* * * *

Something was trying to pull her out of a deep sleep, something tickled at her brain, trying to break through the almost comatose state that held her in suspended animation. She stirred, conscious of her body moving sluggishly. Her head thumped as she tried to drag open her eyes. The thing that had disturbed her was a noise—a jarring, grinding noise that had no place in her world at Ainsley House.

She rolled over and stared up at the ceiling. The light fitting trembled. In fact, the whole room vibrated and the noise became a thumping, pounding rumble. Recognition smacked her. It was the sound of big machinery grinding and grumbling.

She rolled out of bed, and staggered to the door.

"Wade, wake up! Wake up! Something is wrong," she shouted.

As she flung the door open, she heard a faint whistle and the rattle of a chain. The room disintegrated around her. The force of the explosion knocked her backwards and she landed hard. She rolled over quickly and covered her head as lumps of plasterboard rained down on her and shattered glass peppered her bare skin. Kitchen utensils, bits of cupboard, and food fell all around. As silence snapped into place, she peeped over her arms. The lacy kitchen curtains billowed out from what was left of the window frame. Most of the neat, functional kitchen was gone. Wade crouched at her side.

He grabbed her arm. "We've got to get out. They're demolishing the house!" he bellowed.

Then it loomed. First the shadow, then the solid metal reality of the wrecking ball. It sliced through the air straight toward them. Wade pushed her to the floor and threw himself over her. The ball missed them by inches. The roof and walls rained down, lumps of wood and old ceilings filled with dust.

"Keep down, love, crawl to the door. Have to get out," he yelled in her ear.

She dropped her head and crawled as fast as she could toward the door that led to the stairs. There was another bone jarring thud, a screech, and crack that hurt her ears. Half the apartment roof was demolished right over her head. Dust rose like an angry horde of locusts to block out the faint cool morning light. She screamed and screamed until the dust blocked her throat and she could barely force out a croaked cry for help.

Together they commando crawled toward the door of the flat that now hung drunkenly on its hinges. Kayla clawed it open with bleeding fingers. The wrecking ball swung back, taking the remainder of the kitchen wall out. There was a huge gaping bite right through the middle of her home. She turned away from the devastation and dragged herself onto the landing. She ignored the stinging, bleeding puncture wounds all over her body, some of which were still embedded with glass. Right beside her, Wade was barely recognizable, bleeding and covered in dust. Together they half walked, half crawled down the stairs, each supporting the other. Below them, the reception area was as yet untouched, but the next blow smashed the fine timber balustrade of the landing into thousands of jagged pieces. Heavy timbers rained down. Bright stars burst in her head as a lump of railing cracked down hard on her skull. She heard another thump. Wade slumped against her, a huge block of wood across his shoulders. Together they tried to lift it off him, but it was wedged tightly across the stairs.

"Go, Kayla. Get out. Leave me," Wade yelled. "Go."

More timber crashed down. Wade pushed her away from him. "Go now!"

She wanted to resist. To scream no, but she recognized her only hope of saving him was to stop the bastards wrecking her house.

She scrambled down the remainder of the stairs, almost slipping in her own bloody footprints. Her head throbbed and the room spun. She shook it to clear the fuzziness. In the hallway, she wrenched open the metal gun cabinet by the front door. She curled one hand over the barrel of a shotgun and with the other snatched up a handful of shells. By the time she had the door open, both barrels were loaded. She stepped, totally naked, out on the verandah, aimed, and squeezed the trigger. The force of the discharge almost unbalanced her. Her shot went wide. She aimed again and squeezed the trigger. The front window of the machine swinging the wrecking ball shattered into a million pieces.

"Back off! Halt! If you don't stop now, I will blow your bloody head off," she yelled. She had already jammed two more cartridges into the double barrel. Her heart pounded so hard she thought it would burst out of her chest. She staggered toward the machinery.

She fired the gun again, taking out the back window.

There was sudden deafening silence.

"You bastards! One move and I will blow your heads off!" she screamed.

The man in the cab sat frozen, his hands high above his head. "Don't shoot, Miss. Don't shoot. I am only doing my job," he whimpered.

She glanced over her shoulder just in time to see a large black SUV roar from behind the coach house. She lifted the gun and squeezed the trigger. The back passenger window disintegrated in a shower of glass. She pulled the trigger again, but the car was already too far away. She reloaded and aimed it back at the man in the cab.

In the distance, she could hear sirens.

Now police cars, an ambulance, and a Faxton Constructions work car streamed up the drive. Four men jumped out of the Faxton truck — Ryan, Toby Silverton, and two other burly blokes in shorts and T-shirts.

"Wade's trapped inside on the stairs," Kayla cried. She was hurting all over and tears welled up and spilled down her cheeks.

Ryan and Toby raced inside as the constable took the shotgun from her trembling hands.

"It all right now Miss, just hand over the gun," the young constable said in a soothing voice, "and perhaps you should have this." The constable held out his uniform jacket.

She let the gun be taken from her, pulled on the proffered coat, then slowly turned and walked toward the house. Her heart still pounded and her stomach clenched. She was petrified of what she would find. As she put her first foot on the steps, Toby and Ryan squeezed through the door with Wade supported between them. Blood dribbled down his face from a gash on his forehead and he was supporting his right arm.

He gave Kayla a rueful grin. "There are benefits to being hard headed sometimes," he mumbled.

"Yeah and dressed, boss. Here, take my shirt," Toby said.

Moments later, Wade all but fell into her arms, one strong arm went around her waist, and he clamped his mouth onto hers in a desperate kiss.

Now she was really sobbing.

"Don't cry, Cinderella, I'll fix your castle," Wade said.

"No, Wade. It doesn't matter anymore. We are what matters, you and I and the fact that we're alive."

With Wade rescued, Ryan immediately took charge of the wrecked building, and the machinery, while the police controlled the rest. Despite his protests, Wade was bundled into one ambulance and she in another.

Her admission through the emergency department was a blur of pain and patches of blackness, her body trembled uncontrollably with shock, and tears flooded her eyes and poured down her cheeks.

* * * *

When she was next fully conscious and opened her eyes, she saw Wade dozing by her bed in a wheelchair, various wounds patched up with bandages. On the other side, Simon sat watching her, his face haggard and gray. She stirred. Her head throbbed at the minute movement and a small involuntary whimper slipped out past her parched lips. Simon was up instantly, handing her a cup of ice with a dribble of water in the bottom. Wade's eyes flew open. She raised her head a fraction and sucked through the straw. Then lay back exhausted by the tiny effort. She hurt everywhere.

Wade leaned forward and took her hand. He held it gently, rubbing his thumb up and down and over her knuckles.

"Kayla, my love. I'm so sorry. I never thought they would use the equipment."

She tried to shake her head, but instantly abandoned the attempt in a blast of pain. "It's not your fault, Wade. Are you all right?"

"I'm fine, just a few scratches and a dislocated collar bone. The doctor says you have a bad concussion, fortunately there was no sign of a skull fracture."

She tried to nod, but it hurt so she lay back now. There was more she wanted to say—to ask. But she could not form the words. She let her eyes close.

When she next opened them, Wade was still there, watching her intently.

His hair was tousled, the cultured three day growth was now a full on beard. His eyes were dull and bloodshot below the deep frown that furrowed his forehead. Even his mouth showed lines in the corners as if he hadn't smiled in a while.

She looked directly at him. "How bad is the house, Wade?"

He shook his head and her heart jumped into an erratic beat.

"It's not too bad, Kayla. Most of the damage was confined to your flat."

"Phillip is so determined to knock the place down. He believes it will free him, but there must be more to this, otherwise how can they justify the lengths they have gone to. What happens now, Wade? Will you continue the demolition?" she asked.

"No. I'm packing up all the contents and putting it in secure storage to protect it from vandals and the weather. My men have put temporary scaffolding up, and tarpaulins to protect the exposed walls. There will be no demolition until this matter is resolved."

"Oh, Wade."

He climbed awkwardly out of his chair and leaned over the bed. He brushed his lips across hers in a fleeting caress. "We *will* resolve this, my love, and we *will* have a future together."

* * * *

Three days later, Kayla was discharged from hospital and joined Wade in a beachfront suite at the Hilton. The police came three times for statements and updates. Apparently the coroner was finding it hard to prove Abrial and Pierre had been murdered because all their injuries could have been caused by falling. It was different with the shipwreck, because they had survived. The police were frustrated because Tenney, Mitchell, and Rossi had gone to ground. They suspected that one or more of the three men could be responsible for the deaths of Pierre and Abrial, and they knew they had tried to kill Wade and Kayla. Seville had co-operated with them, but they could not substantiate any criminal activity on his part.

They were almost ready to go to dinner when there was a loud knock on the door. Wade opened it cautiously and found Edgar Seville standing on the step, his swarthy face dark and unsmiling.

"What do you want, Seville?" Wade asked.

"To give you this, Faxton. You going to let me come in or am I considered that much of a pariah I have to do business on the front doorstep?" His voice was deep and gravelly, but had no signs of anger.

Kayla backed up and slipped into the bedroom, half closing the door. She had no desire for Seville's company.

"You can tell your little lady she has nothing to fear from me," Seville announced.

Wade stood back and let Seville squeeze through the opening.

"This is for you, Faxton—a legal document releasing you from the completion deadline on the contract. It was Mitchell's requirement, not mine. I want nothing to do with knocking that bloody house down right now."

"Oh come on, Edgar. It wouldn't be the first time you've sailed close to the edge on a deal," Wade retorted.

"Yeah, you're right, Faxton. Me and your dad did some right ole dodgy deals and had some shady friends, but I draw the line at murder. I got the damn cops crawling all over me about that couple they found in the cellar and your little misadventure on the high seas. And now with the rogue demolition attempt on the house, I can't breathe for the damn cops."

Wade perused the papers Edgar Seville had handed him. "So is this document canceling the contract? I would stand to lose a great deal of money if it is."

Seville reached out and patted Wade's arm. "Hell no, Faxton. I still want you to build the place, but I want it nice and clean. Do you hear me, missy? I know you're in there. I want this deal nice and clean," Edgar yelled.

"What if the house can't be demolished, Edgar? What then?"

"Then, Faxton, you go back to the drawing board and find and secure a suitable site at your own cost," he replied.

The door slammed behind Seville as he made a sudden exit from their suite.

Wade sank into a chair as Kayla emerged from the bedroom.

She came up behind him and placed her hands on his shoulders, caressing them gently through the light material of his shirt. "Is it good or bad, Wade?"

He studied the letter. "To be honest, Cinderella, I don't have a clue. The removal of the completion deadline means we have time to sort all this out, but if the house can't be demolished then I have to both find a new site and pay for it."

"Wade, I meant it, out there on the island. Just demolish the house. It is not that important anymore."

He stood, turned and took her in his arms. She lay against the warmth of his body as he held her. She felt his breath on her ear.

"You're such a liar, Miss Mackenzie. I saw the expression on your face when you saw the destruction. You love that damn house," he mumbled against her neck.

She pulled away from him, tears welling in her eyes. "I do love the house, Wade, but I love you more. If the house needs to be sacrificed for our love, then so be it."

"Don't worry about it right now, my love. The house is safe for the time being, but while Tenney, Rossi, and Mitchell are at large, you aren't." He squeezed her shoulders lightly. "You need to think, Kayla. There has to be more to all this than just the house. I know it's worth money, but not worth two murders and two attempted murders."

"I don't know," she said.

Wade shook his head. "We need to confirm who the debtor was. David Richards has been asking questions, but no one will give him a straight answer."

"There is only one person left who can unravel this. Elizabeth Carven. Grab the keys, Wade. Maybe confronted by both of us, she will choose to remember the McLeod Family Trust."

Chapter Eight

The house appeared deserted. There was no car in the drive and the blinds were halfway down. Wade parked by the curb. Kayla took his hand, drawing warmth, strength, and courage from the contact. Her heart beat faster and she found herself almost creeping up the driveway beside him. She was uneasy. Nothing was obviously out of place, but something was wrong. Her foot slipped a little on the loose surface of the drive. She glanced down. Glass. Shattered car window glass.

"Wade, look."

He squatted down beside her as she picked up several of the small pieces.

"Phillip, Tenney, and the other guy have been here," she said.

"Could Elizabeth Carven be in on this?" Wade asked.

Kayla frowned at his suggestion. "No. No, surely not."

"Then maybe she is in danger or..." He broke off before he verbalized the worst case scenario.

They stood as one and moved quickly to the windowless side of the house. Wade slipped his arm around her shoulders. "Perhaps you should stay out here, love."

She shook her head. "No, Wade, I am not letting you go in there on your own. What we do, we do together," she said.

He kissed her—a short sharp kiss—and took her hand in his. There was no answer to their knocking on the front door. Kayla's breath came in jerky gasps as they waited.

Wade tried the large window by the front door. It opened without a sound. He climbed in, his long legs making easy work of the height. When Kayla struggled to scramble in, he smiled at her efforts, grabbed her around the waist, and lifted her into the room. It was obvious someone with untidy habits had been living there. Takeaway food containers lay all over the coffee table. The cushions were chucked on the floor and the place smelled stale.

She followed Wade so closely she was almost glued to his back, as they slipped out into the passage. The kitchen was in a similar trashed state as the lounge. They crept on past a single bedroom that had obviously been used. The next door was shut. Kayla felt a tingle of apprehension. She clutched Wade's hand. He squeezed it in reassurance then without warning, he kicked the door open with his foot. It cracked back against the wall as it flew open. Both Kayla and Wade jumped back from the opening, but no one barged out or fired a gun. They both peeped around the corner.

"Oh no. Mrs Carven," Kayla wailed as she caught sight of Frederick Carven's widow.

The elegant, elderly woman was bound to the chair with rope. Her mouth was gagged with material. Tears poured down her haggard, ashen face.

Wade leaped forward to untie her. He threw his phone at Kayla. "Call the police, Kayla, and an ambulance. Then get her a glass of water."

As Elizabeth Carven sipped the water, Wade pulled the quilt off the bed and tucked it around her.

"I'm so sorry, Kayla. I'm sorry. Really I am," Elizabeth Carven muttered over and over.

"Shhh, Mrs Carven. Shh. Don't go worrying about things now. Let's get you safe then we can sort everything out." Kayla embraced her and the older woman laid her head on Kayla's shoulder.

Elizabeth Carven was trembling with shock and distress, hot tears streaming down her face. Wade kept watch out of the window, in case Tenney and Mitchell returned, but already Kayla could hear the sirens screaming closer.

* * * *

Despite her ordeal, Elizabeth Carven recovered quickly and they were summoned to the hospital early the next morning. Simon and Corey Thomas, the younger partner of Carven, Thomas, and Smith, were already there, and David Richards arrived shortly after them. Kayla was confused. Why was Simon here—and Corey Thomas? Kayla stared intently at Elizabeth Carven, wondering why she had denied her knowledge of the trust.

The older woman returned her steady stare. "You are angry with me, Kayla, and rightly so," she said soberly.

Kayla nodded, even though Elizabeth Carven had not been expecting a reply. Conflicting emotions kept Kayla silent. She didn't want to rashly lash out with the anger and frustration she felt toward the older woman before Elizabeth Carven had a chance to explain herself.

"You are justified in your anger, child, and I am sorry for turning you away when you first came to me. I have much to answer for, but when I refused to speak of the matter, it was for the sole purpose of protecting my own reputation. Since Frederick's death, I have received several threatening letters, each warning me to stay silent and not to speak to you or the police, otherwise they would reveal my past to our friends, acquaintances, or even the media."

"Your past, Mrs Carven?"

"Please call me Elizabeth. Yes, Kayla. Your grandparents knew and Frederick, of course, but I have worked very hard to bury my sordid background, because for me it meant rejection or acceptance by Frederick's family, friends, and peers."

"What could be so terrible that it would see you ostracized?" Kayla asked.

Now Elizabeth smiled, a sad, reflective smile. "I had a terribly rough childhood and to get away from it, I married a handsome, young man. But he was a drinker and with the drink, he was violent. He beat me, sometimes half to death. I took it for two years then one night, after he beat me senseless and then came back for another go, I shot him point blank with his hunting rifle. I was convicted of manslaughter. Eloise paid for Frederick to be my lawyer. Frederick and I fell in love during the trial. He waited for me to be released and then we were married. Only Eloise and James knew about my past before I married

Frederick, but somehow someone else has dug it up and, although I knew it was wrong, I stayed silent. Forgive me, Kayla, but I was so afraid of losing all I had worked so hard to build up, and I no longer had Frederick to protect me from gossip and ostracism."

"Remember, Elizabeth, things are different now. We don't tolerate domestic violence, and battered wives have a legitimate defense," Corey Thomas said.

"Corey, you are a caring young man, but I don't think you understand my world — the world Frederick and I circulate in. It's not very forgiving. Now, I shall begin at the beginning. Kayla, you, of course, will know some of this, but there is more you don't know and I'm sure some of it will be painful for you. So please bear with me." Elizabeth eased herself against the pillows. "After the accident, Eloise was left to bring you up. She often said she was too old to cope with child rearing, but she did a good job until you turned into a rebellious teenager."

The heat of embarrassment and guilt rushed up Kayla's face. Elizabeth reached out and patted her hand.

"She loved you, Kayla. But it wasn't until Peter Tenney, fresh out of prison, turned up and seduced you, that she really began to have concerns. He had constantly threatened to get his revenge on the family for sending him to prison. One day, she caught Peter snooping in her private papers. He laughed at her when she told him to get out. He told her he was just checking to see what his baby would be worth when its mother was dead."

"What? I never told him I was pregnant." Kayla almost squealed.

Elizabeth ignored her outraged question. "His ultimate plan, right from the start, was to have a child with you and when you died his child would have the Mackenzie money."

"But..." Kayla fell silent. She didn't know how to address this.

"I do not understand either, Kayla, why he thought he deserved such compensation. After he was sent back to prison and you terminated your pregnancy, Eloise hoped that would be the end of it. She still couldn't rest easy, though, so she asked Frederick to prepare three trusts. As her sole direct descendent, Kayla, you were to inherit everything, but because — and forgive me, Kayla — you were a wild young thing back then, she decided to keep many of her assets secret. She did not want men...bad boys like Peter Tenney, chasing you just for your money."

Kayla was conscious of Wade's warm palms on her shoulders. "I don't understand?" she muttered.

"Kayla, Ainsley House and the trust fund that came with represent about a third of the assets the McLeods, Mackenzies and Campbells had accumulated over the last two hundred years," Elizabeth announced with quiet dignity.

Kayla squirmed in her seat. "A third?" she said.

Elizabeth patted her hand. "Yes. We will firstly talk about Ainsley House, as this is the item in dispute right now. Eloise badly wanted Ainsley House to be a museum of pioneer memorabilia in honor of her grandparents and other early pioneers, so she bequeathed it to the town with you retaining control and a lifetime tenancy through the trust."

"But why didn't Frederick register the trust deed?" Kayla demanded to know.

Elizabeth Carven shook her head. "I am not sure. The documents were drawn up and signed by all parties, but at that time, I had a serious heart attack, and then—whether he forgot or did it deliberately, I cannot say—they were never registered." Elizabeth glanced around at the three of them. Her face was still and pale. "I always knew that Frederick was a little too fond of gambling—horses, poker and blackjack at the casino, but we always had money and I didn't pay much attention. He was always discreet. I had no idea how deep my husband had gotten himself into the underworld of gambling—illicit high stake card games and borrowing from money lenders."

Now she pulled out several crackly pieces of paper. Tears glistened in her eyes. "There has been speculation that Frederick's untimely death was not an accident as recorded officially, but a suicide. No-one but I knew for sure. I found his suicide note in his briefcase, which he left home the night of the fire."

"Elizabeth, I'm sorry you have to go through this," Kayla said.

Elizabeth held up her hand. "No, Kayla, this is partly of my making so I must fix this mistake. I will not bore you with the personal things he said to me alone but the part that is relevant says this... '*I have betrayed my sacred trust as a lawyer and a friend to service my own weakness to a master greater than any – gambling. I am sorry to those who will be affected by my selfishness and criminal acts. My hope is that I will find forgiveness in God's eyes.*

"*I confess that in the fiery heat of a poker game, with a hand I believed foolishly could not lose, I tendered Ainsley House to match Hugo Faxton's bet. George Mitchell and I were so sure but in the end, Faxton had the upper hand, through honest means or otherwise, and Ainsley House was lost to me. I tried several avenues to retrieve the property, but to no avail. Peter Tenney had always sworn revenge on me for my pursuit of his incarceration and it is he who orchestrated the game that was to be my downfall. Phillip is also servant to a demanding master – drugs. It is through this that Tenney drives him. George is also greatly troubled by our monstrous deed, but I feel he is subject to his son's authority in his continuing illness. For myself, I cannot live with my actions. Elizabeth dearest, I leave you with the originals of the documents so that when it does come to light, and indeed it will, you will overlook your loyalty to me and do what must be done to right my wrong...'* There is more, but it is not relevant..." She stopped and raised her eyes from the crumpled note she held in trembling hands. Tears welled in her eyes. "And I have those documents here that prove Ainsley House belongs to Kayla." She pulled them out of Corey's briefcase and handed them to Wade.

When Wade was seated once again, he cast his eye over the papers. He handed the documents to David, standing quietly by the door. He scanned them and nodded to Wade.

"David has decreed these documents are authentic so to save all the hassle of the courts, Faxton Constructions is withdrawing its interest in Ainsley House as of this moment. What the consequences will be, I am not sure," Wade said quietly.

"It's so unfair," Kayla murmured.

"Kayla, it is what you wanted – to save the house." He smiled at her with a sad sort of sympathetic smile.

Her lips trembled as she looked up at him. "I know and I still do, but it seems unfair that you will bear the brunt of other people's criminal activities."

"Life isn't always fair, Kayla."

"What if you can find another property, Wade?" she asked.

He smiled faintly. "It's not so easy, Kayla. I invested four point five million in Ainsley House and Seville's project. I do not have the money available to replace the input of Tenney and Rossi."

"But, Wade, the money from Tenney and Rossi must be mine. The money Phillip embezzled from my trust fund. You are welcome to it all."

Wade pushed himself up out of his chair and closed the gap between them. "Oh, my bewitching Cinderella." He hauled her out of the chair and pulled her hard against his chest and planted a kiss full on her mouth.

She wrapped her arms around him.

"Sorry, my love. It is going to take more than that to save this."

"Now, you two, please sit down, I am not finished yet," Elizabeth said sharply.

Chastened, they sat.

"The other two trusts?" Kayla asked.

"Yes, Kayla. Eloise had a large property portfolio that brought her in a considerable income. She divided the properties into two trusts each with three trustees — Simon, myself, and a senior partner, other than Frederick, of Carven, Thomas, and Smith. Both were similar, made up of a mixture of small and large properties. You are the beneficiary of both trusts, Kayla, but there are conditions attached. If your personal situation at the age of twenty-five was judged by all three trustees to be unsuitable, you would only be able to access the income from the trusts. If your life was deemed suitable, you would be given total control of both trusts. The age of twenty-five is discretionary. If you predeceased Phillip, then of course all three trusts would go to him under the same conditions unless, of course, he had committed a criminal act and then all assets are divided between the four charities listed." Corey handed over two thick manila envelopes. "On the front, Kayla, you will see the accounting for each trust and their individual values, as of today."

As Kayla examined the figures the real reason for Phillip's greed became apparent. "Oh my God. Now it all makes sense. Phillip wants everything. By getting rid of me, Phillip inherits. And Peter Tenney controls Phillip by his drug habit, and therefore, the money. Peter gets his revenge after all."

"Corey, Simon, and I have decided you should take control of all your funds now. With Frederick gone and George incapacitated, you already have control of Ainsley House. The one condition we put on it is that you make a will immediately that cuts Phillip out of the picture completely, as he has proven himself to be a weak-minded, jealous, grasping thief."

Corey Thomas held out a single page document. "I have taken the liberty of drawing up a draft. If it is suitable, you can sign it here and now."

She took the paper, still struggling to comprehend the full consequences of this meeting. She read her will. It was simple. All assets to be sold and proceeds to be divided between the four charities listed in Eloise's trust deed with Phillip George Mitchell specifically excluded. She picked up the pen and added another charity, signed it, then handed it back to the lawyer.

He read her amendment and smiled. "The Children's Cancer Foundation—a very worthwhile cause, Kayla."

And it was finished.

* * * *

With her envelopes clutched tightly on her lap, she stared through the windscreen. She didn't know what to say to Wade. He made no attempt to get out of the car as they pulled up. They sat in silence until he reached out and gripped her arms in a firm hold. He leaned closer. His eyes were shadowed, his full lips drawn down in a tight line. Warmth radiated from him and her breath caught in her chest as she stared into his eyes totally hypnotized by his animal magnetism.

Then she was crushed against the hard muscles of his chest, his grip tightened on her arms as he lifted her just a fraction toward his seeking mouth. He claimed her lips with a hard commanding pressure, seeking and finding consolation in savoring the taste of her. She parted her lips and he immediately plunged his tongue into the moist recesses and she welcomed his penetration with an entangling caress of her own. She needed him, wanted to taste him, to be drunk on the aphrodisiac of his masculinity.

He moaned. "I love you, Kayla. I want you. But I don't know how to get past this right now." He broke away. "I need some space. Some time alone, to work out what options I have."

"Wade..."

"Wait here for me, Kayla. It will be all right," he muttered.

She slipped from the car, shut the door, then entered the hotel suite without a backward glance. It cut deep that her win had caused Wade so much grief and placed him in such a difficult situation.

The room felt cold and empty without Wade's presence. She made a coffee and opened the envelopes. She carefully sifted through each property in the two trusts. Many meant nothing to her, but it didn't take long to match some of them to the land titles. She grabbed a map of Port Lincoln and began to mark the addresses off one by one, becoming more and more shocked as she realized the significance of this portfolio. One huge parcel of land at the Lincoln Cove Marina caught her eye. She opened her laptop and logged into Google Maps. She studied the satellite pictures of the area and matched it to the document and it gradually dawned on her just what a gem she had in her hand.

She dialed Wade's number. When he answered, she jumped straight in, determined not to give him a chance to wriggle out of this.

"Wade, is your helicopter available?"

"Maybe, why?"

"What are you doing now?" she asked.

"Researching site options," he said.

She heard the rough edge to his voice. "Well stop that, organize the helicopter, and meet me at the airport in half an hour. Can you get flight clearance over the town and surrounds?"

"Maybe. Kayla, what is going on?" His tone was almost pleading.

"Just meet me there, Wade. Please. Trust me on this one."

"Fine. I'll be there," he grumbled. He didn't sound at all enthusiastic as he conceded to her request.

She heard the sharpness of stress, the touch of impatience in his voice, and she intended to soothe it away and put the spark back.

She made four phone calls informing David, Corey, Simon, and Elizabeth to make themselves available at two this afternoon. She arranged for David to have a room key and call the other investors.

Wade was late and she was already pacing up and down the tarmac impatient to spring her surprise.

As Wade pulled up, Kayla climbed into the helicopter.

He paused by the open door. "What are you playing at, Kayla. I have things to do."

She patted the seat. "Stop grumbling, Wade, and get in. There is just a short window of opportunity between commercial flights."

He sighed heavily, his full mouth thinned into a stern line, his eyes dulled with tiredness and frustration.

He had barely clipped his seat belt by the time they left the ground. He looked at her, his expression stern. "So are you going to tell me?" he asked.

She smiled. "No." They flew west across town. "Tell me what you see, Wade."

He gazed down at the land sliding slowly past. "Land, sea, pristine beaches, the Marina."

"Yep. Tell me Wade, what could you do with the land below?"

"Kayla." He growled her name, his eyes flashing sparks of anger now. "I don't own the land and don't have the wherewithal to buy it right now, even if it was for sale. Do you realize how much land on the edge of the channel is worth?"

"Actually, I have no idea," she said. "Tell me how much *you* think it's worth. Say that piece down there. It would be perfect for the convention center, don't you think?"

"Damn it, Kayla, stop playing games," Wade grumbled.

"I'm not playing games, Wade. Give me an estimate," she insisted.

"Six million, if you could buy it in one piece, otherwise around eight."

"*Really*. Gordon, take us back to the airport please, we've seen enough," she announced.

Wade flopped back in his seat and shut his eyes. "More than enough," he muttered.

They didn't speak on the whole flight back and immediately they touched down Wade piled out to the helicopter and strode toward the terminal.

"Wade, wait. I need a lift back to town."

He slowed and waited for her to catch up. Kayla was barely able to hold her tongue as Wade drove in surly, fretful silence.

As he pulled up outside the hotel she indicated he should follow her inside.

"Kayla, no. This is not a good time."

"Just come inside for a moment. I have something to show you."

He glowered at her, but got out of the car and followed her.

When they entered the hotel room the to-scale model sat in the center of the table. Kayla walked across to the table and began looking it over. Wade trailed after her as she circled the model.

"What the hell is *that* doing here?" he asked as he finally sank into a chair.

"I thought we might need it," Kayla replied, barely able to keep the amusement out of her voice.

"Put me out of my misery, Kayla, please?" he begged.

She knelt down in front of him and took his hands in hers. "I have a proposition, Wade. Promise me you will listen until the end before you make a decision? Please?"

He nodded.

"I spoke to your lawyer and mine about an hour ago. I also spoke to Neil, your accountant, and mine."

He jerked forwards in his chair. "You what?"

"I told them to be here..." She glanced out of the window as two cars pulled up. "About right now," she said.

"Why?" he asked.

"I believe it is always wise to know a business partner's strengths and weaknesses before signing a business deal — correct?"

Now he was eyeing her, his expression full of dark shadows and questions. She could see he wanted to rouse on her and get answers.

"Yes, correct. What business deal?" he grumbled as he glared from her to the model and back again.

"You need a property at least three times the size of Ainsley House to match the combined land you and Seville held for the project and you have to balance the investments of Seville, Tenney and Phillip, for Faxton Construction to complete this project. Right?"

"Close enough," he muttered.

She saw a sliver of interest in his eyes, but also the obvious desire to throttle her.

"What are you up to, Cinderella?"

She laughed shook her head and waggled her finger at him. "Ah, ah, ah, patience, Prince Charming."

He started to rise out of the chair, but stopped when an impatient thud on the door barely preceded David Richards, Corey Thomas and Neil Morgan's entrance into the room. They were almost immediately followed by Damien, Roger and Seville.

Kayla went to stand behind the model. "Good, we are all here. Make yourselves comfortable. Corey and David, can you confirm the legality of what I am about to do?"

Both men nodded. "The paperwork is drawn up," they said in unison.

"Gentleman, you are all familiar with the issues so I won't go over them again. What most of you don't know is that along with my original trust fund, I have inherited a number of properties. Neil has also confirmed that the investments in the project made by Peter Tenney and Vincent Rossi can be traced to Phillip Mitchell and therefore to my trust fund," she announced.

Wade's gaze drilled into her, and out of the corner of her vision, she saw him sitting tensely upright in his chair, his hands curled around the arms of the chair in a white knuckled grip.

"So, in view of that, I put forward the following proposition. In exchange for Ainsley House — which was technically legally inherited by Faxton Constructions — and the two parcels of land adjacent to Ainsley House currently owned by Edgar Seville, I will put forward a suitable parcel of land at Lincoln Cove Marina. By the time the convention center is built, the extension to the marina will bring the channel right across the front of that parcel of land. Ideal for the project, I would say. The whole parcel is slightly smaller than the original, but more than adequate for the approved plans. The value of the marina parcel is double that of the Ainsley House parcel. The additional value will be my investment in the project. Mr Seville, if you are amenable to the exchange, I am sure we can come up with a satisfactory solution."

Seville nodded. "A damn good solution," he said.

Wade's voice was barely a croak now. "I can't let you do this, Kayla."

"Why not?" she asked.

He glared at her. "Because you are not obliged to replace Ainsley House or dig me out of a financial hole."

She walked around the model and sank to her knees in front of him. "Wade, I know that, but this is something I want to do because I love you. This way our love has a chance of surviving — of being given a chance to blossom and grow. Is it not worth it? I think so. Don't you? This is not a gift. It is a business deal — a very profitable one too."

Wade sat there in silence seemingly overwhelmed by the enormity of what Kayla had just revealed.

"Besides, it is a sound business proposition for you and for me. It wasn't your fault you got swindled by Phillip and Tenney in an effort to exact their revenge on me. This way, we win — both of us, in love and business — and they lose."

Wade's phone rang. He answered it. First he smiled then then a grim hardness froze his expression.

"Thanks for letting us know." He shut his phone. "They have Rossi, the third man on the boat, locked up, but so far no sign of Tenney and Mitchell," he said.

"Okay, I think everyone has enough to think on for today. We will leave the rest of our discussions until tomorrow when we can get the architect in to look at the site and get the paperwork processed," Kayla said firmly.

David snapped his brief case closed. "I agree and by the way, Wade, Ryan says he has completed that small job we discussed."

Wade nodded. "Thanks."

Kayla immediately sensed some unspoken communication between the two men, but Wade's face was completely expressionless.

"Okay, Cinderella, out in the car. It's my turn to take you on a mystery tour," Wade said.

A few minutes later they pulled up in front of the house.

She stared in amazement as Ainsley House loomed up in front of them. Lights glowed in the front downstairs windows, the machinery was gone, and the huge gaping hole where the wrecking ball had nearly claimed her life was covered with huge yellow tarpaulins. All the wreckage was cleared away, waiting to be re-cycled during the re-building process, except for the piles of sandstone from the walls.

"But..." she protested half-heartedly.

Wade cut her off with a hissed, "Sh-h-h-h."

He swept her up into his arms and carried her over the threshold. Kayla was amazed. All signs of damage had vanished and most of the memorabilia had been removed. He set her down in the middle of the reception area, took her hand and led her toward one of the large rooms off the reception area. He guided her through the doorway in front of him then came to stand behind her, wrapping his good arm around her waist.

She stood staring at the glowing scene before her. The dimmed lights of the bedside tables cast halos of light over the carefully polished teak master bedroom suite from the flat—the four poster bed with its delicately ruffled bedspread, pristine white and framed by puffy, frilled pillows and drawn back curtains of antique lace.

Her tears welled up and overflowed, pouring down her cheeks as she stared at the scene before her. "Oh, Wade. It's so beautiful. Thank you so much for doing this for me."

She turned and slipped into his embrace.

"I love you, Cinderella, and I've brought you home to your castle," he murmured.

She reached up to kiss him. He promptly covered her mouth with his and ravished its delicate flesh.

He pulled back slightly and asked, "Kayla, will you be this Prince Charming's Princess?"

"Yes, Wade, I will."

He took her hand and led her out onto the decking at the side of the house. The moon rose over the sea, laying a silvery path across the bay. The sky was deepening to navy blues and deep lavenders. At the end of the deck was a table, beautifully set with a white cloth, red roses, and red candles in gold candelabra. A bottle of red wine waited to be served.

"Oh, Wade." She could barely breathe as the emotions welled up.

He kissed her lightly.

"Sit, Cinderella. Enjoy the view and soak up the atmosphere while you await your dinner.

* * * *

They lingered over dessert.

"You planned this before today, didn't you, Wade?"

He nodded.

"You had no intention of knocking this house down, did you?"

"Well, what could I do, my love? Could I do no less than you were prepared to do to salvage our love? You know, Kayla, I never intended to fall in love — to give my heart so fully to another. I was determined not to end up a broken man like my father...but when I met you, I had lost my heart before I even realized it was at risk."

"And now?" she asked as she stood up and went to kneel in front of him.

"Now, I have given you my heart—all of it—and would do so again, to feel like this."

Kayla leaned close to Wade, slid her hands around his neck, and brought his face close to hers. He continued to sit motionless, his face shuttered, but his expression was calm and relaxed, his full mouth curving slightly at the corners. He watched her come closer, but made no attempt to close the gap and kiss her. She was so close she could feel the warmth of his steady breath on her face, and she could smell his maleness barely noticeable through the tang of his aftershave. The familiar scent played havoc with her heartbeat and made her stomach turn backflips. Still he made no move. The chair squeaked very subtly in protest under them as their weight shifted its center of gravity ever so slightly. She linked her fingers behind his neck, entangling them in his hair. She felt herself sinking into the molten honey of his eyes, mapping every line that creased in the corners, every long dark lash. Still he didn't move to close the gap.

She slid her hands down either side of his face, outlining his mouth with a gentle touch of her thumb then cupped his chin so he was looking directly at her before she brought her lips down on his, caressing and exploring their unmoving firmness. She felt him begin to smile. She trailed kisses from the tip of his nose, over his eyes and up to his forehead then back down again. This time she didn't stop at his mouth, but laid feather soft kisses over his chin and along his jaw. She caressed his earlobe with her tongue then kissed down the length of his neck and into the triangle of skin revealed by his open necked shirt. She undid the first button of his shirt then smothered the skin with kisses.

His arousal could be felt under her forearm, but she ignored it, instead sliding her hands along the flexed muscles of his thighs. He watched her every move. His chest rose and fell with small rapid breaths and his Adam's apple bobbed up and down as he swallowed and he dampened his lips with his tongue. She ran her hands, palm down, up his thighs, over his hips and up to the next button on his shirt. She flicked it open then trailed her finger over his skin as she flicked the next one open then leaned forward and pressed her lips on his skin. He took a deep breath and released it slowly on a tiny drawn out moan. As she lowered her head, his desire was very obvious right in front of her. She opened his belt buckle, tugged his shirt out of his trousers, and undid the last two buttons before pushing his shirt fronts apart enough to reveal his whole torso. She knelt up and kissed his shoulders first, before marking a trail down to his nipples which were already erect. She swirled her tongue around each one then sucked on them with a firm but gentle pressure before she trailed more kisses down to his navel. Here she kissed all around it before dipping her tongue into the depths. He gasped and gripped the arm of his chair with his uninjured hand. Their gazes met and she could see flecks of topaz and amber highlighting his eyes and signaling his desire. With nimble fingers, she unzipped his trousers, all the time staring up into his face. He ran his fingers through her hair with the gentlest of caresses. When he released the strands, she pushed aside his trousers and lowered the waistband of his trunks to expose his swollen cock. In its hard, hot state of readiness, it reached for her and she lowered her head and took it into her mouth, slowly sliding her lips down the shaft, flicking the swollen length with her tongue.

"Oh, Kayla," he groaned.

She trailed her mouth up his phallus and watching for his reaction, she stroked her tongue back and forth across the silken surface of his head. His eyes were partly closed and his body was arched ever so slightly toward her, clenching the arm of the chair with his good hand. She lifted her head and smiled at him—a seductive, teasing curve of her mouth—then ran her tongue over her lips before she lowered her head again.

Even in the cloud of sexual awareness that engulfed them, the shuffling scuff of footsteps was loud and intrusive. She paused, her mouth just touching the tip of his moistened cock. She looked up. Fear ruffled across her skin. He put his fingers to his lips. She quickly restored him to respectability and stood, doing up his buttons as she went. He handed her the phone. He mouthed, "Bathroom. Call cops."

She tiptoed to the bathroom and slipped through the door, just as Phillip and Peter came round the corner of the house. She dialed triple zero and ordered immediate police presence for an armed home invasion and an ambulance in case.

"Where is she, Faxton?" Phillip demanded to know.

"Not here."

"Bullshit. I heard her voice—all lovey dovey and smooch smooch," Peter sneered.

"Kayla, get out here now!" Phillip roared.

She waited in the darkness of the bathroom.

"Get out here or I will shoot lover boy," Peter threatened.

She heard the door being kicked open with a violent thud. They were in the house. It was only a matter of time before they found her. It might be better to come out.

"Stop looking. I'm here," she said.

She slipped out of the door and was immediately motioned to stand next to Wade.

Phillip held a pistol pointed directly at Wade. Peter swaggered up behind him. He was also brandishing a gun.

"Stand together, you two," Phillip ordered.

"Phillip, there is no need for this. Give it up. I know you've taken the money from my trust fund. Well you can have it, Phillip. It's not important."

"No, Kayla, the trust fund is not important. Nor is Ainsley House, really. That's Phillip's pet project. It's the rest I want." Peter snarled. "All the riches of the Mackenzies are still not enough to make up for what you lot did to me—destroyed my life, that stinking lawyer and your grandmother. Took my dream," Peter said very, very quietly as he stalked closer. "Did you know that, little rich bitch? Did you? See this." He pointed at his left eye. "See this. It's *glass*."

Kayla looked closer and now she could see his left eye was false. She felt as if he had slapped her.

"How is that my fault, Peter?" she asked.

"You and your family sent me to prison, not once, but twice. You are to blame for the second time—you, the little whore. That's when it got damaged. You know the Air Force don't take half blind pilots. When it got worse, they took the eye. What is it they say 'an eye for an eye or a life for a life'."

He was so close to her she could feel his breath on her. Smell it—beer and garlic.

"I'm sorry for your loss, Peter, but it was never my fault," she said.

Peter punched her shoulder. She was forced to step back. Wade laid his hands on her waist to steady her. Peter pushed her this time sideways so she spun out of Wade's grip and landed on the floor. She scrabbled backwards almost at the base of the damaged stairs. Peter stepped toward her. She scrambled farther backwards onto the first step. Wade moved back with her.

"Your grandmother feared and hated me. And she was right to fear me. You were going to be my ticket to the Mackenzie riches—you and the baby I intended you to have. Instead they put me back in the clink, for raping their little whore. She didn't think a Tenney was good enough for her family, but I made the old woman pay for what she did."

"What do you mean, made her pay?" Kayla asked.

"You should have told me. Kayla. You should have told me you were having my baby. You shouldn't have got rid of it. Then this would not have happened, you know. 'Cause my kid would have had it all. Instead you killed it, you bitch."

Kayla felt like she had been stabbed. "How do you know about the baby? How?" she cried.

"Your grandma told me, after I got out of prison—the night I went to the house. Dead of winter it was, I lured the old girl outside, beat her up a bit. Oh, she told me she made you kill my child. She boasted about it—taunted me. So I left her there to die." Tenney grimaced. "Silly old bag."

"No-o-o-o," Kayla wailed, the pain in her heart almost felling her right there.

"Yes, and soon my revenge will be complete." He was ranting now. Following her each time she slid a bit farther away up the stairs.

Kayla glared at Tenney. "If you kill me now, Phillip won't inherit a cent—not Ainsley House or anything else. I have control of my funds. Damn you, Peter, you will not get my money. You will be going to prison— you and Phillip."

Peter stared at her for a moment then turned to Phillip. "What the hell is she raving about? There is no one else to inherit, is there?"

Phillip watched Peter for a moment, but made no attempt to answer his question. Then he stared directly at her and she saw the madness on his face. His eyes had that glazed-over, heavy lidded, red rimmed look of recent drug use and his intent was evident. He intended she should die.

"I don't care, little cousin. I will not let you have Ainsley House. It must be destroyed. Destroyed before I can have peace. Don't you see, little cousin? This house is a constant reminder. I need peace, Kayla. I need to stop the recriminations," Phillip shouted at her.

Phillip waved the gun, indicating Wade should move up beside her. She climbed to her feet and he put his arm around her as they retreated up the stairs. Both men followed, step by step.

"You should have both died out at sea and saved us this trouble. When I've dealt with you, I am going out there to finish knocking this damn house down. Do you hear that, little cousin?" Phillip screeched.

"Damn you, Phillip, go on. Go knock it down. I'll sign it over to you. Free hold all of it and you can have the money you embezzled from my trust fund too. Have it all, both of you, if that's what you think will make it right for you…if it's what you need to assuage your bitterness—to make up for all the perceived wrongs," she ranted in a shrill screech.

"Perceived wrongs, little cousin?" He waved the gun, his finger unsteady on the trigger. "It's too late for you or anyone to make up for the miseries my family visited on me—the guilt trip—over twenty years, Kayla. No forgiveness, and I wasn't even driving. My father never let me forget that I had taken the love of his life away from him. Your grandmother twisted the knife every chance she got because I killed both her daughters. And that damn lawyer, Carven? He worked every legal angle to see Peter and I served time. It was great to see him brought to his knees—to have him beg and plead with me to get the house back from Hugo. And my father? Well, he finally realized I had the upper hand. He knew I was dipping into your fund, but refused to sign the documents for transfer of the house, so I did. Pretty good forgery, if I say so myself. Poor Father got himself so worked up, he had a stroke. That made it easier and easier to kill him when he tried to tell you, Kayla."

"You killed Uncle George?"

Phillip nodded.

"Oh God, Phillip, how could you? Your own father."

"Believe me, it was easy. He was my tormentor for twenty years," Phillip snapped.

Kayla huddled closer to Wade. "And is killing me going to be easy, Phillip? I haven't been your tormentor for twenty years."

"No, little cousin, I regret having to kill you, but you are the one thing stopping me from wiping Ainsley House off the face of the earth. The huge insurmountable obstacle between me and peace. You should have just stayed out of it like I told you. If you hadn't come back early from Scotland, Ainsley House would have been gone. I would have made a packet and re-paid your trust fund and no-one would have been any the wiser. But no, you had to 'save the house' and 'respect her wishes'. If you had just done as you were told, it wouldn't have come to this." He aimed the gun directly at Kayla. "Back up the stairs, little cousin."

Wade stepped in front of her. "Mitchell, stop this. I will not let you kill Kayla."

Phillip chuckled. "You think you can stop me, Faxton? I'll just shoot you first then. Yes, that would be better. She can see you die first."

Peter frowned and moved closer. "Shut up, Phil. We don't want to shoot them. It's meant to look like an accident or you won't inherit. Back up, you two," he ordered.

Now they were on the landing and there was nowhere to go except off the edge of the gaping hole left by the wrecking ball.

She felt Wade's fingers poking her in the waist. He was trying to tell her something. She moved in the direction he seemed to be pushing her and ended up with a tangle of ropes just touching her hair. The guns stayed trained on them as they edged nearer to the gaping hole. Wade poked her a bit more. She took another couple of sideways steps. He tightened his grip. She stopped and he patted her lightly on the bottom as he took his arm away. She knew he was up to something, but wasn't quite sure what. Whatever it was, he would need a distraction. She peered down and pretended to be petrified.

"Please, Peter, Phillip. Please don't do this. You can have everything, all of it," she wailed.

"Just get on with it, bitch," Peter hissed.

She fell to her knees. "Please, Phillip, I'm your cousin." She began to howl. "I don't want to die."

Both men stepped forward, intending to push her over the edge. For a split second they took their stares off Wade.

There was a rattle of ropes and pulleys and the tarpaulin shook and dropped. It covered them. One of the guns discharged. An agonized yelp rent the air. Kayla leaped up, grabbed a plank of wood leaning against the wall and began belting the two lumps under the canvas. Wade jumped on the one farthest from the edge, tore the canvas off and landed several well aimed punches on Peter's face. Kayla kept hitting the other lump, as Phillip tried in vain to get untangled from the tarp and escape her hefty blows. There was a scream, a thud, a gunshot, and the tarp lay flat.

Kayla felt sick. Phillip had just fallen off the edge.

She turned to find Wade and Peter scrabbling in the tarpaulin, as they wrestled for possession of the gun. Peter's expression was maniacal. Wade's was twisted with effort and determination. Kayla walked up behind Peter. She swung the plank and cracked him across the back, once. He kept fighting. She hit him again, catching him across the back of the neck. He dropped onto the yellow tarp and lay still. His eyes were open. His gaze darted from her to Wade. She saw fear in them and was glad he was afraid. The rest of his body lay inert.

As Wade leaned over to check for a pulse they heard sirens in the street below and the sound of many boots thudding up the stairs. "You haven't killed him, Kayla," Wade said as he straightened and turned to face the police.

* * * *

As the police took over the scene Wade guided Kayla downstairs to the office. She couldn't stop shaking and she noticed Wade's hand was not quite steady as he took the mug of tea from the young constable.

"It's over, Kayla. You're safe now." He pulled her so close to him she was almost on his lap and he wrapped the blankets provided closely around both of them.

"I thought we were both going to—"

His lips covered hers, silencing her words. Then he was showering tiny kisses all over her face. "It's over, love," he murmured.

She laid her cheek against his chest. He encircled her in a tight possessive embrace. She laid her hand on his thigh and felt the tension in his muscles. She caressed it lightly, and after a while she felt the muscle relax under her touch and he leaned back into the deep leather sofa.

It was past midnight by the time the police had photographed the scene, taken copious notes, and collected evidence. Peter Tenney was diagnosed with a broken neck. Phillip was dead from the combined injuries of the fall and an accidently self-inflicted gunshot wound.

"Now you two we need to find you a bed for tonight," the detective said.

Kayla shook her head. "No Detective we are going to stay in our home tonight."

"I don't think that is a good idea, Miss."

"Detective we will be safe now—with the Peter and Phillip out of the way."

The detective frowned at them, then shrugged. "Fine. I can't force you to leave, but I can forbid you to go past the yellow tape. It is my crime scene and I don't want it messed with."

"No problems, Detective, we'll confine ourselves to the ground floor until you say otherwise."

The detective and several of his men moved toward the front door. Wade went to see them out when the detective stopped in the doorway. "I'll have further questions about this matter so I suggest you don't leave town without advising me."

"We won't," Wade and Kayla chorused in unison.

"Goodnight then."

At last they were alone. Wade swept her up into his arms and strode into the bedroom. With one hand he pulled back the covers. He laid her on the crisp white sheets before he tore off his shirt then leaned down and undid her blouse, pushing it back to expose her lacy bra. Neither of them spoke. There was no need for words. Each recognized the need in the other — a desperate need to make love, to be joined, to confirm life, to reaffirm their love in the face of death.

"I thought I was going to lose you," Wade muttered, as he impatiently tugged off her bra, dropped his trousers, then knelt on the floor beside her. He leaned in and suckled her breasts, and laid scorching kisses and little nibbles all over her breasts, shoulders, and neck.

"Oh, Kayla, my love."

At his slightly frantic fumbling, she lifted her hips and helped him pull her shorts off.

It was almost a sense of relief to feel his naked skin pressed against hers. He fondled her breasts then eased his hand between her legs. A searing need burst into a raging inferno inside her. His desire was obvious and she urged him to take her. She had to have him right now. She lay back as he moved above her and she guided his hard throbbing shaft to her moist pussy. Without pausing, he thrust into her. She cried out and abandoned herself to the seething sensations in a head to head race with her lover to reach the dizzy heights of passion. They melted together as they burst over the edge of a frenzied sexual climax, their joint cries shattering the silence in the room and the fear in their minds.

They lay joined for a long time. Kayla struggled to regain equilibrium and breathe in the bone melting aftermath of their impassioned sexual joining, but slowly the fever diffused and mellowed. Still tingling with passion, but drained and sated by the frantic coupling, Wade withdrew from her body but still clung to her and she was glad because she was vulnerable to the horrors that lingered on the edge of her mind.

To Kayla their togetherness was an unspoken confirmation of their love and their life and when Wade kissed her, so commandingly, like he would never be parted from her she knew it would all be okay. Neither of them made any attempt to talk. Kayla knew they would discuss the whole debacle later, but for now there was no need. Each knew what the other thought and felt. The horror was over, Ainsley House was safe, and they had a new business partnership to build and grow. But what was most important was their passionate, new love had survived the nightmare battle for their lives. Wade tightened his embrace and Kayla cuddled closer fully enclosing their forever love that would carry them forward together.

About the Author

Cassandra was a closet writer for several years before she got brave enough to share her work with anyone until she joined Eyre Writers Inc, a creative writing group in the seaside town of Port Lincoln and really began to improve.

Her first book was a 100,000 words family saga novel, but after a workshop on 'How to write a Mills and Boon', she embarked on a new direction—writing the romance novel.

After being made redundant from the job she loved in 2011 she became a carer for her frail, vision-impaired mother and turned to fulfilling her dream of becoming a writer.

When Cassandra's not writing she enjoys spending time with family and friends, especially her mother, and her three wonderful adult children and two adorable grandchildren.

She also enjoys egg decorating and carving, reading of course, painting and cooking.

Cassandra Hawke loves to hear from readers. You can find her contact information, website details and author profile page at http://www.totallybound.com.

Totally Bound Publishing